We're all a little BROKEN

you are enough

BOOK 1

A NOVEL BY

TIFFANY ANDREA

Paperback ISBN: 978-1-990724-03-9
Hardcover ISBN: 978-1-990724-04-6
eBook ISBN: 978-1-990724-05-3

Cover Design by: Burden of Proofreading Publishing featuring Graphics by JemStock via CanStockPhoto

Interior Graphics by Yupriamos

My mother, Bethea.
Thank you.
Thank you for your understanding and compassion.
Thank you for being as dedicated to my passions and interests as I was.
Thank you for fighting to give us as much time together as you could.
Thank you for teaching me to love with all that I am.
Thank you for sharing all of my triumphs, failures, successes, and heartaches.
Thank you for always believing in me, even when I deviated from what you knew was best.
LYM MYM, Momma

Preface...vii

My World.. 1

You're Crazy.. 7

Street Of Dreams.. 13

Down On the Street.. 19

Too Much, Too Soon... 26

Right Next Door To Hell...................................... 32

Look At Your Game, Girl..................................... 37

New Work Tune... 42

I Don't Care About You.. 49

Don't Cry.. 56

Sorry 61

Out Ta Get Me 65

Since I Don't Have You.. 71

Patience 77

Think About You... 84

Appetite For Destruction 96

Breakdown 101

Yesterdays... 108

Human Being.. 113

Welcome To the Jungle 120

There Was a Time 126

Ain't It Fun 133

Reckless Life 139

It Tastes Good, Don't It? 145

This I Love 151

Nice Boys.. 158

Heartbreak Hotel 162

One In a Million... 168

Anything Goes.. 174

Knockin' On Heaven's Door.................................. 180

November Rain 187

Shadow Of Your Love 193

Civil War.. 200

Shotgun Blues 207

Perfect Crime 213

The Plague... 219

Used To Love Her 223

Better 227

So Fine 233

It's So Easy 240

Bad Apples 245

Attitude 252

Confession 257

Estranged 262

You Could Be Mine 268

New Rose 274

The Garden 279

Sweet Child O' Mine 284

Acknowledgements 289

Special Thanks 291

Also By This Author 294

As a lifelong sufferer of Generalized Anxiety Disorder, I set out to write this book to give others like me comfort in knowing they aren't alone in their wild and sometimes frustrating thoughts. I wanted to create a body of work that normalized those invasive thoughts and feelings, which sometimes feel like a tiny jerk walking around on your shoulder, telling you all the ways you're failing or how things can go wrong. To my fellow sufferers, you are not alone.

To those who don't deal with anxiety or depression, Zara might annoy you. Trust me, anyone who deals with anxiety finds it just as annoying. So, all I ask is that you approach this book with compassion and take a glimpse into an anxious mind.

I'm adding a trigger warning, but if that doesn't apply to you, skip on ahead to page one. Thank you for reading.

This book addresses issues such as Anxiety, Panic disorders, depression, suicidal thoughts, and sexual assault. Though it addresses these difficult issues, I tried to do so in a way that wouldn't open old wounds, but rather explore the impact they can have. That being said, if any of those issues could be difficult for you, please reconsider reading this story.

If you are ever feeling concerned for yourself or a loved one, please reach out for help. Take care of yourself, take care of each other, and always remember, we're all a little broken. We all need help sometimes.

I stand here, staring at Tyler down on one knee. This shouldn't surprise me; I knew it was coming. He asked me to be here for this moment, but seeing Quinn jump into a passionate embrace after accepting Tyler's proposal, I can't help but think my life doesn't look how I thought it would by now. From the look of joy on Quinn's face, I can tell this man is her soulmate. A soulmate doesn't appear to be in the cards for me.

What if you never find someone? You're almost thirty. Your time is running out. Your mom and sisters were all married by your age. You're destined to be a spinster forever.

The promenade at the Parry Sound waterfront is basking in the glow of the early autumn sun, which gives the streets a cozy warmth—a direct contrast to my own internal battle. The waves are crashing against the concrete pier. Tourists and locals are gawking and clapping at the scene that has unfolded, and the string quartet Tyler hired is playing the melody of a song I don't recognize, but holds significance for the happy couple. Everything is perfect. So, why do I feel like my stomach is a maximum-security prison for the Hulk, and he's determined to escape?

I plaster on my most convincing fake smile for my best friend—a smile that looks like I am suppressing my gag reflex. Quinn needs me to be happy right now—which I am. I'm simply drowning in the disappointment of my own life. I force the thought out of my mind. My romantic failings can be my focus later tonight, with a bottle of wine and some Oreos. Who am I kidding? Probably an entire package of Oreos.

After she finishes jumping up and down, crying, and kissing her future husband, Quinn walks toward me with a questioning look in her eyes. Her long, satiny, wheat-blonde hair is blowing in the breeze, intensifying her halcyon appearance. She's one of those people you look at and feel jealous of their external beauty, but can't dislike her because she's the kindest human you've ever encountered. "Did you know about this?" She stretches out her hand toward the array of flowers and string quartet.

I fiddle with my silver necklace, which displays my initials, ZRL. "I did. Tyler called a few weeks ago and asked me to help him arrange everything. I'm so happy for you, Amiga."

"I can't believe you kept this a secret! You kept me in the dark. I thought you were seeing someone when you blew me off last week."

My face flushes. "You know I'd never keep something like that from you. No romantic prospects for me." The feelings I was already struggling to keep at bay intensify as I voice that reality.

"Thank you so much for your help, Zara. I couldn't have pulled this off without you," Tyler chimes in as he approaches Quinn and me. They are a perfect match for each other. He's the epitome of tall, dark, and handsome with his Spanish ancestry and friendly demeanour. He smiles at me, creating wrinkles around his deep brown eyes, and I can feel Tyler happiness radiating from him.

"Of course, Ty. I got as many pictures as I could on my phone and used yours to record video. Your parents are all going to be ecstatic. I'm sure they'll want all the photographic evidence."

Quinn laughs. "Don't remind me. I bet Mom will have me dress shopping by the end of the week."

"I don't doubt that. The sooner, the better. I can't wait to make you my wife." Tyler stares at his future bride with enough lust in his eyes to set anyone in our proximity on fire.

"Oh. My. Gosh! I am going to be a wife!" Quinn jumps into Tyler's muscular arms for another kiss.

It's time to make myself scarce. This is getting awkward. I am happy for them, but I don't want to overstay my welcome here and interfere with their celebration—nor do I have the emotional stability to watch them express their love so publicly, knowing I'm going home to packaged cookies and a potted plant. These two are the epitome of sunshine, and I'm standing here like a solar eclipse.

I give them both a warm smile—at least, I think it's warm. "Congratulations to you both. I'm going to head out so you two can celebrate without a third wheel." I turn to make my escape but swing back around to face my best friend. "Call me later to fill me in on how your family takes the big news."

"I love you, Zara. This won't change anything. Ty knows it will always be me and you against the world." She leans in to give me a hug as Tyler smirks in our direction.

"Oh, Quinny. It's you and Tyler against the world now, but I'm okay with that. I've always been able to count on you both. This is a step for you two."

It's a good thing I drove myself so I could set up before Tyler and Quinn arrived. If I had to stick around, the gushing and fawning of the newly engaged couple would have nauseated me. I hug Tyler, then say goodbye to him and Quinn before venturing off in search of my car. Alone.

Where did you park? What if you lost your keys somewhere? You better find them before you get to your car so you don't get mugged.

I scan my surroundings as I march toward the parking area with intention. I note the small shrubs and manicured gardens, but only to check if someone is lurking behind them. Sure, I probably look like I'm a wanted felon evading capture, but in reality, I'm your average anxious millennial, trying to survive day-to-day life.

A bench on the edge of the parking area looks to be the perfect place to stop and get myself organized. I sit on the forest green bench to rummage through my Mary Poppins bag for my keys. Being prepared for anything has its downfalls. I could probably find a baby zebra in here if I look hard enough. It's unfortunate I can't find any money.

Do you have your phone? You better make sure. All of Quinn and Tyler's engagement photos are on there and if she can't post those pictures on social media by tonight, she will be furious. Or, if you don't have your phone and something goes wrong, you can't call for help. Something bad will happen.

I pull my arm out of my purse from elbow-depth with my phone in hand and breathe a sigh of relief. The thought of Quinn being upset with me is too much to bear. She's been my best friend for a decade, and I'd be lost without her. Sure, things have changed over the past four years since Tyler entered the picture, but he is a great guy and they are, without a doubt, head over heels in love. He has been so understanding anytime I have needed Quinn at my side. Married life shouldn't change that, but I need to be more independent and let her live her life. I don't want to be a burden to her—to them. Good news is I found my keys by myself. At least I managed something alone.

Once I confirm I have my essentials, it's time to head home. I have plans—plans to binge on high-calorie treats and TV show reruns.

Now I need to find my car; my lime-green Prius. I chose the bright colour intentionally to minimize the chances of losing it in a parking lot or blending in during a snowstorm. You can never be too prepared for Canadian winters.

I arrive at my car, which I parked under a streetlamp in case we were here past dark. It may only be three o'clock in the afternoon, but I wasn't taking any chances.

Do a walk around of your car to check for anything suspicious—stalkers in the backseat, flat tires, lost kittens, or missing children.

I open my driver's side door after completing my visual inspection of the car; no missing children hiding underneath. Good, good. I climb into the seat, lock the doors, and start the ignition. The hum of the engine is reassuring—it sounds normal.

My grip on the steering wheel is hard enough you'd think I need to hang on to stay inside the vehicle. I check my rearview mirror, put the car in reverse, and slowly back out of my parking spot.

Another car is coming this way. Back out quickly so you don't hold them up. They will be so angry if you delay them. Hurry! Hurry! They're waiting. You're making them wait.

Before I stop my car from her backward momentum, I throw it into drive; she growls in protest. A pat on the dashboard and a muttered apology will hopefully satisfy her enough to get me home without breaking down. I'll stress about her retaliation the entire way, though.

I focus on the road ahead—something I can't seem to do in the proverbial sense—as I signal to turn right onto Bowes Street, scanning all directions before proceeding. Once approaching the highway on-ramp, I turn off the radio so I can focus. I need to hear the outside world. My heart rate increases as I join the weekend's highway traffic.

Keep two car lengths back. Check your rearview mirror. Listen for sirens. Watch that car in your blind spot. Adjust your speed to go with the flow of traffic, but not too fast.

Forty minutes later, I merge into the right-hand lane with plenty of time before I exit onto Muskoka District Road. My heart rate steadies. I'm almost home.

Home is safe.

Once I exit the highway, I continue the additional fifteen kilometres to my street as I think about Quinn and Tyler's engagement. I am ecstatic for them, albeit a tad jealous. I'm jealous their lives are moving onto the next step I have longed for. Jealous they are so perfect together and always have each other's support. Jealous they feel safe enough to be vulnerable.

This means they're going to have a wedding. You're Quinn's best friend, so she's going to ask you to be her maid of honour. You'll have to plan a bridal shower and make a speech.

By the time I reach my condo building, my heart could hammer a nail. I'm paralyzed with the fear of the unknown and uncontrollable. Weddings are high on my list of panic-inducing activities. Quinn will understand if I tell her I can't be the maid of honour. Right? Will she even ask me?

You are a terrible friend.

Anxiety. My real BFF. She never leaves my side.

As I sit on the off-white sofa in my 700-square-foot, sparsely decorated third-floor condo, I try to convince myself everything will be fine. As a lifelong introvert, when I started my sophomore year at university, I didn't have a single friend. Sure, I interacted with people during my freshman year, but only when group assignments forced me to. None of the students I teamed up with were the type of people I could see myself developing friendships with, so I didn't try, but I was okay with that. Truth be told, there wasn't a person in the world I would have sought a friendship with at that time in my life. I was so used to keeping to myself—being alone was safer.

Along came Quinn. During our first month of classes that year, I had a Developmental Psychology class that required us to pair up for a project; one with a presentation component. My two worst classroom fears; well, maybe second and third behind ripping my pants and everyone seeing my panties.

She took me under her wing and spent endless hours trying to pull a confidence out of me I was sure she'd never find. She hasn't yet, but that doesn't stop her from trying. My friendship with her has only been outlasted by my relationship with anxiety, but Quinn has never made an issue out of playing second fiddle. She's my best friend, and if she asks something of me, even if it's out of my comfort zone, I'm going to do it. For her.

Crippling anxiety will not stop me from making sure my best friend has the greatest day of her life. I can't promise I won't look sweaty and frazzled in wedding photos, but even if my capacity on that day is holding her dress while she goes to the bathroom, I'll do it.

The last time anyone photographed me without crippling anxiety was in a sonogram. My inability to function like most people has prevented me from getting close to anyone other than Quinn. I even keep most of my family at a distance.

Sure, I dream of finding romantic love someday and hope to have what my parents have—a happy marriage for over forty years. Romantic opportunities are few for me, though. For now, I am focusing on my career—get this—as a youth counsellor.

I work with "troubled" youth to help them process trauma and grief. It is a very taxing but rewarding job. My biggest struggle, however, is trying to detach myself from their problems and not bring their issues home with me. In reality, I need a dump truck to carry my emotional baggage because I am not wired to be unfeeling; I retain every emotion of each of my clients. I think part of what makes me a successful counsellor is the empathy I have for them, which comes at a cost. At least I hope I'm successful.

Probably not. Your coworkers and clients are merely tolerating you because they're aware you are emotionally fragile and they don't want to hurt your feelings.

I try to shake off the feeling of failure, but it won't leave; it never leaves. It's time for wine. Drinking a bottle of wine at 4pm on a Saturday, alone in your home, right after seeing your best friend get engaged is totally normal, right?

Self-medicating with alcohol is never a good idea, but today it's necessary. Standing in my kitchen, I open a bottle of Soave and pour more than my fair share into a glass.

Quinn is engaged; she's getting married. She is going to have a wedding—a huge wedding because everyone loves her. No big deal. What could go wrong? My breathing is fast and shallow as I torment myself with my constructed version of a future reality.

Where are the Oreos?

You haven't been eating healthy. You're never going to find a man with that muffin top. Plus, you need to look good for Quinn's wedding. They'll have pictures online and all over their house for decades.

I tear open the package of Oreos in hopes the sound of my chewing will drown out my relentless internal dialogue. Instead, Oreos remind me of my mother, who both introduced and enabled my addition to them, so my nagging thoughts move on to what a failure I am as a daughter. I haven't spoken to her in over a week.

What if something is wrong and you don't know because you haven't called?

Sigh. I pick up the phone and dial my parents' home phone number, figuring I might as well inform my mother about Quinn's engagement. Maybe she can offer some comfort to ease my nerves about the wedding. After three rings, there's still no answer.

She usually picks up by now. Something is wrong, and because you haven't called, she won't know you love her.

"Hello," my mother says after five rings.

"Mom, hi! Are you okay?"

"Yes, Darling. Everything is fine. Why do you sound so panicked?"

"Oh, no reason. You took longer than normal to answer the phone." I breathe a sigh of relief at hearing her confident, cheerful voice. "I wanted to call to check in, and I have some exciting news."

"Please tell me you've got a boyfriend! Oh, I knew something was up these past few weeks. Tell me all about him." My mother, Alanna Levy, never one for subtlety, has been begging me to "settle down" since I was eighteen. Eleven years later, it hasn't come close to happening, so my sisters have deemed me an Old Maid, destined to remain single forever.

"No, it's not me. Quinn and Tyler got engaged. I was busy the past few weeks helping Tyler set everything up. He proposed at the town dock in Parry Sound. Once she answered, he had a string quartet play the same song that was playing when they first met at the gym. It was sweet."

"That's nice Darling. I am so pleased for Quinn." She utters her words with little enthusiasm. "When will it be your turn?" Now, her tone is a little on the harsh side of her range.

You'll never be good enough. Being single means you are an unwanted failure. No one wants a failure. Not even your own mother.

I release a defeated breath. "Mom, I am not good at dating. If it's meant to be, it will happen." I try to sound hopeful, even though I don't feel it.

"Well, Darling, put yourself out there. It's a new age. There are so many dating apps, or you could meet someone in a club. Maybe try going to the gym; that worked for Quinn." Mom's pitch is increasing with each word, so by the time she's finished her rant, she sounds like Minnie Mouse.

"I'm twenty-nine years old. It's not that easy. I am not going to a club. I don't trust dating apps, and the gym isn't my scene."

Too much sweat, small talk, and ogling.

"That's your problem. You never step out of your comfort zone, and you've become a hermit. You might as well go to the Humane Society and adopt fourteen cats. When I met your father, it didn't happen by sitting around waiting."

"You met dad in High School. Besides, why does it matter so much if I find a boyfriend? Can't I be happy on my own? You talk about a new age, and part of that new age means women can be strong and independent on their own."

"But are you?"

"Yes, I am independent. I bought my car and condo. I live alone and don't depend on anyone. I have a good job and—"

"No," she interrupts. "Are you happy?"

Cue the serotonin. Increase stress level. Unplanned questions mean unplanned answers. Why do people always go off script?

Deep breath. "I… I am happy, for the most part."

"Listen, Zar. I'm not saying you need a man to be complete, but I know you want to have a relationship. It will never happen if you don't at least *attempt* to get out of your comfort zone. Your father and I are proud of you for all you've accomplished on your own, but I'm your mother and I want you to be happy."

"Your concern is touching." That almost sounded sincere. "I just don't want to force something and end up miserable in a marriage like Lexi or Noa."

"Your sisters are not miserable, but you're right; they aren't as happy as they could be. I respect you for waiting to find the right person, but promise me you'll try. Do something that pushes you beyond your invisible barriers. I'm not getting any younger."

"You're fifty-nine. You're hardly at the age you're going to expire at any moment."

"I'm no spring chicken. Can you please, just promise me you'll try? Your father would love to walk his baby girl down the aisle someday before he can't remember where he left his dentures."

I laugh at her comment. My father, Frederick, is sixty, but after working as a firefighter for over thirty years, he is still in great shape for his age. "Okay. I'll try. After all of Quinn's wedding planning is in order, I'll try to make more of an effort to put myself out there."

"Love you, Darling."

"I love you too, Momma. Tell Daddy I said hello and that I love him, too."

"I will. We'll talk soon. Please tell Quinn I said congratulations. Bye, my beautiful girl."

Beautiful? Who is she kidding? You are a grey sprinkle on a rainbow cupcake. Plain Jane. You have miles to go before you even hit mediocre.

Where's the wine?

As I lie in bed, with a pretty wicked buzz from the half bottle of wine I drank, I can't stop thinking about what my best friend's wedding will entail. Is she even going to ask me to be her maid of honour? I mean, she knows better than anyone how I struggle to be in crowds of people, and especially being the centre of attention.

What if you fall flat on your face walking down the aisle? What if Tyler pairs you up with an unfortunate best man? What if you forget to untuck your dress from your pantyhose after your inevitable bathroom trip?

This is a disaster. Maybe if she asks, I can decline.

No. I will support my best friend. I will step out of my comfort zone, like I promised, and I will be there for the woman who has always been there for me. Nothing bad will happen.

But what if...

Sunday morning, I wake up, feeling as if I haven't slept at all. I'm not sure I did. My head is throbbing—likely on account of the wine binge—and I need some caffeine. Anxiety could use a little boost today.

One can never be too careful in preventing an unnecessary electronics fire, so I always unplug unused small appliances; once I plug the coffee maker in, I wait for the water to heat. My new favourite breakfast blend better do the trick to help me survive the day. While my coffee percolates, I check the fridge for something to eat. Oreos for breakfast after having them as a main course last night is probably a bad idea.

All I have left in the fridge are two eggs, some ketchup, and a DIY facemask I found a recipe for online but lost interest in before it "worked its magic." Delicious. I'll have to add grocery shopping to my otherwise empty agenda for the day.

Grocery shopping on a Sunday? The store will be so busy. You might not even be able to find parking. Most of the stuff you need will be sold out, then you'll have to wait in the long line to buy half of the items you wanted. Don't forget about the small talk you'll be subjected to.

After considering the downfalls of weekend shopping, I decide I'll grab some things tomorrow after work. Today, I can pick up something from the deli that will suffice for lunch and dinner. Oreos are fine for breakfast.

Leave the house? What if you get hit by a car walking down the street? What if you get into the deli, and while you try to decide what you want, people assume you are waiting in line, so everyone is standing behind you waiting for you to order? They'll be so angry with you.

I think the deli delivers.

Just as I take my coffee mug from the coffeemaker, my phone lights up. It doesn't ring, nor vibrate, because both sounds make my anxiety level spike.

I glance down to see who is calling and realize it's my sister Lexi, who is seven years older than me. At thirty-six, she has three kids and has been a stay-at-home mom since her oldest child Hollis was born eight years ago. Her husband, Lorenzo Luna, is six years older than her and not my favourite person in the world. My sister went from Lexi Levy to Lexi Luna. Her middle name is Olivia—she is LOL. She does everything *but* make me laugh out loud.

"Hi, Lexi. To what do I owe this pleasure?" I lean back on my kitchen island; I'll need all the support I can get to survive this conversation.

"Wow! Would it kill you to dial back the sarcasm?"

"It just might. What's up?"

Lexi calling me without a reason never happens.

"Just calling to check on my baby sister. I saw on social media that Quinn and Tyler got engaged. I thought you'd be feeling a little sad because you're still single."

Subtle jab.

"No, I'm *thrilled* for them. I can be happy for her without needing the same thing myself."

"Of course, of course. I shouldn't have assumed." She takes in an audible breath. "I know you're a modern woman who is career driven and happy being single."

"Yes, I'm fine with how my life is right now." If I say it enough, maybe I can convince myself.

"How is your job?" she asks, as if she is trying to be interested in my life for once.

"It's going fine, thanks." Time to put her out of her misery because I know talking about anyone but herself is painful for her. "How are the kids? And Lorenzo?"

Her tone notably changes to one of triumph. "They are all doing wonderful. There's nothing like being a mom, you know? Oh, I didn't mean it like that. I just mean, it's the greatest joy in life. I couldn't be happier." She says that last statement with a bit too much enthusiasm, as if she's practiced saying it a thousand times while driving home from her kids' soccer practices.

"That's great, Lex. Listen, I really need to get going. I have to go run some errands and prepare for some meetings this week, but call anytime, okay?"

"Sure Zara. I'll tell my hubby and the kids you say hi."

I roll my eyes. She loves to say "my hubby" as if she has to clarify which Lorenzo she is referring to. "Okay, thanks. Bye!" I can't hang up the phone fast enough. Conversing with my sister shouldn't be torture, but she is so fake, it's exhausting.

Where are the blasted Oreos? Forget her. I don't need to live her life to be happy. I am going to live my own life, my own way! Starting today.

Right after my Oreos.

I sit at my kitchen island, chomping away on my twistable treat, staring vacantly at my kitchen sink. Am I letting life pass me by? Is my anxiety causing me to miss out on the things that would make me happy? Maybe everyone has a point. I've spent so much time living in fear, drowning in worry, I can't force myself to live in the now.

I could survive on a delivery order, but I feel like it's time for me to take control of my life. It's time for me to venture outdoors without a specific purpose; to expose myself to sunlight without being forced.

What if you expose yourself to the sun too much and you develop skin cancer? Melanoma is serious. What if you don't pay attention and you get run over by a taxi? What if a gang shootout starts and you get caught in the crossfire? Home is safe.

Some fresh air will be good. It may even help me sleep tonight, so I'll be well rested for my meetings tomorrow. I don't have to prepare for any meetings today, like I told Lexi. That was just the first excuse I could come up with, so I didn't have to listen to her pretend she's living in domestic bliss. Of course, I had everything prepared days ago. That's not something I would leave until the last minute!

So instead of wasting my day inside, I'm going outside. By choice.

I. Can. Do. This.

I enter my bedroom, that I have thoughtfully decorated as my own peaceful sanctuary, and open the door to my wardrobe. What does one wear to go outside just because? Track pants? No, that's too sloppy. None of my jeans fit, thanks to Oreos, wine, and my constant cravings for mac and cheese. Leggings. Women are always walking around in leggings, looking cute. I settle on a pair of solid black cotton leggings, a taupe tunic top with a high neck and long sleeves, and my comfortable below-the-knee black boots. My hair is uncooperative, so I brush it and let it do its thing. Who am I to argue?

Why do I look like a potato? Like I'm actually trying to star in a french fry commercial right now. Ugh. This is going to have to do. It's not like I am going to see anyone I know. I need to get out the door before I change my mind. I am doing this.

Make sure you unplug the coffeemaker. Check that all the windows are locked. It would be a perfect opportunity for a serial killer to sneak in while you're out.

After catering to anxiety's checklist, I grab my small shoulder bag, ensure I have my wallet, cell phone, and keys, throw the strap over my head and strike out the door. I am really doing this; acting like a proper adult.

I take the stairs to the lobby and I'm not sure if my heart rate has increased from the paltry amount of physical activity, or from the thought of being in the outside world.

A deep breath helps slow my heart rate before I exit the building onto the sidewalk. It's a beautiful, late-September day. A deep inhale of the fresh air calms me enough to walk in the deli's direction. One foot in front of the other; just like the other outdoor humans.

The deli is about one kilometre from my home, so I consider taking the long way to get in a bit more exercise. Certainly, after my recent indulgences, I could stand to burn a few extra calories.

I glance around at the buildings lining the street, the curated gardens, and the people happily walking along the sidewalks. The street is not overly busy, as I'd expect for a Sunday, post-tourist season. Distinct aromas from the various restaurants invade my senses, so I analyze each one to see which my stomach responds to. This isn't so bad. Everything is fine.

Several hundred metres down the road, walking through an area full of white-collar businesses, I reach a real estate office on the corner. I decide I'll turn right and walk an extra block because this fresh air business is kind of nice. I walk past the edge of the building when I hear a wretched squealing sound and feel a searing pain through my body. Before I can comprehend what is happening, I'm on the cold ground on my back. Ow.

B icycle brakes. The sound was bicycle brakes.

"Oh my gosh! I am so sorry! Are you okay? Can you hear me?"

I am lying on the sidewalk with my entire body in pain. The gentlest hands reach behind my neck to raise my head from the concrete.

Looking directly into my own green eyes are the most enthralling eyes I have ever seen. It's as if they are kaleidoscopes of colour—mossy green speckled with a light celery shade. They belong to a deep, tender voice that asks again, "Are you okay? Can you hear me?"

"Am I dead?"

He laughs. "No, you're not dead, but you're probably going to be sore for a few days. I am so sorry. I normally never ride on the sidewalk, but they are doing construction, so I was trying to get around it." He pauses, then asks, "Can you get up? Let me help you."

A bike. That can be filed away under "things that might go wrong outside."

The stranger attached to the beautiful eyes and sexy voice places his arms underneath mine and first moves me to a seated position. From here, I can better see his chiseled jaw and full lips as he squats beside me; he's remarkable. Once I am steady, he lifts me up to stand, but leaves his hands on my arms for support. I am mortified, but his touch is so comforting, I almost forget what happened.

"Um, thanks."

"I can't apologize enough. I feel terrible. Please let me make it up to you."

"Oh, no. I'm fine." I am not.

"Do you need to see a doctor? Is anything broken? Please, what can I do to help? Can I get you something to drink?" His eyes dart from side to side. "If for no other reason than to spend some more time with a beautiful stranger. I'm Zach, by the way. Zachary Haynes." He rambles almost as much as I do. Why is it so adorable when other people do it?

I look behind me, wondering who he could be talking about. Beautiful stranger? He can't mean me. His first impression of me was seeing me lying on my back on a public sidewalk, dressed like a potato. I run my fingers through my hair, which is an anxious habit I have, but in this instance, it's because my hair *is* a tragic disaster. I look down at his crumpled bike. "It seems you were headed somewhere in a hurry. Don't let me keep you. I'm totally fine." I try my best to fake confidence in that statement.

He looks disappointed. "I was out for some exercise. I have nowhere else to be. I mean, aside from nearly killing you with my bicycle. We could have skipped that part. Can I buy you lunch? Try to make this meeting less of a debacle?" He waves his hand down toward his bike, then at me, reminding me of our minor mishap.

Who even says debacle? That's suspish. You'll end up on Murder Mystery, and Makeup *if you don't get out of here. What would someone like him ever want with someone like you? He is model-level beautiful, and you are a walking calamity. Say something so he doesn't feel guilty anymore.*

"Oh, no. It's fine, honest. I'm just out for a walk. I'll head back home. Don't worry about me." I'm spitting out brief sentences in rapid-fire succession, trying to ease the awkwardness. Awkwardness that is me—he is perfect.

"Can I at least make sure you get home okay? You had quite a fall, and it would be the gentlemanly thing to do."

He is too good to be true. He must be a serial killer who preys on unsuspecting potatoes by using his good looks and captivating eyes—he's like Ted Bundy. Abort. Abort. Get home to safety. Do not let him follow you home. Home is safe.

"No, no. I insist. I am completely fine. No doctor, no lunch. I'm going to walk myself back home. Have a good day, Zachary Haynes." I turn and walk away.

"Goodbye," he says. Then whispers under his breath, "Beautiful stranger."

Maybe I should have asked if he hit his head in our collision. I am not even remotely beautiful. Quinn, now she is beautiful. Every time she dragged me to a party or a get-together, people always flocked to her magnetic personality while I'd search for the family dog to sit in the corner with, refusing to socialize or even drink anything. Beautiful is not a word I would ever use to describe myself. Average. Tragic. Clumsy. Awkward. But never beautiful. He is a serial killer.

Monday morning, I wake up feeling like a bus hit me. I mean, a bicycle levelled me; that's bad enough. I expect a busy day at work with meetings and client visits. One of my most "troubled" youngsters, Chelsea Wells, is coming in for an appointment today, and I always feel emotionally drained after our encounters.

She is only fifteen, yet she has been through more trauma than most people face in their entire lives. We're slowly working through her issues, but she is riddled with anxiety because of everything she has been through. My anxiety helps me to be empathetic toward her, and I am trying to give her coping mechanisms to handle her PTSD. Those who can't do, teach.

I get out of my cozy bed, slide my feet into my bunny slippers, and head toward the kitchen. My condo always feels so lonely in the mornings. I have resorted to speaking to my ivy plant, but it's not like she has anyone else to talk to or somewhere to go. She's the only thing I can keep alive aside from myself—and that's questionable.

Coffee is not an option today because I need my mind focused. A nice peppermint tea should do the trick. I fill the kettle and place it on the stove, then retreat to my bedroom to choose what to wear. I always try to look professional, but not overstated because my young clients need to view me as approachable. A dark-grey pencil skirt and an emerald-green blouse will do. A pair of practical kitten heels complete today's look. I lay everything out on my bed and once I hear the kettle whistle, I rush back to take it off the stove, then make my tea in a travel mug.

After a brisk shower, I dress in the clothes I have already chosen. I pull my long, chocolate-brown hair into a quick bun, smooth a tinted moisturizer over my face, and put on some lip gloss. I glance at my deepening worry lines around my eyes and on my forehead. Yesterday I was a potato; today I'm a pug.

My schedule dictates I have more than an hour before I'm supposed to start work, but today I'm going early.

Grab your reading glasses. You don't want to be in a meeting and not be able to read your notes. Make sure you've turned the stove off. Lock the windows. Don't forget your keys, phone, and wallet. Brace yourself for the dangers of the outside world. There's no telling what could happen today.

After checking the window locks, I stop at the stove to confirm it is off. The first three times I checked have not convinced me. Phone, check. Wallet, check. Keys? Where are my keys? I don't have time for this. I rummage through my purse, confident I had them yesterday when I returned home. It occurs to me to open the door and look in the hallway. To my horror, I left my keys in the lock overnight.

Anyone could have walked in. There might be someone hiding in your closet. Someone must have taken the keys and made copies so they can break in while you are least expecting it.

I try to calm the panic rising within me by being logical, but anxiety is anything but logical. It's fine. I'm fine. The keys didn't move. Nothing bad happened.

Good thing I didn't let the mysterious serial killer, Zachary Haynes, follow me home. He really was dreamy, though. I mean, what a way to go.

I hate to admit I stayed awake thinking about him for far too long last night. Maybe I should have taken him up on his offer for lunch. I promised my mother I would try. No, I said I would try after Quinn's wedding plans were in place. For now, I will focus on my friend; she needs me.

She doesn't.

I push the vision of those magical green eyes out of my head, grab my keys from the door after triple checking that I've locked it, and make a mental note to contact building maintenance for a new deadbolt. A single girl in a low-crime, small city can never be too prudent.

Calm washes over me as I turn my car on, and everything sounds normal. The idea of getting into a rolling death trap every day will never be easy for me, but it's less stressful than taking public transit. I tried.

Check your mirrors. Monitor your blind spots. Stay in the lane-of-least resistance. Keep your distance and monitor the crosswalk signals. Watch for bike riders.

My thoughts drift to one specific bike-riding person.

I shake the image of Zach from my head as I drive to work. Thoughts of him creep back in as a sweet love song plays quietly on the radio. Zach and Zara. Zara Haynes. Zara Rihanna Haynes. I like the sound of that. What are the chances we'd both have "Z" names? "ZZ Haynes, Zaza, Zachara?"

Get a grip. You'll never see him again. Even if you do, you rushed away from him as if he were a leper. You blew it.

A sigh of frustration escapes my lips as I turn into my office building's parking lot. My office is on the tenth floor of a fifteen-storey building. Our counselling services are nestled in amongst accountants, lawyers, various brokers, and other businesses. The main floor has a small coffee shop, but I avoid it like the plague. Standing in line, making small talk with coworkers, is not my idea of a relaxing break.

Then it occurs to me, I forgot my tea. I was so distracted by my keys and potential break-in that I left my travel mug on the kitchen counter. Now I have to stop at the coffee shop after all. Thankfully, I arrived twenty minutes before anyone else, so I likely won't have to speak to anyone other than the cashier.

Decide what you want and calculate the cost before you get to the counter. Make sure you have the correct change so you don't keep people waiting. No one likes to be kept waiting when they're about to start their workday—especially un-caffeinated.

I dig through my wallet and find a two-dollar coin. I'll give the change as a tip.

Waiting in line behind two other customers, there's something familiar about the man ordering. I ignore the thought and mentally chastise myself for obsessing over a complete stranger.

What kind of pathetic woman falls for a man after he runs her over with a bicycle? You need to keep your distance from people. You're a hot mess.

As the man at the front of the line grabs his coffee and turns around, I let out an unintentional sound of surprise that sounds a bit like a feral cat.

Zach.

Zach stands there, staring at me as if he's found water in a desert. Why is he looking at me like that?

Why is he here? Did he follow you? You've never seen him before and suddenly, he shows up at your workplace? This is really suspicious. Sound the alarms! Serial Killer.

He approaches me after he has taken a moment to remove the shocked look from his face, but I'm certain I still look like I'm trying to catch flies with my mouth.

"Hi! What are you doing here? How are you feeling? Are you okay?"

I blink several times. He's not a figment of my imagination. "Wow, that's a lot of questions at once. What are *you* doing here?"

He smiles the most knee-weakening smile I have ever seen. "I work here. The mortgage brokerage on the sixth floor… uh… that's where I work."

"I… I've never seen you before. My office is on the tenth floor."

"I've never seen you before, either. I would have remembered. Are you new here?"

"No, I've worked here for five years. I started here shortly after University. I don't hang around much, other than for work. Interoffice mingling isn't really my thing."

That was an over-share, Zara.

"Well, that explains it. I only opened my business about eight months ago." He makes no effort to hide the fact he is scanning me head-to-toe. "Will you let me buy you a coffee today? It's the least I can do. You must be feeling sore."

"Um… you've already paid. I don't want to be a bother. I came prepared." Like a loser, I hold up my toonie.

"Can I buy you a coffee another time, then? I'm not only asking because I feel guilty for knocking you to the sidewalk. I would genuinely like a reason to see you again."

I stand there, feeling a bit surprised. Was this man honest with me about his intentions? Are there actually men who do that? Aside from my father and Tyler, I didn't think they existed. But is he being honest? Or is he trying to earn my trust so he can slaughter me and preserve me in formaldehyde?

He can't be interested in you. He's seen what a hot mess you are. It's a pity coffee. Or a ploy.

Feeling defeated as my internal dialogue fills me with doubt, I ask, "Why?"

He looks surprised again. Winning girls over must be easy for him. He looks like what rom-coms call "a panty-melter". "I find you interesting, and you haven't even told me your name. It's just a coffee. What do you say?"

I give him a half shrug and cross my arms. "Okay, I guess. Maybe tomorrow. I really have to get to work to prepare for my day."

His eyes light up as he smiles at me. I'm not sure if he truly meant what he said about being interested in me, or if he is trying to charm me so he can murder me. Only time will tell, because as I look into his eyes, I can't bring myself to resist him, even under potential threat of death.

"Tomorrow sounds great. Same time, same place?"

A feeling of giddiness bubbles up in my belly, so I struggle to calm it. "Perfect." And boy, he is perfect.

If something seems perfect, it's usually too good to be true. Don't let your guard down. You're going to get hurt.

"So, what do I call you?" he asks as he brings my train of thought to a halt.

"Oh, I'm sorry. Zara. Zara Levy."

"Zara. That's a beautiful name. I'll look forward to our coffee tomorrow, Zara." He smiles and turns toward the stairs.

I wonder if he takes the stairs instead of the elevator every day; that explains why he is so fit. My lazy behind could benefit from a few flights of stairs too, but who am I kidding? I work on the tenth floor. The few times we had fire drills, I almost took my chances inside.

A smile plays at my lips as I try to contain my excitement, but a quick anxiety check squashes any threatening smiles.

Is this a date? What will you wear? What will you talk about?

Shut up for one minute. Let me enjoy this moment.

"A large peppermint tea, please," I say to the cashier. I suddenly have the feeling I can take on the world. Okay, maybe not the world, but at least some awkward conversation or eye contact.

I survive the ascent to the tenth floor with no conversation. I step out of the elevator into the eerie silence of my department and make my way to my office. It's not a glamourous corner office, but it is my personal space that represents how hard I have worked to get here. I've decorated it with cozy, modern finishes, trying to make it feel comfortable without feeling sterile. I am proud of this room, and grateful to help young people here.

My desk chair creaks beneath me as I swivel back and forth, sip my peppermint tea, and think about tomorrow morning. I wish I could hit the fast-forward button on this day so I can see Zach again. There's still a few minutes before I need to dive into work, so I decide to search Zach online. Without any social media—despite Quinn's protests that I should "join the other twenty-somethings in this century"—I can only look up his professional information via a search engine.

My search pulls up results for **Zachary Haynes Mortgage Broker Muskoka**.

"Sweet mother of..." I say, under my breath. He is even more beautiful in photos. How is a person that photogenic? He is exquisite. That sandy blond, unruly hair, his chiseled jaw, just a hint of facial hair, and kissable lips (not that I would know); the man is a ten. But, beyond his looks, he's kind and polite. So far.

He is out of your league. He's a mortgage broker—his world is finance, and yours is feelings. You have nothing in common and you'd never fit into his world.

I'm so immersed in my internet search, drooling over this unattainable man, I don't notice my boss enter until he's standing behind me, looking at my computer screen.

You are an embarrassment to yourself. You are the reason they have to put directions on shampoo bottles. If your brain were dynamite, there wouldn't be enough to blow your nose.

"Oh, hello. Good morning, Sir. I didn't hear you come in." I try to minimize my internet tabs. Thirty seconds too late.

"I suspected as much. You looked quite engrossed in whatever you were doing. I called your name."

"Sorry, Mr. Stafford. I was looking up someone I met earlier." There's no point in trying to cover my tracks, because my face will betray me with a flush of colour.

"That's fine Zara. You aren't on the clock yet. I was coming to see if you've prepared for our staff meeting this morning. I need you to give a brief report on how your clients are doing and ask if you need any recommendations for any of them."

"Right." I look at Mr. Joseph Stafford, who is about fifty years old, slightly overweight, and has a unibrow that makes him look like he is permanently scowling. All that aside, he is a wonderful, understanding boss, and I am honoured to be working with him. "I'm all ready, Sir. I prepared my notes on Friday. See you in the boardroom at 9:30?"

"Yes, that's great Zara. I'll continue my rounds, and you can continue," he says, waving a finger toward my computer screen, "whatever it was you were doing."

"Uh, thank you, Sir. I'll be getting to work now." I favourite my internet search so I can come back to those pictures later.

Time to open my case files to review for the meeting that will be in just over an hour, and prepare for my clients scheduled this afternoon. I pull up Chelsea's file notes and my heart clenches.

Social services took Chelsea in when she was young, but at fifteen, she has yet to be adopted and will probably age out of the system in a few years. I intend to do as much as I can for her in that time. She has deep-rooted trust and abandonment issues, in addition to PTSD.

They sent her to our office many years after her ordeal, and I have been working with her for over four years now. She has made some great strides and I am proud of her, but I know it's weighing heavily on her mind that she will be with no support in the not-too-far future. I wish there was more I could do.

For the next forty minutes reading through client notes, adding notations, and researching different treatment options. Maybe today we can have a breakthrough.

Our office "mother", Adele, always insists on having healthy snacks available as opposed to more traditional options of croissants or doughnuts. Carby goodness is my preference, but I grab an apple from the office kitchen on my way to the boardroom fifteen minutes early. My waistline appreciates Adele. Tastebuds are undecided.

I examine my seating options upon entering the boardroom and settle on an optimal position. One would assume, after five years of working here, I'd have a particular spot, but after each meeting, I come up with new criteria for the ideal seat. Today's list: proper line of sight to Mr. Stafford, distance from my nearest neighbour, and a direct path to the door in the event of a fire. Check, check, and check.

The room is bland, with stark white walls, a large table void of style, surrounded by standard black office chairs on wheels—some in better shape than others. The wall of windows might let in some light, but the ugly blinds are always closed, leaving the only light coming from the broken slats filtering slants of sunlight through, and the fluorescent bulbs overhead. Today it seems we are in luck; none of them are flickering.

I sit down, spread my notes in front of me, double check my pen is working, and bite into my apple. I become absorbed in rereading my notes for the thirteenth time. Turns out, chewing apple drowns out commotion because I was blissfully unaware that my coworkers had filed into the room. By the time I look up, the room is full, and Mr. Stafford is in his position at the head of the table. Thanks, anxiety. Way to be mindful of my surroundings.

What do you do with your apple core now? Just hold on to it. You don't want to draw attention to yourself by getting up. Add "proximity to garbage can" to your seat-finding checklist.

My focus is directed at Mr. Stafford, who is giving a review of company policies—no inter-office dating, no bullying, matters with clients are confidential and are not to leave the office; blah, blah, blah. Nothing new. All the while, I'm fiddling with my browning apple core, stressing over what I should do with it.

Two other counsellors make their presentations, and as expected, no one feels the need for any second opinions. They claim all is going well with their clients.

What is wrong with you? Are you even capable of doing this job? Everyone else is here acting like adults, and you're warming the seat, contributing nothing.

"Miss Levy, would you like to present?"

"Of course, Sir." I stand and straighten my skirt as best I can with an apple core in my left hand and try to muster up a modicum of confidence. "I am currently seeing forty-two clients, ranging in age from seven to fifteen. Everything is progressing as expected, but I have a few requests for second opinions."

"Proceed," Mr. Stafford says with a reassuring nod.

I fight the urge to toss my apple core at the garbage can from a distance. "My first request is for my youngest client, Isla Harding. As I said, she's seven, but she is having significant sleep issues because of night terrors. I have given her and her foster parents some techniques to help and counselled her extensively, trying to get to the root of the issue, but she remains very guarded, as if she's scared to open up. Does anyone have any experience in a situation like this?"

My hands are shaking and my heart is pounding in my ears when I look up to see all eyes on me. After a few seconds, someone chimes in.

"You're telling me you've worked here for what, five years, and you have no experience getting a child to open up to you? What have you been doing?"

My heart might explode out of my chest as my stomach purges my partially digested apple if I don't hold myself together.

He's right. There's no reason you shouldn't be able to handle this case on your own. If you were any good at your job, you'd have that little girl sleeping by now. You should do everyone a favour and quit.

I blink away my tears as I turn to face the chastising voice of Mr. Patrick Kennedy. A well-built Italian man in his mid-forties, who lately has been so full of resentment toward anyone whom he perceives to be more successful than him, or more well-liked—which is everyone. A tapeworm holds more appeal.

Deep breath. "Mr. Kennedy, with all due respect, it's not as if I have no experience with getting children to open up to me. This young client is a troublesome case, and I suspect there's something going on that she is afraid to share. She also deals with social anxiety, so getting her to divulge anything is a challenge. With no evidence of anything untoward, I can't approach the authorities." I take another breath and strengthen my resolve. "So, what I'm asking my colleagues, you included, is if you have any advice on how to proceed. Anything *new* I can try that I may not have thought of."

"Miss Levy is right, Pat. We aren't here to question each other's effectiveness. We're here to make each other *more* effective for the benefit of our clients. So, I would appreciate if you kept your unhelpful remarks to yourself." Mr. Stafford looks at Patrick, setting his unibrow in a firm line.

If looks could kill, I would be dead after the glare Patrick sends in my direction. Instead of shrinking back into my seat, I hold his gaze and try not to let him intimidate me. The sweat dripping down the small of my back would give me away in an instant, but I don't back down.

The friendly voice of our office gossip, Mrs. Erin Copeland, breaks through the tension. "I think you know exactly what you have to do. Continue earning her trust, speaking to her, and when she feels ready, she will open up to you. There's not much more you can do for her beyond that."

That's not what I was hoping to hear. "I think you're right, Erin. I wanted to see if anyone had any specific advice or personal experience that would help, but I presume she needs time."

Patrick is still glaring at me when I look across the table. The weight of his stare unnerves me—but that's not difficult.

Mr. Stafford attempts to move the meeting along. "What are the other cases you wanted to discuss, Zara?"

I sit back down and wave off the question. "Not to worry, Mr. Stafford. I've figured them out."

The meeting continues for another forty-five minutes. When Mr. Stafford dismisses us, he asks Patrick to stay behind. This can't be good. I've never known a person to hold a grudge better than Patrick Kennedy, and it appears I've hurt the man's ego. He's always been short with me, but I've yet to be a recipient of his outright hatred before today. I'm not the first one in the office he's had an issue with, though. It's not true what they say about a woman scorned; Hell hath no fury like Mr. Kennedy.

I throw my brown apple core in the garbage can on my way out of the room, avoiding eye contact with Patrick.

Once I'm in my office, I work to busy myself to avoid thinking about what conversation is happening in that room. It's out of my hands—but that doesn't mean I can keep it out of my head.

Why didn't you figure that case out on your own? Are you totally useless?

My anxiety is overtaking me and it causes me to feel physically ill. I sip on some of my lukewarm tea from this morning, which reminds me of Zach. I pull up the search from my favourites menu and look at his handsome face. Even if he never wants to speak to me again after our non-date tomorrow, at this moment, his virtual presence is calming.

He'll find someone better. You're not worth the time or effort.

B y 5:30 in the evening, I am standing in line at the grocery store checkout. It is the last place I want to be right now, but unless I choose to eat fast food or delivery all week, I figured I should pick up some essentials. Oreos, check.

Please don't make eye contact, please don't make eye contact. Just stare at the floor with a grumpy face and no one will bother you.

When it's my turn to check out, the cashier scans my items and engages in her obligatory small talk. "Hi, how are you?"

Her name tag says Gertrude, which is quite an old-fashioned name for a sixteen-year-old girl. Part of me wants to say, "Listen, Gertrude. I'm not in the mood for small talk. Bag my groceries and put the Oreos on top so I can reach over and eat some on my way home, would ya?" But I don't. Instead, I reply "I'm good, thank you. How are you?" Like I care. No one is ever honest during small talk.

"Oh, I'm okay." She glances at me as if she's checking that I'm listening, when really I'm considering slipping a plastic bag over my head. "I'm stressed because of school, work, and my social life. You know how it is."

Um, no, Gertrude. I don't *know* how it is. What is this social life you speak of? Perhaps part of your problem is that you can't read facial cues, because I am aware of what my face is saying. "Of course." I plaster on my best fake smile. I must look terrifying, because Gertrude suddenly doesn't seem too interested in talking to me. Mission accomplished.

"That'll be $67.84."

I blink and scan the list of items on the computer screen. Wow, that adds up fast. "Debit, please."

Please don't decline. That would be mortifying.

Not wanting to hold up the line, I rush to grab my bags of groceries, throw them in the cart, and snatch the receipt from Gertrude the second "approved" flashes on the screen. I'm off toward the exit like my keister is on fire. It's home time.

Home is safe.

Once I load everything into my car and perform my routine inspection, I climb in and ease out of my parking spot. Suddenly, my car rings. Quinn is calling.

"Hey Amiga, how are you?"

"Hi, Chica. Why do you sound weird?"

"I'm in the car; just leaving the grocery store. How was the rest of your weekend?"

"It was amazing. We called our family Saturday night, and they were all thrilled. My mom was beside herself and can't wait to get things going, so I was wondering if you'd come dress shopping on Saturday."

"Of course! Anything for you." I giggle.

"Oh, good. My maid of honour needs to be there to help me find *the* dress."

I'm a bit gutted she asked someone else to be her maid of honour. I truly thought she'd ask me, but I guess she knows it would be too hard.

"You need your maid of honour there for sure. Who did you choose?" I try to hide my feelings of rejection.

"Girl, are you for real asking me that? You, silly! There's no one else in the world I'd want up there, other than you."

My tears flood my eyes and as soon as I'm safely pulled into my parking spot, the floodgates open. I bawl like a baby.

"What's wrong, Chica? Do you not want to be in the wedding party? I realize it's a lot to ask of you, but I wouldn't be asking if I didn't think you could do it. You're so much stronger than you think, Zara, and I want you up there with me." Quinn's normally measured and confident voice expresses a touch of panic, and I hate myself for making her worry.

"They're not bad tears. I've had an emotional roller coaster of a day and being there to support you when you marry the love of your life couldn't make me happier," I blubber through my tears.

"I knew I could count on you. Don't be afraid to tell me if things are too much for you, okay? I don't want you becoming overwhelmed and retreating into your hermit-hole."

"For you, I'll find a way to manage."

"You need to find that same confidence in doing things for yourself, Zar. Slowly but surely."

I debate for half a second to tell her about my coffee-date, or coffee-non-date, in the morning, but decide against it to spare myself the embarrassment when Zach inevitably bails on me. I'll talk to her about it after. Chances are, I'll need her help to analyze every glance, word, and breath *if* he shows up.

It would be rude to tell her you have to go to put your groceries away, even if you call her back. But you can't risk shutting the car off and disconnecting her, either. Sit and wait. Don't be rude. You don't want her to be upset with you.

"I'm trying, Amiga. I promised my mother, after her incessant nagging, that I'd make more of an effort after your wedding."

"What?" she shrieks.

"What, what?"

"You are not waiting until after my wedding, Zara! You are going to try now. Life is short. You can't keep waiting to put everyone else first before you go for what you want. You know after my wedding, something else will come along to distract you, and you'll put it off again."

She's right. It's what I always do. I use helping others as an excuse not to put myself out there and potentially get hurt. It's an effective, but lonely defence mechanism.

"Okay, I'll make more of an effort, but I won't force anything. I want to see how things go and take it one day at a time." But I'm not mentioning Zach yet.

"I accept those terms." She laughs. "I am so proud of you, Chica."

I blush at her words, feeling childish that my friend needs to tell me these things. Even when she knows I'll never believe a word.

"Thanks. I'm sorry to cut you short, but I need to get these groceries inside and make myself something proper to eat. I've been surviving on Oreos for two days."

"How long have you been sitting in your car waiting? Why didn't you say something?"

"It's no big deal... maybe five minutes. I didn't want to cut you off. Text me or call when you have details for Saturday, and I'll be at your beck and call."

"You're ridiculous, Zara Levy." She chuckles again, so I know she didn't mean to offend me with that statement, but I'm well aware I'm ridiculous. "I'll talk to you soon."

"Bye, Quinny."

After struggling inside with my groceries, I set everything on my kitchen island and immediately search my condo for anything out of place. Home might be safe, but that doesn't mean it's impervious to threats. Once I know there are no burglars or kidnappers lurking in my closet, I can put my groceries away in peace without panicking over every sound that permeates my condo's walls.

Sesame-ginger ramen is on the menu tonight, so I prepare a package of noodles, steam some vegetables, and top it with a pre-made sauce. I settle in on my sofa and flip the TV on to watch reruns of shows I've seen countless times. The familiarity of old shows eases my anxiety because I know what the outcome is. It doesn't matter what the subject matter is, as long as I know how it turns out at the end. It's the unknown that terrifies me.

Halfway through slurping down my noodles, my appetite disappears. The unknown of what will happen tomorrow when I meet Zach, along with my new duty as Quinn's maid of honour, has proven to be too much for my nerves. I take deep, calming breaths, trying to ease my panic.

I fail. My worry over the potential problems that could arise is too powerful for logic to compete with. My life would be so much easier if I could rationalize the crippling panic away, but I have yet to achieve that level of skill.

Maybe someday, but today is not that day.

s this what people talk about when they say "it's fate"? Zach crashing into my life—literally—just as I told my mom and Quinn I'd branch out of my comfort zone? I've never believed in fate because it implies things that happen to us are predestined and, if that's the case, what's the point in trying? I guess it's too soon to tell, but it wasn't too soon for me to stay awake all night worrying about it.

Once I shower, I get dressed in the outfit I chose last night. I opted for a cream-coloured blouse with black buttons, black tapered slacks, and pointy-toed heels that match my shirt. I feel sophisticated and comfortable without looking like I'm trying too hard.

Today, I add a little extra to my makeup routine by putting on some muted eyeshadow, mascara, and a more vibrant lip gloss. I blow-dry my hair and wear it down with its natural waves. Looking at myself, I acknowledge this is as good as I'm going to get.

Girls like you—damaged girls—don't get happy endings, so don't get your hopes up. Why did you agree to this? You should have come up with an excuse, like you always do. It's too bad you can't text him to cancel with an irrational excuse.

I shake off the feelings of inadequacy that plague me and open my purse to check for the day's necessities. Everything is accounted for. I need to follow up with maintenance regarding my new door lock. They didn't seem too thrilled yesterday when I called, but I pay a small fortune in condo fees, so if they won't let me change my lock, they better do it for me.

It's time to do this—try something new. You will not die. It's just a coffee in a public café. Maybe he is a terrible conversationalist, and you won't even be interested in him. Maybe he has disgusting feet. Maybe he indeed is a dreamy serial killer, and your internal torment will be over soon.

It's more likely he is a fully functional human being capable of holding a conversation, and you'll be the one to blow it.

I arrive at work about fifteen minutes earlier than necessary. I am torn between sitting in my car like a creeper or going inside the coffee shop to wait like a creeper. Option A, or Option B. At least if I go inside, I can pretend like I have something to do.

My car's lights flash as I press the button to confirm it's locked. My shoes are already hurting my feet, so the entire day wearing them will be a chore. Quinn convinced me to buy heels, thinking they would make me more confident and, I admit, they are pretty, but it doesn't make me confident when I am walking around like a baby giraffe, fresh out of the womb.

What I see when I enter the coffee shop takes my breath away. Zach is standing inside waiting; he's waiting for me. When he spots me, he smiles the most beautiful smile I've ever seen. His green eyes sparkle under the fluorescent lighting, and I notice for the first time how white his teeth are. He's wearing a navy button-up dress shirt with the top button undone, charcoal slacks, black shoes and belt. His sleeves are unbuttoned and rolled up to expose his sinewy forearms. He's fit, but not bulky. He is flawless. Perhaps aside from his murderous ways—to be determined.

"Hi," I squeak.

"Good morning, Zara," he says with an even bigger smile than before.

The inside of my stomach is being tickled by butterflies—or raging stomach acid. Po-tay-toe, po-tah-toe. What is happening to me? My eyes dart around the room, taking in the coffee-themed décor and sparse fake plants. I'm struggling to find the right words to say. "Good morning, Zach. You're here early." This is the best I can come up with.

"I am always early. I figured if you came a bit early, I would get extra time with you, and if not, at least I had plenty of time to make the staff here uncomfortable."

The laugh that escapes my lips is mortifying. He doesn't seem repulsed—rather, amused. "I was debating whether I should sit in my car, or come inside and wait, so I'm glad I came in. Saves you from looking too suspicious."

"Me too." The man winks at me and I never knew smile lines could be so sexy. "So, what can I get you? Coffee? Let me guess. Grande medium roast, two cream, one sugar?"

"Wow. That's an excellent guess. Completely wrong, but I'm impressed."

"I've lost my touch. I worked as a barista through college and high school, and I got pretty good at guessing people's orders. In all fairness, I am really distracted by the beautiful woman in front of me."

Beautiful woman? Is this guy high? Ignore that statement.

"I'll have a peppermint tea, please. I restrict my caffeine consumption because it fuels my anxiety, which I don't need help with."

You idiot, he didn't need to be informed of that. You could have stopped at "Peppermint tea."

To my surprise, he says, "That makes perfect sense. My mother had Generalized Anxiety Disorder, and she used to say the same thing."

"You say 'had.' Why past tense?" I ask before my brain can stop my mouth.

"Uh, she passed away many years ago. Let me get our drinks, and then we can sit and talk. Do you want to find us a seat?"

"Surely there are enough chairs in here, we don't need to share a seat." I wink at him and I'm not even sure I recognize myself right now. Who is this flirt in my body? Did I flirt my way out of an awkward conversation?

"Well, that sounds like a plan for a future date." He turns to place our order with a smirk on his face.

My cheeks are so hot I could cook an egg. I need to calm down before I embarrass myself any more. He's going to get the wrong idea if I keep flirting. Girls probably go back to his place on their first date, and that is not who I am.

He arrives at the table with our drinks and an assortment of baked goods. "I wasn't sure what you'd like and clearly I'm not good at guessing, so I got a bit of everything."

"Oh, Zach." I pause mid-sentence to berate myself over how that sounded. "Um, you didn't have to go to that much trouble. Thank you."

"No trouble. It gives me some insight into you. I can tell a lot about a person based on their pastry preference."

"Is that right? Well, clearly, I eat my fair share of pastries." I point to my waistline, drawing his attention to my soft midsection.

Why are you so awkward?

"I'd say it's the perfect amount, then." There's enough conviction in his words, I almost believe him.

Well, he doesn't know you yet. Anyone can put on an act for a day. He'll see through your veil of flirtatious comments and fake confidence soon enough.

I release an audible sigh and stare at the pastries. My appetite disappears again. "I'm not a big eater in the morning, but maybe I can take one for later."

"No deal. If you don't want to eat one now, you'll have to come to my office to have one with me later." His smile is so bright and genuine, I'm finding it hard to abstain from turning into a doe-eyed fool.

"Already planning a second date, are you?" As soon as the words come out of my mouth, I wish I could stuff them back in.

You're an embarrassment to yourself.

"This is just coffee… and tea. When I take you on a date, it won't be where we work."

"*When* you take me on a date? That's presumptuous."

"When. So, when do you think we can make that happen? I know you barely know me, but I enjoy your company and I think that's a good place to start. How about Saturday?"

I rack my brain thinking about my plans and remember I never have plans for the weekend. My social life is non-existent. "Saturday sounds doable."

"May I be so forward as to ask for your phone number so I can contact you with details?" His tone is comically proper, as if we've transported to the 1800s—minus the phone number part.

"Zach, you already asked me on a date. My phone number is hardly crossing a line. Hand me your phone and I'll input my number."

He smiles while he leans to one side to retrieve his phone from his back pocket. He unlocks the screen and passes it to me. His wallpaper photo is of him and a beautiful blonde on a hiking trail. My stomach sinks and I try to push aside the sickening feeling in my gut.

You're not the only one.

I finish inputting my number, but leave off the final digit. If he tries to call me, and we run into each other at work afterward, I can tell him it was an honest mistake. If he's interested, he can dial the ten possible phone numbers to get in touch with me.

The change in my demeanour doesn't escape his notice as I hand his phone back to him.

He is a player who's used to women giving him what he wants. Desperate women will jump at the chance to have his attention, so he doesn't even need to hide it anymore.

I try to hide my growing upset and anger. "Well, thank you for the tea, Zach. I have a lot on my schedule for today, so I better go."

He appears startled. Maybe he's surprised I'm not falling for his Prince Charming bit. "Oh, sure. Sorry if I kept you. Will I see you later?"

Our potential pastry meet up slipped my mind. "Probably not. I should watch what I eat. My best friend is getting married soon and I don't want to look like *The Michelin Man* in her pictures."

Just. Stop. Talking.

"You're beautiful, Zara."

Shoot, he's good. I believe him. If I didn't know better, I might have fallen for it. He must have a lot of practice at this.

"I'll see you around then, Zach. Thanks again for the tea." I stand and rush out of the coffee shop as fast as my baby-giraffe legs can carry me.

Of course, the first man who has shown any interest in you in years is a playboy.

As the elevator doors close, I struggle to come up with a reasonable excuse to skip our date on Saturday. Then I remember I promised Quinn I would be available to help her go dress shopping. Perfect. I can't let my best friend down. If Zach goes to the trouble of calling me, I'll politely decline and tell him my plans slipped my mind. This will work out fine. Enough of Zachary Haynes.

Saturday arrives, and I didn't see Zach the rest of the week. That may have had something to do with me showing up to work at the crack of dawn to avoid him, which meant I didn't sleep for days because I had an unrelenting fear that I'd oversleep my alarm and be forced to face him.

Today, though, I'm meeting Quinn, her mother, and her younger sister, Paige, at a bridal boutique downtown. It didn't even occur to me when Quinn asked me to come dress shopping that she also wanted me to try on dresses. This whole bridal party thing is becoming more real, and each passing day increases my stress level. Is it possible to top up a worry metre, or does it just keep increasing forever until you spontaneously combust?

Only time will tell.

I shaved my legs, put on a proper bra and deodorant, and tossed my shapewear in my purse. Standing next to Quinn and Paige, who both resemble female models, is going to destroy what little confidence I have. I can only hope I look as unremarkable as I normally do, and no one glances in my direction.

The bridal boutique is called *Don't Stress for The Dress. As if that will stop anyone from stressing. Doesn't work for me.*

I circle the block, looking for parking, when I notice the bridal boutique has a small lot in an alleyway behind the building. These are times I am grateful for my tiny car. The spaces are tight, but I manoeuvre in with a slightly elevated heart rate.

Lock the door three times, just to be sure. This alley is kind of sketchy. Scan the area for anyone hiding behind a garbage bin or in between the buildings. This looks like a prime kidnapping location.

I knock at the back door of the boutique, and a posh middle-aged woman opens it. She welcomes me and asks, "Do you have an appointment, Darling?" Her use of the pet-name "Darling" reminds me to call my mother later.

"Yes, I'm supposed to meet my friend, Quinn Ayala, here at 11:00."

"Oh, yes, Quinn. She's already in the showroom with her mom and sister. You must be the maid of honour."

"I am, yes. Zara."

"Lovely to meet you, Zara. Oh, you three are going to be such a pleasure to dress. You will make a beautiful bridal party!"

"Quinn and Paige are beautiful." I'm not included in that category.

"Zara!" Quinn shouts from around the corner. "I'm so glad you're here!" She squeals with delight and embraces me in a hug. I suspect Quinn has taken full advantage of the mimosas on offer.

"Paige, Mrs. Ayala, it's nice to see you again." I glance up to see Quinn's beautiful blonde family members suppressing their laughter. Chances are, they're laughing at Quinn's exuberance, but it's possible the source is my awkward facial expression.

"Zara, Dear. Please call me Ren. We've been over this. You're family," Quinn and Paige's mom, Lauren, requests with a friendly smile.

"Sorry, Ren." I need to move this conversation past the lengthy, awkward introductions. "So, what do you want for your dress, Quinny?"

"I haven't even told you. We're getting married in four weeks!"

"Four weeks? That's so soon."

"I'm aware! We've been together for so long we don't see the point of a long engagement. We looked into some venues we liked and one of them had a cancellation in four weeks. So, we all need to choose a dress from the rack. We can get them altered, though."

"Wow. I'm a bit in shock. Here I thought I'd have the chance to lose some weight first. I don't want to be your frumpy maid of honour."

"Zara, none of that! You are beautiful, and you don't need to lose a single ounce. We'll find a dress that makes you look like a princess, and you're going to be the belle of the ball."

"Quinn, I'm sure it's me that's supposed to be giving *you* a pep talk. I'm already a terrible maid of honour."

Quinn glares at me so hard I feel like her eyes might burn me. "Zara, I swear on this stack of bridal magazines, if you don't stop talking down about yourself, we are going to have a problem."

I can tell she's not playing. Buzzed Quinn means business.

"Right, sorry Amiga. You know it's my default mode."

"Well, not on my watch. So, what colour do you think we should choose?"

Quinn will end up hating you if you pick the wrong colour. Defer. Let her decide.

"Well, for an October wedding, which you always wanted, you might as well choose the colours you dreamed of. Create your dream wedding."

"I never thought about colour schemes before. Let's see what they have in stock in the right sizes for you and Paige. We'll decide from our options."

We browse the bridesmaid dresses and I am overwhelmed. I glance at Quinn, who is scanning through the racks, and she looks like the happiest woman in the world.

She turns to me and says, "Hey, can I ask you something?"

Ah, the anxiety starter pack in word form. What could go wrong?

Why did the chicken cross the road? How much do you weigh? What was the best thing before sliced bread? Do you feel lonely? Where is a good place to hide a dead body? What is the meaning of life?

She takes my hands in hers and blows out a grounding breath. "Take a breath, girl. I wanted to ask what's your favourite feature about yourself?"

Her question surprises me. This is harder to answer than where to hide a dead body. Does she mean something I like about myself?

Your fingers are an average length and thickness. Your hair sometimes cooperates, and thanks to significant dental work, your teeth look decent.

"Um, my fingers?"

Quinn gives me a blank stare, which I return, equally confused.

"Chica, it's hard to find you a dress that accentuates your fingers. Please don't tell me that's the only thing you can think of."

"Well, I don't particularly like my fingers, but I thought I should give you an answer. I didn't understand the direction you were going with that question. Can we find a dress that makes me invisible? Like a brown dress and I'll stand in front of tree trunks? Ooh, or a nice Autumn leaf print? I don't want to ruin your wedding day."

Quinn heaves a sigh and looks as if she's about to cry. We have reached the next phase of brunch drunk; overly emotional.

"Zara, you couldn't ever ruin my wedding day. I wouldn't care if you looked like a 300-pound pigeon. You are my best friend and I want you up there with me. I only asked because I want *you* to feel beautiful."

"I'm sorry, Amiga. I am ruining this. Are you sure you don't want Paige to be your maid of honour? She'd be better at it."

"What will it take to convince you that you're the person I want for the job? There's no one else, Zara. You're my BFF. My ride-or-die. The Thelma to my Louise. The Skywalker to my Obi Wan. I'm not doing this without you."

Obi Wan? Seriously? "I'll try to be better, Quinn. I just don't do well with the unknown, and there are so many 'what ifs' piling up in my brain, it's making my head spin."

"I know. Sit down for a second and let's see if we can tick some 'what if' questions off your mental list."

We seat ourselves on a tufted upholstered bench on the far side of the showroom. I stroke the velvet fabric back and forth, changing the colour from a deep blue to a shimmery cobalt with each swipe. It doesn't ease my nerves at all.

After a few seconds of painful silence, I blurt out, "What if I trip and fall while I'm walking down the aisle?"

"If you trip and fall, I'll rip off my dress and run around stark naked as a distraction, okay?"

She says it as a joke, but I'm sure she would.

"What if Tyler's best man is a handsy creep when he drinks?"

"I can 100 percent confirm that his best man is a well-behaved gentleman and doesn't even drink. He's drop dead gorgeous. If I weren't a taken woman, I'd take a run at him. Maybe you two will hit it off."

"Drop dead gorgeous isn't in my league."

"Zar, you really underestimate yourself. You are a classic beauty with a heart of gold. Any man would be lucky to walk into a room with you on his arm and come home to you every night." Quinn grabs my hand and makes intense eye contact with me. "I want you to be confident that for every 'what if' you come up with, I'll have a solution. Everything will be fine, okay?"

I choke back my tears as I question how I got so lucky to have this wonderful human as my best friend. My only response is a nod.

She jumps up from her seat. "Okay, let's find our dresses! We better sort this out today so they'll be ready for my big day!"

After a swipe of my eyes to get rid of the lingering tears, I stand beside the future Mrs. Ochoa. "Let's find your perfect dress. Ty won't know what hit him."

After two hours, we've found a dress for each of us. The bridesmaid dresses are black, floor-length gowns with wide straps and a plunging neckline. This may be the first time in my life I'm happy to be well endowed—it's your time to shine, girls. There's also a high slit up the long skirt over the right leg. Quinn insists the slit will make it easier to walk, but I have my doubts. It looks like a perfect opportunity to tangle myself in misfortune.

Quinn's dress is a stunning white gown with a lace bodice and sleeves with beading overtop. The skirt is a simple satin A-line that beautifully enhances her figure. Tyler might not make it to say, "I do," because she looks stunning.

Ren purchases an elegant mother-of-the-bride dress and jacket in a champagne colour, which she seems quite happy with. She always had a very tasteful style sense. Quinn always told me I dress like her mother; I take it as a compliment.

After we check out, we say our goodbyes at the front door because Quinn and Tyler have an event to get to. Quinn hugs me so tight it makes shapewear feel like pyjamas, but I enjoy every second. She is my favourite human.

Now you have to get to your car in that shady back alley. Look around for anything suspicious. Don't follow an Oreo attached to a string. It's a trap.

Why is my anxiety so ridiculous? Like I'd follow an Oreo on a string. Well… no… I probably wouldn't.

I walk back to the alley, checking behind dumpsters and under vehicles. As soon as I hop in my car, I speed off toward home.

A few minutes into my drive, my Bluetooth rings through the car speakers. I don't recognize the number.

What if it's an emergency with your parents? What if it's one of your clients who needs help with something? What if police arrested Lexi for starting a riot, protesting Starbucks' prices and she's calling you to bail her out?

I press accept. "Hello?"

"Zara? I'm glad I finally got a hold of you. It's Zach."

'm momentarily frozen—which is a big problem because I am driving. A car behind me honks, and I notice too late that I've drifted into the lane to my left. I give an apologetic wave and hope the person doesn't drive past me whilst giving me the finger.

Avoid eye contact at all costs.

"Zara, are you okay? Are you there?"

"Sorry, yes, I'm here. I'm driving."

"I'm sorry if I caught you at a bad time. Turns out you missed a digit when you entered your number into my phone, and I've been texting no one all week. I called six people before I got to you."

"Oh, really? My bad. I didn't notice." My tone is unconvincing.

"So, can I pick you up around seven tonight?"

"Listen, Zach. I don't want you to get the wrong impression. I'm not one of those girls who falls into your arms and overlooks whatever else is going on."

"What? I never assumed you were 'one of those girls' and that's not what I want. I enjoy your company, and I'd like to experience more of it."

My teeth are digging into my bottom lip as I clench down, trying to distract myself from what I need to do. "I don't think I'm the right girl for you. You should focus on the woman you have." Before I lose my nerve, I disconnect the call. I wish I had a flip phone so I could slam it shut with conviction. Instead, I settle for the touch screen, so I bend my finger back, hanging up with force.

Right away, my speakers are ringing again. I don't answer. He calls three more times in a row before I pull into my parking lot, but I refuse to speak with him anymore. I was fine before I met him, and I'll be fine without him now.

Were you fine before you met him?

I sit in my car in the parking lot outside my building and sob. It's not because I'm upset with Zach; I'm upset with myself. Do I have "take advantage of me" tattooed on my forehead?

I can't seem to get a grip, and I don't even understand what the real problem is, so I can't talk myself out of it. A panic attack is looming when I decide to call Quinn. I tap the screen on my car, but I can't see through the tears, so I only hope it's her I'm connecting to when it starts to ring.

"Hey, Chica. Miss me already?"

All I can do is cry. I can't speak. Can't move. Can't see. I feel like I'm breathing through a snorkel, but someone keeps putting their hand over the top. My heart is ready to jump out of my chest. I'm sweating, and I can't make it stop.

"Talk to me, Zara. What's happening? You're scaring me."

Now you've made things worse. This was supposed to be a happy day for her, and you're ruining it because you are weak.

She doesn't need you. With a friend like you, who needs enemies? Just hang up.

So, I do. I hang up on my best friend to save her from my mess. She's better off without me; I can't keep dragging her down.

I continue to break down in my conspicuous vehicle and only hope no one can see through my tinted windows. I have no concept of how long I've been sitting here when I hear a knock at the passenger door.

You look terrible. This is so embarrassing.

I look over to my right, but my vision is blurry. A mane of champagne hair surrounding an ethereal face is outside the window, and I know my saviour is here. I unlock the doors and Quinn drops into the passenger seat. Her arrival sparks another wave of sobs as I cry into my hands. She leans over to put her arms around me and starts rubbing my back.

"Okay, I'm here. Take a deep breath for me. In for three. One, two, three. Hold for three. Good. Now breathe out, one, two, three. Do it again. In... hold... out. You've got this. Now start relaxing your muscles. Relax your fingers. Zar, you're a rockstar. Relax your arms. There you go."

I release the tension in my body and begin to calm. Quinn has a lot of experience in seeing me through panic attacks. This has probably happened 100 times in the ten years we've been friends. I can go months without having a single attack, but then as soon as something feels out of control, they come at me fast and furious. I was hospitalized on four separate occasions because of attacks I couldn't get control of; each time leaving me more ashamed than the last.

"Talk to me, Chica. Tell me what's wrong. Is it the wedding? I'm so sorry if you feel like this is too much."

"No, it's not that. I promise." The skin around my nails is raw from picking at it, but instead of making eye contact with Quinn, I continue inflicting harm on my innocent fingers.

"I'm worried about you. What's going on?"

"Do you want to come inside and talk for a bit?"

"I can't. Ty and I were on our way to that event for the gym when you called. I was already late getting home from dress shopping."

My stomach sinks. That slipped my mind amid my panic.

Selfish. You are ruining her life. You constantly interrupt her plans, you can't support her when she needs you, and you don't add any value to her life.

"I... I'm so sorry, Quinny. Please go. You can't be late on my account."

"None of that matters. I'll always come running, but I don't want to keep Tyler waiting too long, either."

You can't keep depending on her. She has other obligations, like an actual adult.

"I'll be fine, I promise. I was due for a breakdown. Work was getting to me, and I hadn't been dealing with it."

She squeezes my hand, undeterred by my bleeding cuticles. "You have the biggest heart of anyone I've ever known, but you have to make sure you're taking care of yourself. You know the saying, 'you can't pour from an empty cup.'"

"I'll take it easy tonight and tomorrow; make it a point to fill my cup, okay? Now, would you get on with your date, please? I can't have Tyler mad at me for ruining your afternoon."

"He'd never be mad at you for having a bad day."

Is that even true? Or is that something someone says so they don't sound like a selfish jerk? You're a selfish jerk, Zara. Everyone is sick of you.

I swallow down my self-loathing and choke out what needs to be said. "Well, I'm fine now. Thank you for coming to my rescue. Go, enjoy your event."

"Okay, but please call me if you need me. I'll be out of this function so fast."

That's the last thing I want. I don't want to be a damsel in distress she feels responsible for anymore.

Just to please her, I say, "I will. Thanks Quinn."

With that, she blows me a kiss, opens the door, and hops back into Tyler's car. A moment later, they disappear down the road and toward their happy afternoon together.

I finally work up the nerve to get out of the car and make my way inside. Most days, I take the stairs because it's only two flights, but my panic attack zapped every bit of juice my energy bank had in reserve, so I walk to the elevator.

When I get out on the third floor, I see a yellow notice taped to my door.

Have your mortgage payments not been coming out? Are you being evicted? Has someone complained about you being too noisy, or about your random bouts of crying in the parking lot?

I breathe a sigh of relief when I realize the notice is for a new deadbolt on my door, which is scheduled to be replaced on Wednesday. It's a good thing I plan on staying home for the entire week. I have sick days saved up, and right now, I can't face the world. I'm just *that* pathetic.

I call Mr. Stafford's office around 7am on Monday morning. The least I can do is let him know I won't be in to work for a few days, but speaking to him directly isn't something I can manage at the moment. I'm bound to cave at the slightest hint of disappointment in his voice. A voicemail solves that problem, and I only hope he doesn't call me back or question my motives.

Coward.

An overwhelming sense of guilt consumes me over not seeing my clients this week because they're dealing with their own struggles too, but like Quinn said, "You can't pour from an empty cup." My cup isn't particularly helpful, even when it's overflowing, but it's not going to be any use empty. I keep reminding myself that mental health days are important, and, at times, necessary, but that doesn't lessen the self-loathing plaguing me.

You're a disgrace to your profession. Selfish. Useless. Worthless.

I don't know what to do with myself anymore. For the most part, I love my job, but I feel like it's selfish of me to keep doing it. Should these kids, who have already been through so much in their young lives, have to suffer with my mediocre counselling, too? Am I doing it for them, or to give myself some sort of validation so I don't feel worse about my own issues? As if that's even possible. Whatever. I don't have the emotional capacity to handle my own issues and my clients' right now. Nor do I have the desire or ability to face Zach for a while.

You're going to have to see him, eventually. What about poor Chelsea? Look at everything she's been through, and you can't even pull yourself together to help her? Isla made some strides last week, and you're throwing it all away. Pathetic.

Pull yourself together. I spent the entire day yesterday in bed, only getting up to answer the door when the food delivery guy came. One can only hope I never see him again because I looked like I should have been scaring crows away from crops.

I huddle up in a sherpa-lined fleece blanket on my couch and flick on the TV. While I sleep the day away, I need some noise to distract me. Plus, it distracts from these pains of guilt — is it "pains" of guilt, or "pangs" of guilt? Whatever they are, I'm feeling all the pangs I can manage. If you can call hiding in your house avoiding all your adult responsibilities "managing."

Slipping into unconsciousness for a while is the only way I can deal with my feelings, so I curl up and attempt to nap. My brain is on overdrive, flipping through the "Ways Zara is a Screw-up" catalogue, reminding me of my endless list of failures. Sleep doesn't come easily with tears pooling in my eyes, but before my Netflix menu asks if I'm still watching, I fall asleep.

Two hours later, I wake, feeling more exhausted than I did before. I decide to get up to make a cup of tea, then check my phone. Zach texted me and I question whether or not I should read it, but you know what they say about curiosity and the cat.

Zach: I came to work early this morning and waited for you in hopes we could talk. I didn't see you arrive. I'd like to talk with you if you'll give me the chance.

That's a big nope. I'm not going to make myself someone's mistress. I will never be the other woman, the side piece, the dirty little secret. His dreamy eyes will not sucker me into compromising myself.

His text message releases pent up anger and frustration in me that makes me realize I am a grown woman! My anger is directed at myself, not him. Nothing should have ever stopped me from providing the necessary care for the kids I'm tasked with helping. My own failings and fears shouldn't matter when it comes to them, because they need to be my priority. I will not hide out in my home, neglecting my responsibilities. I am strong and independent. Tomorrow morning, I am going to get up and go to work with my head held high.

For the rest of the day, I sit on the couch, eating leftover takeout, watching true crime shows on Netflix, and trying to convince myself I will survive when I go back to work. I also attempt to do things I tell my clients to do when they are feeling out of control. Meditate, take a bath, and write in my journal that is designed for people with anxiety. It includes writing prompts to deal with intrusive thoughts and to help focus on more positive things. Focus on reality, you could say—somewhere anxiety doesn't like to exist. Today I wrote about small but satisfying victories I've had. It may not help in the long term, but it does for the time being. Today, I am living in one-moment-at-a-time survival mode.

Once I finish writing, it's almost 9:00pm. I rarely go to sleep so early, especially not after having a nap, but my brain battling itself all day has been exhausting.

As it turns out, going to bed and going to sleep are not the same thing. I may be tired, but my brain is not. The same thoughts overtake me from my nap earlier and I lie awake, hyper-aware of every sound or flicker of light.

Why is your heart beating so hard? Something serious is wrong. Did you hear that sound? Is someone trying to break into the building? The shadows in your room are moving around too much. Someone is out there.

I try to release the tension in my body, and in the process, I decide on one thing I know for sure: I'll be going to work extra early tomorrow.

Tuesday morning, I'm attempting to get ready for work, but my burning rage at myself has subsided and I am questioning my resolve. I should go into work today and not sit at home wallowing in self-pity, avoiding my problems, but ignorance seems so much easier.

Home is safe. You should stay home. Nothing bad happens at home. When you leave the house, bad things happen. What if the maintenance man changing your lock is secretly a stalker who places inconspicuous cameras around your condo so he can watch you walk around in your pyjamas? But what if you stay home, and you're here alone with him?

Just smile, breathe, and go slowly. Nothing can combat anxiety like action. I can't conquer my worries by sleeping them away. Move forward. This day will be fine. I can do this.

An hour earlier than necessary, I arrive at work. If anyone asks, I'll say I came early to catch up on things I missed yesterday. That sounds plausible and isn't a bad idea.

My attempts to get in the back of the building prove fruitless, so without another option, I walk around to the front. As I pull the lobby door open, my eyes are drawn to Zach. That would have been enough to have my anxiety causing a ruckus in my stomach, but the worst part is, he's not alone. He is wrapped in an embrace with the gorgeous blonde from the picture on his phone. Before I can tear my eyes away, he plants a kiss on her forehead and she turns to leave.

She's coming this way. She is coming this way! Run! Hide! Do anything, but don't let her see you. You do not want to come face-to-face with the woman who is better than you in every way.

I stare at her as she walks my way, noting how she moves gracefully. I can't help but think she looks far too young for Zach;

it's not my place to judge. There's not a line on her face nor a hair out of place, which makes me even more self-conscious about my bulldog jowls and worry lines. Her clothes are stylish and look designer. What could he ever see in me if he can have her?

She's closed the gap and I'm still standing here with my hand on the door handle, like I've suddenly forgotten how to work a door. I have. The next logical step would be running back to my car for cover—and a good cry.

No. I will not cry over him. He is a nobody to me. I will walk in there with my head held high... and pray that he's already gone to his office.

The stunning blonde is exiting as I walk through the first set of double doors. Of course, she holds the second door for me, gives me a movie-star smile, and says, "I love your ballet flats!"

Trying to mask my shock at hearing her lyrical voice, I mutter, "Oh, thank you. They were on sale."

"I love a good deal. Have a good day." She giggles, and it sounds as soothing as a bedtime lullaby.

I hate her. She's beautiful, stylish, and worst of all, she's nice. Like a younger Quinn. Gorgeous. Has everything going for her. Near palpable charisma. If champagne cosplayed as a human, it would look like this woman in front of me.

You could never hold a candle to her. You wouldn't stand a chance next to someone like her even if the lights were off.

Tears threaten to spill from my overtired eyes, but I don't allow them to. A man I had one coffee date with is not worth crying over. I'll stay focused on the fact he ran me over with his bike.

I scan the lobby and spot Zach in the coffee shop. He's placing his order, so I rush past to the elevator. Thankfully, at 7:30am, elevator traffic is nonexistent. My entire body relaxes as the doors close. Now I can retreat to the safety of my office and hide there for the day.

As I walk into my office, I hang my purse on the back of the door, turn my computer on, and open the blinds to let some light in. I take a seat at my desk and start scanning through my emails when my office door opens, and someone barges in.

Patrick Kennedy. Perfect.

You're alone with him. He is a big man. You're not safe. Your purse is too far away to grab your whistle. Scan around for something to protect yourself.

I fidget with some things in my desk before my hand lands on the heavy stapler I keep in my top drawer. It won't help much, but finding something keeps my mind distracted long enough to stave off immediate panic.

"What can I do for you, Patrick?" My shaky voice belies my confident words.

"Must be nice to take days off whenever you feel like it," he seethes. He is looking at me with such hatred, it's unnerving.

"I had to take a personal day. I commend you if you've been able to do this job and ever needed one."

"Women are too soft for this job. You get too emotional."

"I beg your pardon? Since when is having feelings a bad thing?"

He lets out a mocking laugh—it reminds me of a Disney villain. "Everyone here thinks you're stupid. It's better for everyone to think you're an idiot than for you to keep opening your mouth to prove it."

I'm dumbfounded by his comment. He closes the door and walks toward me. My heart rate increases and the walls are closing in. I steady my voice by taking a breath, summoning every ounce of false bravado I can muster. "Patrick, I don't understand why you dislike me; I've been nothing but nice to you. If you hate me that much, feel free to leave."

He appears shocked by my boldness. Before I can blink, that shock turns to rage, and he is leaning over my desk, his face only inches away from mine. He is spitting as he speaks, anger pouring out of him. "I don't know why little tramps like you think they can come in here, sleep with the boss, and get whatever they want while the rest of us have to work for scraps."

You should have stayed home; home is safe.

"Enough!" Another voice booms from my doorway, and I realize it's Mr. Stafford.

I stand and move back toward the wall to put some distance between Patrick and me, clutching the stapler in my left hand.

"Patrick, my office. Now!"

Patrick glares at me once again with more hatred than I've ever seen emanate from a human being. I'm shaking, but thankful Mr. Stafford showed up when he did. I fight the urge to call Quinn because I don't want to keep stressing her with my problems. This is something I need to deal with myself.

A short time later, I am struggling to focus on my work. It's been forty minutes since Mr. Stafford and Patrick left my office. My body feels exhausted from the tension I have been holding onto. I am finally feeling calm when I hear a knock at my door.

"Come in."

Mr. Stafford eases his way through the door. I stand to greet him and point to the chair on the opposite side of my desk for him to sit. He looks as if he's going to be sick as he drops himself in the open seat.

"Are you okay, Sir?"

A hint of surprise registers on his face. "Me? I'm fine. I came to see how you're doing."

"Oh, I'm good. No harm done." That's a lie; I'm terrified.

"Well, I wanted to update you on what's happened since Mr. Kennedy and I left your office. Patrick has been on thin ice recently. His wife left him a few months ago, and he's been spiralling out of control. Not that I am making excuses for him, but his behaviour didn't come out of nowhere."

I develop a small amount of compassion for Patrick. "That's understandable. Separation and divorce can be difficult on a person, especially when there are kids involved."

"I appreciate your understanding, but the fact is, his behaviour was unacceptable and cannot be tolerated. His employment has been terminated, effective immediately."

"Wow!" I need a moment to process that. "I hope that isn't because of what happened this morning. The last thing I want is for him to think I caused his firing."

"No, Zara. He has been formally written up twice and been given verbal warnings on several occasions. Last Monday after the staff meeting, I spoke with him again, and since then, he's been very combative. As I'm sure you can understand, we can't allow that here. The clients we deal with need to feel at peace when they come through our doors."

"I'm so sorry for how the situation turned out." I let out an exaggerated exhale. "Hopefully Patrick can get some help and land back on his feet."

"I hope so too." He stands from the white barrel chair he was sitting in, his mouth set in a frown. "I wasn't expecting you back from your personal leave already. Based on your message yesterday, I thought you might be gone all week."

"Well, to be honest, I planned on it. But I knew I had clients scheduled to come in and I didn't want to bail on them or pass them off to anyone else. They need me, so I wanted to be here. Perhaps I'll schedule some time off in the not-too-far future."

"You're excellent at your job, Zara. You always put those in need ahead of yourself. Don't let today's events rattle you. You were not in the wrong, and I'm glad I came when I did."

"So am I. Thank you."

"Let me know if you have questions I can help you with. We'll have to schedule a staff meeting to divide up Patrick's clients to make sure they have continuity of care, so I'll keep you updated."

I smile and nod at Mr. Stafford as he exits my office. He is a wonderful man.

Suddenly, Zach couldn't be further from my mind, and I am grateful for that.

Since my strategy yesterday didn't pay off, my choice today is to arrive moments before my shift is scheduled to start. I don't want to be an easy target in my office again, nor do I want to see Zach feeling up a beautiful blonde.

In theory, my plan was smart. In reality, it doesn't work. I walk into the lobby and see the face of a scared little boy, only that face belongs to a grown man—the most handsome man I have ever seen. Before I can turn and run, we've made eye contact, and he rushes toward me.

"Zara, hi!"

I look down at my feet. "Hey."

He's going to manipulate you. Stay strong and do not give in.

"I waited for you the past two days, but I must have missed you. You didn't answer my texts. After our phone call Saturday, I couldn't get what you said out of my head."

"What part would that be, Zach?" I lift my eyes to meet his and stiffen my posture, crossing my arms over my navy blouse. Fake indifference.

"When you said I should focus on the one I have already. I don't understand what you mean by that."

I'm determined not to fly into an anxious rage. "There's a picture on your phone of you and another woman. Not to mention, I saw you with her yesterday, right in this spot. It's fine, Zach. She's stunning and perfect, and everything I'm not. I don't blame you for choosing her, but I won't be anyone's side chick!" My speech increases in tempo as I progress; my anger stronger than my determination.

He takes a small step backwards as if my rant produced hurricane-force winds creating distance between us.

"This girl?" He pulls out his phone to show me the picture I mentioned. It hurts to see it.

"Yes." Every ounce of indignation in my voice disappears.

She is so much more beautiful than you. He could never be interested in a tragic Plain Jane.

"She's my baby sister, Jasmine."

My face flushes with embarrassment and anger—anger with myself for being so quick to jump to conclusions. I wrote him off as a womanizer when I should have simply asked. This is why I'm not cut out for dating. My anxiety makes me go from reasonable to insane in the blink of an eye.

"Your sister?"

"Yes, she's my little sister. You said you're not 'that kind of girl', and you need to know, I'm not 'that kind of guy' either. I'd never treat you or anyone else as a side chick."

"I... I don't know what to say. I'm so sorry. I shouldn't have assumed."

"No, maybe you shouldn't have, but *I'm* going to assume it's because you've been hurt before."

"That would be a safe assumption." I look up at the clock and realize the time. "I have to get to my office. Sorry for everything." Without making eye contact, I step toward the elevator.

Get out of here and avoid the awkward conversation. Escape. Avoidance is best.

"Hey, why are you rushing off?" His hand reaches out, touching my shoulder as I pass, which, after my encounter with Patrick yesterday, startles me and makes Zach slink back.

Tension is building behind my eyes on account of my whirling emotions. "I told you, I have to get to work."

"No, I mean, can we at least plan to see each other again? Can we have coffee tomorrow morning?"

Why would he give me another chance? I'm a loose cannon. Instead of asking and pushing my luck, I say, "Tea."

"Right, tea. Tomorrow at 7:45? Would that be good?"

He must be really desperate… or a serial killer.

Anxiety is going to have to shut up this time.

"Okay." I do my best to smile, which he returns, and I'm reminded why he's so out of my league. "I'll see you tomorrow." Before I can say anything else stupid, I rush off.

I arrive at my office a few minutes later—late, which never happens—but no one seems to notice. I get to work, though my thoughts are occupied by a green-eyed blond.

Wednesday afternoon, it's about time for my appointment with Chelsea. I love all my clients and work to help them as best as I can, but Chelsea is special to me. She inspires me with everything she has overcome.

I relate to her because I was once a naïve young woman—though not as young as she was when her world was destroyed—and had been very trusting of everyone. I always felt it was best to trust people until they gave you reason not to, but never thought a major breach of trust by one person would result in me being distrusting of everyone.

Chelsea knocks on the door, so I call for her to come in. I greet her with a smile, though I'd much rather be able to give her a hug.

Professional boundaries.

"Hey, Chels. How are you?"

"I'm all right... I guess." Her ginger hair is pulled back in a tight ponytail, displaying her sombre expression.

"Hm. You guess? That doesn't sound too convincing. Why don't you come take a seat and tell me what's up?"

Her shoulders slump as she walks over to the off-white, tufted sofa, and suddenly I feel so relieved that I came in to work to be here for her. Something is wrong.

"So, what's happened in your life since the last time I saw you?"

She pauses a moment. "Well. I'm fifteen now."

"I know. You're a young woman."

Chelsea tells me about the issues she's having at school—the pressures to date, drugs, skipping classes—typical teenager stuff. The problem is, Chelsea isn't a typical teenager with a rebellious streak. She has an instinctive need to follow the rules, and a fear of disappointing people in positions of authority. After what she went through as a child, she is an obsessive rule follower. That's a good thing, in my opinion, but it can be tough amongst a teenage crowd set on bending or breaking the rules.

"Chels, just remember, those other kids have not walked the same path as you, and they live different lives. What they feel is right for them is not always going to be the same as what's right for you. I am proud of you for how you have handled the opposition, and for not letting them decide what's best for you."

After we speak at length about specific comments and pressures from other kids, I'm repressing the urge to spit nails at those little troglodytes who have the nerve to pick on Chelsea because she won't follow them and their idiotic behaviour. I keep myself calm for Chelsea's sake, but I feel a motherly, protective instinct over her. After four years of learning her deepest, darkest fears and secrets, I am so appreciative of having this girl in my life. She is strong enough to move mountains, and I'm sure she helps me more than I help her.

We've gone over specific coping mechanisms she can employ, and I've reassured her there is nothing wrong with her choices.

As our time is running out, I tell Chelsea, "I want you to have some fun too, okay? Nothing you're uncomfortable with, but it's okay to go with some girls to the mall, or for a slumber party. Meet some other students who have more in common with you—ones who focus on their work and don't care about the other teenage drama."

She looks unsure of herself, but squeaks out, "Okay, I'll try."

"I know you will. That's all we can do—keep trying. Take one day at a time."

Chelsea finishes up our appointment by telling me things are going all right with her foster parents. They have said they aren't able to adopt her, so she's pretty certain she'll age out of the system and never have a family. My heart breaks for her.

I stand up to walk her out and remind her she can call me anytime. She is one of the few clients I gave my personal number to so she can call if she's overwhelmed. One thing I've learned through my own struggles with anxiety is that it doesn't matter how bad you are feeling yourself, if someone else needs something, it's infinitely easier to break out of your own head to help them than it is to tackle your own issues.

The delicate, yet fierce, red-headed girl walks toward the elevator, and I smile to myself as I watch the doors close. Today has been a good day.

I don't trust it. Something bad is going to happen. Something bad always happens.

I shake off the feeling of dread and realize it's 3:30. The last hour of my day is reserved for transcribing my notes into my computer to update client files. This part of the process is enjoyable because it allows me to re-evaluate what was said and determine a course of action for our next meetings. Feeling as if these kids are moving forward and their lives have improved a little with each session gives me the motivation I need to keep coming back.

At 4:30, I grab my purse from the back of the door, check for my keys, wallet, and phone. My phone has a voicemail message from a number I don't recognize.

Who knows what that message could be? You should ignore it for a few weeks.

I shove my phone back into my purse, acknowledging that the voicemail icon is a permanent fixture on my home screen now, lock my office door, and walk to the elevator, hoping it arrives quickly. As the large stainless-steel doors slide open, I enter with Erin and Adele, but they each give me a sympathetic smile and don't speak. The only thing worse than an elevator full of people is two people who are afraid to talk to you.

They know what happened with Patrick. Now they think you're a problem-causer who is sleeping with the boss. No one will take you seriously. It's true what Patrick said—everyone thinks you're stupid.

I stare down at my feet until the elevator arrives in the lobby and exit as fast as I can. I need to go home.

Home is safe.

Why won't this lock open? I stare at the number on my door—306—and fiddle with my keys for far too long before I realize someone changed my lock. Okay, this isn't the end of the world. Go to the building manager's apartment and ask for the new key.

Interrupting someone when they aren't expecting you is rude. You don't like when people show up at your door without warning.

When I weigh my options, I conclude I don't have any other choice. The door is locked, and I don't have a key. Go downstairs; everything will be fine.

The unit beneath mine—206—is home to the building manager. He's a peculiar man in his forties, shoulder-length auburn hair with the beginnings of a bald spot who speaks in a husky drawl—a strange trait for a Canadian. I'm not excited about speaking with him, but I need my key.

There is no answer after a moment, so I knock again. No sounds come from the other side of the door and wonder if he's left without giving me a new key. Did he expect me to stand in the hallway and wait for him to return? That's irresponsible and inconsiderate, to say the least. Does he not think I have better things to be doing other than wait around for him? I mean, I don't, but it's rude to assume that.

I consider calling Quinn, but I know Wednesday nights she stays late at the school grading papers because Tyler works afternoons as a personal trainer. My reliance on her must be getting on her last nerve anyway, so it's time to buck up and act like an adult. Come to a solution on my own and get things sorted without my more adulty adult friend coming to my rescue.

My solution: lean my back on the wall and sink to the floor with my face in my hands, as my groan echoes in the empty hallway.

I'm not sure how much time passes, but I've been sitting on the floor for at least thirty minutes, stressing over the germs and filth my clothes and skin are absorbing. Finally, I hear the door open from the stairwell, and Mr. Rodney Harlan emerges. He looks surprised to see me as I struggle to stand with my numb legs and restricted movement on account of my pencil skirt.

"Miss Levy, what can I do you for?"

Each time I hear him speak, I am more and more convinced his idol is Jeff Foxworthy. I love a good "You might be a redneck" joke, but Rodney is the living, breathing epitome of the punchlines.

"I can't get into my home, Mr. Harlan. I was hoping you could help me."

"Are you one of them fancy types that doesn't check her voice messages?" He slides his key into his lock and I resent how easily he gets into his home.

"What makes you ask that?"

"Oh, I left you a message saying I put the key in your mailbox before I left, so you'd be able to get it if I was out."

I know for a fact I had his phone number saved in my phone, so he must have changed his number. On that basis, I'm only accepting partial responsibility for my oversight.

You are so ridiculous, Zara. You made yourself look like a fool in front of a man whose lifelong aspiration is to own a roadside firework stand.

"I'm sorry for bothering you. Thank you for getting my lock changed, and... uh, for the key."

My feet can not carry me away fast enough. I am such a moron. Of course, the unknown number was him. At least I can delete that voicemail message without having to listen to it and it won't torment me for weeks.

The lobby is empty, so I retrieve my mail and new keys. I've always had one for myself and one for Quinn, but I haven't heard from her since she left here on Saturday. I doubt she'd even want the stupid key anymore. If I had a friend like me, I'd want my distance too. Logic tells me she's probably busy with work and wedding planning, but anxiety reminds me, as maid of honour, I should be helping with the latter. She doesn't even want my help.

When I get inside my condo, I have no interest in cooking or eating, so I decide to give Quinn a quick call after all. She doesn't answer, so I assume she's avoiding me. Either that, or she's immersed in her grading. She's been an eighth-grade English teacher for the past three years and really loves her job.

Since Quinn doesn't answer, I call my mom. I haven't spoken to her for ten days, but she understands I go through phases and don't have the desire to talk on the phone. That's one thing she doesn't make me feel guilty about. Usually.

"Hello, Darling."

"Hi, Momma. How are you?"

"I'm better now that I've heard your voice. I was getting worried that I hadn't heard from you."

Worrying everyone is your purpose in life.

"I'm fine. I had a few taxing days at work and needed to get a handle on things."

"Is everything all right?" She's paused whatever she was doing when she answered, which tells me she's more worried than her voice conveys. My mother is a going concern and doesn't stop for much.

"You know the job. It's emotional and sometimes it's hard. I also had a confrontation with a man at work and he ended up being fired."

She gasps. "What kind of confrontation? He didn't hurt you, did he? I swear I will march to his front door and beat him senseless with a bag of onions."

"Wow, Momma. I'm fine. It wasn't a physical confrontation. I guess he was going through some personal things and took it out on me because I was the only one in the office. My boss showed up and handled it. No need to resort to violence, but I appreciate you uttering empty threats on my behalf."

"Not empty at all. In a heartbeat, my Darling. I'd face an assault charge with a smile on my face if someone ever hurt you again."

She's always going to see you as a defenceless, broken little girl.

We talk for about thirty minutes—mostly about Noa and how amazing her kids are. Noa is a decade older, and I've always had the feeling she resented me. We were never close; that hasn't changed as we've gotten older. Noa and her husband, Henry McNamara, have two honour-roll children, twins, Sophie and Caleb. They are fourteen, attend a private school, and are being groomed to take over their father's shipping and receiving company someday.

They may be smart for their age, which one would expect given they have attended a prestigious private school their entire lives, but I've never seen either of them smile. Even Chelsea, who has lived through real-life nightmares, still finds reasons to smile. It makes me sad for my niece and nephew, but in my mom's eyes, they're perfect.

"Okay, Mom. If you talk to Noa before I do, please tell her I send her and the family my love. Hopefully, we'll be able to see each other soon." That sounds like a reasonable thing to say, but I could go the next five years without seeing my sister and not be bothered. When I'm around her, even my anxiety gets anxiety.

"Sure, my Darling. I'm so happy to have heard from you. Please call more often. Or better yet, come home to visit. Your father and I miss you."

"I'll try to get home one weekend soon. I promise."

"Oh, before I forget, speaking of promises, how are Quinn's wedding plans going? And have you made any progress on the promise you made the last time we spoke?"

I debate whether to tell Mom about my second attempt at a coffee date in the morning, but she'll make it into a bigger deal than it really is. I don't want to answer to her if things don't go well, or worse, if they do. "After Quinn's wedding, Mom. They're getting married three weeks from Saturday. They decided they didn't want to wait."

"That's wonderful. They've been together long enough; there's no sense dragging out an engagement."

"That's what they figured." Because most people aren't afraid of adult decisions and commitments. "Kay, I'm going to go make something to eat, have a bath, and get to bed early. I love you."

"I love you too, Darling."

Once I take a few breaths to recover from our conversation, I contemplate what I'll have for dinner. My grocery stock is running low. Options are limited. Oreos?

No. You have to keep on track for Quinn's wedding. You do not want to be bursting the seams of your dress.

I whip up a quick vegetable omelette instead. Being a vegetarian, omelettes are often my preference for a weekday dinner.

After I eat, I pour a glass of wine and run myself a bubble bath. My condo bathtub is not spa-worthy, but it does the trick when I need to partake in a little self-care. Some of my lavender and mint bubble bath will be perfect. As the flesh-melting hot water is running and the bubbles are threatening to spill over the sides of the tub, my phone lights up. It's Zach.

My heart sinks.

He's cancelling your coffee date. You are more trouble than you are worth. He can't be bothered with someone that jumps to conclusions in a single bound. If repulsing people were an Olympic event, you'd be the gold medallist.

Anxiety convinces me what the content of that message says, so I don't need to read it.

I climb into the bath that's hot enough to turn my skin pink, sip my wine and try to let the water relax me. It doesn't help. The only way soaking in a bath would release the tension in my body is if it were full of hydrochloric acid.

As I climb into bed, my phone lights up with another message from Zach. I should at least glance at them before deleting his number. No sense dragging this out.

Zach: I'm looking forward to our teatime in the morning.

I'm shocked that his message is reassuring and not him bailing on me.

Zach: Good night, beautiful. I'll see you tomorrow.

Is he texting the right number? Is it possible that he's gotten my number confused with some other beautiful woman? I'm not confident he intended that for me, but I reply anyway.

Zara: Good night. See you tomorrow.

For the first time in a long time, I'm excited for the next day.

Morning arrives and I get up earlier than normal. Partly because I can't sleep anymore, and partly because I want to give myself extra time to look half decent. I need more time than I've estimated to achieve that, though.

I have a quick shower, blow-dry my hair, add in some beachy waves with my curling iron, and put on some basic makeup. Zach has already seen me on a regular day at the office multiple times, so while I want to look nice, I want to appear carefree—which, of course, is the opposite of how I'd describe myself.

My self-consciousness is breeding self-doubt faster than a fluffle of rabbits. Breathe.

I throw on one of my favourite work dresses. It's a long-sleeve, burgundy peplum dress that falls above my knees. It's a bit scandalous for workwear, but it's professional enough to pass off the shorter hemline. I'm as ready as I'll ever be.

Before leaving, I perform my usual leaving the house tasks, triple-check everything, then try to calm my nerves with a few deep breaths before putting on my shoes. Nude, easy to walk in heels finish my outfit. I walk out the door—then check three times to make sure it's locked. Everything is fine.

When I arrive at the office building a short time later, I realize how nervous I am. I've been clenching the steering wheel so tightly I have to lift my fingers back one at a time to release them from their death grip. My shoulders are aching from having them pulled up to my ears. I don't know how anyone enjoys doing this whole dating thing… and this isn't even a date.

Deep breath. Don't focus on the future, Zara. Whatever happens, everything will be fine.

Nothing ever works out "fine." The next disaster is around the corner.

I force myself to walk to the entrance, reminding myself to breathe and not make a fool of myself. Again.

Zach is already inside, waiting. When I catch his eye, I notice his mouth drop open for a quick second. He walks toward me with his trademark smile, bigger than I've ever seen it.

"Wow. If you look this good for work, I can't wait to take you on an actual date."

"Oh, um… It's nothing special. Just workwear."

"Well, consider me a fan of workwear."

I blush and note his appearance. He's wearing navy-blue slacks, cognac dress shoes, and a white, button-down shirt with the sleeves rolled up—apparently this is part of his signature style. He looks effortlessly sexy, with his perfectly messy hair and a hint of whiskers on his face.

You're double A and he's the big leagues. If people see you together, they'll wonder if you're his housekeeper. You're not good enough for someone as perfect as him.

Zach interrupts my thoughts before I can succumb to a full downward spiral. "I ordered you a peppermint tea. I hope that's okay."

"That's great. Thank you." I scan the area, noting several other patrons here already. "Are you sure you want to sit in here?"

"Why? Would you rather sit outside?"

"Well, no. I mean, people will see you in here with me."

He raises one eyebrow. "Why would that be a problem? I have no issue with other people being jealous I get to sit here and speak to the most beautiful woman in the building."

Oh, puh-lease. "Zach, you don't have to feed me your lines. Please, be honest. I can handle it." No, I can't.

"I'm not feeding you any lines. I've only known you for a few days, but I can see how incredible you are. Most people become so proud they can't see their faults. You, on the other hand, are so humble, you can't see your greatness. It's my mission to help you see."

On the verge of tears, I choke out, "I don't want to be some pet project for you. I'm sure you have better things to do."

Zach lets out an intentional exhale, reaches over to take my hand, and pulls me toward the nearest table with our two drinks sat atop it. We sit down in adjacent seats without him releasing my hand. He's looking into my eyes with a concerned expression. "You're not a pet project, Zara. I can't explain it, but since the moment I ran over you with my bike, you have intrigued me. When I turned around the next day to see you here, of all places, I couldn't believe my luck."

I don't even know how to respond, so I nod. A smile threatens to escape, but I suppress it so I don't appear too eager. I don't want to be a pet project, but I don't want to be an easy target either. The promise I made to my mother flashes in my mind, so I decide to make an effort. Breathe.

"So, now that we've settled that," he says with a wink, "tell me about yourself."

I'm so used to keeping myself out of any kind of spotlight, I'm not even sure where to start. What kinds of things do people say when they talk about themselves? Do I tell him I'm a tragic disaster who only lives to work and hide out at home? My hobbies include eating my weight in packaged cookies and watching reruns of TV shows because the familiarity eases my anxiety? "There isn't much to learn."

"I doubt that. Tell me about your job, your family, where you went to school."

"Are you a private detective, Zachary Haynes?" I can't stop a playful smirk from appearing.

He looks at me with delight in his eyes. "I want to learn everything there is to know about you."

"Well, I work on the tenth floor, which I'm sure you've noticed is the *Caring Conversations* office. I'm a counsellor and work with young people deemed 'troubled youth' by the foster care system."

"Wow, that's admirable. Suddenly, my job feels insignificant."

"Not at all. People need somewhere to live. Having a home is important to a person's identity. Don't sell yourself short."

He focuses his smiling eyes on me for a few long seconds. "See how easy it is for you to see the good in what other people do? You need to do that for yourself more often. The fact you work with 'troubled youth' makes me even more convinced that you're as amazing as I thought."

I allow his comments to pass unacknowledged. "Well, anyway. I have two older sisters, Lexi and Noa. They've both been married for over a decade and have five kids between them. My parents are still happily married after forty years and live not too far away, in Bala."

"So, you have a big family. That's a real blessing."

"I suppose. I'm not close to my sisters. They were always in a different stage of life than me. We have different goals, and they are both the type that think their way is the only right way. It can be exhausting not living up to their standards."

Way to unload your family drama on the guy. If he wasn't ready to head for the hills already, he will be now.

"Sorry. I shouldn't have said all that. Yes, it's nice having a big family." I tuck a lock of hair behind my ear, focusing my eyes on my takeout cup.

"You don't have to be sorry for being honest. Tell me the truth, not what sounds nice."

"I appreciate that. But please, tell me something about you before I blurt out any more awkward truths."

He laughs. "What do you want to know?"

"I'm aware you have a sister, Jasmine, who's stunning, by the way. What about the rest of your family?"

He tenses at the question. "I've been beating guys away from Jas since she turned thirteen. She's going to college for fashion design, and dreams of starting her own clothing line for women of all sizes."

"That's admirable to use her talents to be inclusive."

"She's a good kid, but she hates when I call her a kid since she's twenty now."

"She's a lot younger than you."

He laughs again, and if it's possible to fall in love with a laugh, I have. "Because I'm old? Eleven years. I just turned thirty-one."

"Thirty-one and you've got your own mortgage brokerage. That's impressive."

"Not as impressive as helping young kids find their way in life." His kind smile could pull me in, but I glance away to keep from melting.

The clock on the wall of the coffee shop indicates it's 8:27. We've been talking for almost forty-five minutes and I have to get to work.

"I'm so sorry, Zach. I have to get to my office. Thank you for the tea and the chat. I appreciate it."

I stand to leave, and he pushes his chair back so fast it almost falls over. He reaches a hand out and places it on my arm. "What are you doing tonight?"

"Oh… uh… watering my plant, maybe? I'm not sure how to tell if she actually needs water."

He tilts his head and slants a smile across his face. "How would you feel about me taking you out? Nothing that will take you away from your plant-mom duties."

"You don't have to do that."

His tilted head straightens as he raises his brows. "Are you saying that because you don't want to go, or you don't think I want to?" He places a calloused palm on my forearm and I wonder how a mortgage broker earned such rough hands. "I want to take you out, Zara. If you'll let me."

"Take you out?" Like a mafia hitman? He's a serial killer.

To say I'm nervous would be a gross understatement. As pathetic as it is, in my twenty-nine years of life, I've only been on a handful of dates. This is so far out of my comfort zone, a NASA telescope couldn't find it.

My dear mother encouraged me to ask myself, "What's the worst that can happen?" That's a terrible question to present to an anxious introvert because our imaginations run wild and take a lot of creative liberties in coming up with horrific—albeit unlikely but plausible—scenarios. What if my outfit catches on fire? What if a beam from the ceiling comes detached for no reason, falling and crushing me, but not killing me right away so I die a slow, painful death waiting for emergency crews to rescue me? Or what if I get sucked in by Zach's charms and he breaks my heart? That's the worst of all.

Clinical strength antiperspirant isn't strong enough to combat the stress sweat issues I'm having, and my royal blue silk blouse is paying the price. Before I'm even ready, I have to change. How am I going to survive an entire evening?

I settle on a black cotton long-sleeve shirt and a pleated leopard-print skirt. Black should hide my sweat stains. I hope. As much as I wanted to try to look nice, my stress level is impeding every effort, so my hair and makeup are a disaster. Zach is going to regret insisting on this.

A knock at the door ratchets up my heart rate, and instead of walking to answer it, I stand in place, scanning my surroundings. My condo was clean when I started getting ready. Now it appears as if there was a struggle—which, of course, there was. Me, struggling to come to terms with doing normal adult things.

Deep breath. I walk to the door and peek through the peephole, spotting the profile of this man I can't understand. What could someone like him ever see in me? He seems rational and successful. Put together and… normal. I'm none of those things and never will be.

Instead of staring at him like a creep, I step aside to pull the door open, and I'm met with a gorgeous smile.

"Hi." Zach is dressed in charcoal jeans and a burgundy v-neck, long-sleeve shirt. The colour makes his green eyes and tan skip pop.

"Hey. Uh… hi. Hello."

Why are you like this?

Zach chuckles, making heat rush to my cheeks. I don't need him to laugh to prove I'm a loser, incapable of normal conversation.

"You look beautiful. Are you ready?"

"You too. I mean, you look nice. Obviously you're ready." This is not off to a great start. "I'm sorry. This is weird for me. Not you… you're not weird. I'm weird."

Make it stop. Shut your mouth. Quit while you're ahead.

"Relax. No pressure, okay?"

Easy for him to say. "Let me get my shoes." Anything to turn away and hide my blushing face for a minute. I dig my nude heels from the closet, but immediately discard them because I don't know if we'll be walking, so I trade them for a pair of low black wedges.

"Okay, ready."

"Perfect." Zach smiles at me again, making my racing heart flutter. He's dangerous.

A large part of me wants to do another tour of my condo to make sure everything is locked or unplugged but I can't bring myself to make him wait. I'm already enough of an inconvenience, I won't hold him up any longer.

Locking the door is non-negotiable, though. That, I take my time with and check twice before following Zach to the stairs. "Um… so, where are we going?"

"That's up to you." Zach pauses on the landing between the second and third floor, forcing me to stop two stairs above. It's an unusual perspective looking down at him. "Whatever you're comfortable with." He reaches a hand up in offer, so I hesitantly place my hand in his.

"Ice cream?"

A devilish smile overtakes his face. "Ice cream sounds great."

We exit into the parking lot, where Zach leads me to his silver BMW X3 and opens the door for me. Such a gentleman. Still, I have an overwhelming fear of going to an unknown location with a man I barely know. Being secluded in his vehicle with no way of escape terrifies me. So much so, I can't get in.

"Hey, what's wrong?"

"I… I can't do this."

Zach's face twists into a pained expression. "What can't you do?"

"Th… get in there. I can't get in there with you." I can't even look at his face.

"Hey. That's okay. I said whatever you're comfortable with, and I meant it. Do you want to take a walk?"

That, I think I can do. "I'm sorry. A walk sounds fine."

He takes my hand again, and we walk toward the front of my building, onto the sidewalk and head toward the ice cream shop. My pounding heart relaxes, but still responds to his touch.

We arrive at *The Ice Cream Dream,* which borders the river running through town, and a young woman greets us with a smile. "How can I help you?"

I order a single scoop of Oreo ice cream, naturally. Zach orders a strawberry milkshake, and we find a seat on a bench bordering the walking trail along the water.

"You look really excited about that ice cream." Zach smirks at me before taking his straw in his mouth and his cheeks caving in from trying to consume the thick milkshake.

"Honestly, I wish it were socially acceptable to survive on Oreos. Or… you know… possible."

"I'm sure there is plenty of calcium and protein there."

Instead of assuming he's having a laugh at my expense, I feel a sense of ease sitting beside him and I giggle. Like a socially awkward, lame, overgrown child. But still, I giggle and it surprises me. "I appreciate your support. Don't encourage me, though. I'd be content as an Oreo-eating hermit."

He appears contemplative for a moment before he speaks again. "I think the world would be missing out on something great if you were a hermit."

What would they be missing out on? A helpless female who can't do anything right?

Just like that, my anxiety is back, taking control of our conversation. "I… I don't think anyone would miss me."

Zach swings his arm around me, placing it around my shoulders. He's so effortlessly affectionate, I'm struggling to keep up with him. He says what's on his mind, and doesn't hold back in finding something nice to say. There's nothing I can offer him in any capacity. I'm struggling to survive, spending my energy combating my thoughts, and he's gliding through life, finding success in all he does. At least, that's how I see him from the little time I've spent with him.

"I'd miss you." His words feel out of place after thirty seconds of silence, but it just confirms what I was thinking.

"You barely know me. You should quit while you're ahead."

"I guess the only way to convince you that I'm here because I want to is to prove it to you." Zach leans his head down to mine and I freeze.

He won't take no for an answer. Get away while you still can.

My thoughts are going a mile a minute as his lips graze mine. Anxiety flees for a split second as his touch sends a pulse of electricity through my body, but before I can sink into a world of euphoria, they come flooding back.

My flight instincts activate, causing me to push Zach away. The taste of his strawberry milkshake lingers on my lips. I stare at him with wide eyes, my chest heaving from panic. "I have to go."

"Zara, wait! I'm sorry."

Blood is thumping in my ears as I attempt to jog down the path toward home. Zach is calling my name from behind me, but a glance over my shoulder confirms he's not chasing me. He looks crushed.

You're incapable of being around people. Forever making yourself look like an idiot.

What have I done? I need to get home.

Home is safe.

By the time I unlock my door and slink in behind it, my heart rate has decreased, but my self-loathing is at a near all-time high. Anyone who thinks anxiety is a mental problem underestimates its ability to destroy a person physically, too. It is a full-service, life-controlling ailment that impacts every waking moment.

Now it's gone and ruined any potential with Zach, which only tells me I'm not ready to date. Nobody deserves to be saddled with someone who can't manage a kiss. A kiss. Something that should be sweet and invigorating, is instead terrifying.

Poor broken Zara. What have you done?

Last night, my emotions were bouncing between self-pity, frustration, and complete sorrow. I didn't answer Quinn's phone call or subsequent text message. If I answered, she'd hear the emotion in my voice, then she'd want to know what was wrong. The issue, aside from not wanting to burden her with my problems, is what she'll say. She'd be practical. She'd advise me from the perspective of someone who is sympathetic, but doesn't truly understand how all-consuming anxiety can be.

Listening to her advice would mean making changes in my life, and that terrifies me. It's easier for me to instruct other people how to improve their own lives, but digging myself out of my situation is different. That's not something I'm ready for.

Quinn is the only person outside of my family who knows what happened to me. If I tell her about Zach, she's going to tell me I overreacted, that not everyone is out to hurt me—things that, logically, I agree with, but can't accept. She'll encourage me to go tell Zach the truth and see if anything develops between us. But I can never tell him the truth. No one can ever learn the truth.

He would never understand. He would never see you the same.

With the sun slanting through my bedroom curtains, I get out of bed, dragging my feet. I don't even bother with my bunny slippers today. I force myself to shower and brush my teeth, but those two tasks take every ounce of energy I have. Today, I am going through the motions, trying not to have a breakdown. I sit on the edge of my bed until the last possible moment before getting dressed, then pull my hair into a messy bun.

Just stay home today. No one will miss you. It's not like you do anything useful.

For a moment, I debate giving in to my inner critic. My hands are clammy, and the hairs on the back of my neck are standing up. It's the constant feeling of dread looming over me. No, it's just anxiety.

Let's get this day over with. It's almost the weekend. I can survive one more day.

It's 7:20 by the time I get to the office. I'm over an hour early, but I had to arrive before Zach would, so I'd be sure to avoid an awkward encounter. I deleted the texts he sent last night without reading either one.

I rush across the marble floor, toward the elevator, without even glancing at the coffee shop. I don't want to risk making eye contact with Zach if he is there. The elevator doors open after I press the button for the tenth floor. Breathe. I should be in the clear now.

The office is silent as I exit the elevator, but my body tenses. Something isn't right.

Something bad is going to happen. You should have stayed home. Home is safe.

After a decade of crippling anxiety having my body on high alert for no reason, I convince myself it's in my head. I go into my office, close the door, and hang up my purse on the back— where it always goes. I walk across the small room to pull the blinds up and take advantage of my west-facing windows while the sun isn't glaring in. When I sit at my desk and power on my computer, I lean down to grab files from the bottom drawer of my filing cabinet.

As I hear the welcome chime of my computer, I sit up to look at the screen, but I'm greeted by the furious face of Mr. Patrick Kennedy. I nearly flip back in my chair as I roll it away from him. He's standing on the opposite side of my desk but rushes around toward me. He doesn't speak a word, but it doesn't appear he's here to talk.

I scramble to stand in hopes I can use the chair as a barrier between us, but he's coming at me full tilt. Before I can react, he grabs my blouse with both hands, shoves me against the wall, and pins me with his body.

My efforts to scream are useless. Fear grips me and I can't make a sound. There's no one here to hear my cries for help, anyway.

He's going to kill you if you don't fight him. You better think of something or he'll make you pay for what you did. This is your fault.

"Patrick." I don't want to enrage him, so I stop before I say anything else.

"You stupid woman. Did you really think I'd let you get away with what you did? Get me fired because you are sleeping with the boss, and I found out? I shouldn't be the one punished because you're a filthy whore."

My face scrunches in response to his accusation, but I plaster on a neutral expression so I don't upset him more. His accusation couldn't be more wrong. "I don't know why you think that, Patrick, but I've never slept with Mr. Stafford." The de-escalation protocols we studied in university replay in my mind as I contemplate what to say.

"Bull! There's no way an idiot like you comes in here and gets special treatment without doing something in return. Why does Joe always defend you then, huh?"

"I... I'm not sure, Patrick. Why don't you let me go, and we can talk about this? Maybe we can have a meeting with Mr. Stafford and work something out. You're going through a lot personally. I understand."

"You don't understand jack," he spits. "No talking is going to fix this. I'm ruined, and I'm going to take you down with me."

My heart is pounding so hard now, I'm on the verge of passing out. Patrick reaches one hand up to place it around my throat, but I let out a scream before he takes hold of me. I scream for my life, finally able to force out a sound above a whisper. It doesn't seem to do anything other than anger him because he places his other hand over my mouth. His knee is holding my legs in place, while his huge frame presses me into the wall. My arms are free, but I don't have enough room between us to push him away.

The entire world is closing in around me as my vision blurs. I'm going to die. I failed to protect myself again.

Flashes of light start dotting my darkening vision, when all of a sudden, I slump to the floor. Patrick's enraged body is no longer holding me up.

Once I catch my breath, I scramble backward to look at the scene before me. My computer is broken to pieces on the floor. Patrick is bloody and unconscious behind my desk, and I see Zach's concerned face rushing toward me.

"Zara, are you okay? Are you hurt? Let me look at you."

I crawl backwards a bit more, not wanting him to come near me. The panic in me overflows, and I can't contain it anymore. Within seconds, I am a blubbering mess. I can't see, I can't breathe, I can't control my heart rate. Sweat is dripping down my skin, but at the same time, I'm freezing cold. Hysteria takes over and there's little I can do to come back from it. I've been here before.

Zach is on the phone, but his words are cut off by the sounds of blood pumping through my body. "Please hurry… ambulance… tenth floor."

Everything around me fades.

The ride in the ambulance gave me enough time to grow increasingly uncomfortable with what just unfolded. Zach was asked to stay behind by the police to give a statement, and I'm grateful for that small mercy. The last thing I want is him fussing over me. Maybe not the last thing, but it's low on my list. Why was he even in my office at 7:30 in the morning? Is he stalking me now? I doubted he'd want to see me after I ran away from him yesterday. No scenario I come up with makes sense.

Why can't he just leave me alone?

My arrival in emerge is stressful. No matter how many times I tell the doctors and nurses I'm fine, they insist on keeping me for observation because this isn't the first panic attack I've had that caused me to black out. Yeah, thanks for the reminder. Since each attack drains the energy from me like a leech, I don't have the mental fortitude to argue, so I agree to let them run some tests. I could save them a lot of trouble by informing them I'm a crazed lunatic for no apparent reason, and there's no cure for my insanity.

They place me in a curtained room in the emergency department, leaving me alone with my thoughts. That's always a fun time. I wish I had my phone so I could have a distraction, but I'm assuming it's still in my office. I wonder what Mr. Stafford is going to think. He'll probably conclude I'm more trouble than I'm worth. Random days off and "personal emergencies" are hardly going to win me any favours.

I don't know how much time passes or how many times I've been poked or prodded, but a familiar face peeks around the curtain. "Hey, can I come in?"

No less than ninety-nine percent of me wants to say no, but that would be rude, and the handsome green-eyed rescuer in front of me is at least owed a thank you.

"Sure."

He steps inside the curtain, tugging it closed behind him. "I brought you some Oreos." He waves a package of birthday cake Oreos in front of him. "How are you feeling?"

"That's a loaded question. Are you okay?"

His eyes pop wide. "I'm fine. Nothing some ice on my knuckles won't fix. I'm... uh... I'm sorry I didn't get there sooner."

Why would he think it was his problem to fix? It's my fault for not being able to protect myself. "Why were you there at all? After last night, I thought..."

He stares at the floor, shifting his weight, with his hands shoved in the pockets of his grey slacks. "I wanted to say sorry for that, too. I shouldn't have—"

"No, that was my fault. There's just... I don't know how to explain it." No way am I telling him the truth. "I have history. It makes me... stupid."

"Zara." His gaze meets mine, but none of his usual confidence is present. He looks as scared as I do. "You weren't stupid. You don't have to explain your history to me if you don't want to, but I'd like to explain mine."

I gesture toward the chair beside the hospital bed, inviting him to sit. "You don't owe me any explanations either, but I'll listen."

Zach drops himself into the vinyl chair and leans forward, resting his elbows on his knees. He closes his eyes for a moment, lifting his hand to rub his chin. "I'm a twin."

How do I process that information? Our conversation has taken a sharp turn in an unknown direction. My least favourite direction. "Woah. I didn't expect that. There are two men as gorgeous as you walking around?" Blush overtakes my cheeks after outing my attraction to him.

"No." He stares across the room at the beeping heart monitor that assures him I'm still alive. "That's how my story starts. When we were fourteen, my brother Leo and I were riding our bikes home from a friend's house after dark; something we'd done 100 times before. We would go to our friend's houses to play video games or to the ball field to play baseball—typical fourteen-year-old stuff. On that night, when we were riding home, Leo was about thirty feet in front of me. We would almost always ride side-by-side, but that time, I was riding farther back. We rounded the second-last corner before our street, when a car came speeding toward us, and without warning swerved across the lane Leo and I were riding in. The car missed me, but I ended up crashing into the side of it and flew into the yard of a nearby house."

"And Leo?"

Zach shakes his head, his eyes brimming with tears. "The car struck him directly. The driver was drunk and walked away without a scratch. It knocked me unconscious, and I didn't wake until a few days later in the hospital. They put me in a medically induced coma because of brain swelling. I was lucky my mother always drilled into us the importance of bike safety, so I was wearing my helmet because it saved my life. When I woke up, my parents were standing beside me, and I could tell by their faces something was wrong. My mom threw herself over me and started crying like I had never heard a person cry before."

"Zach, I can't even imagine."

"You know how they say twins have this special connection? Well, Leo and I had that. From the second I woke up, I couldn't feel it anymore. I knew he was gone."

The obvious pain on his face makes tears run down my cheeks.

"Anyway, after we buried my brother, my mom changed. She was so grief stricken, she spiralled into a deep depression. She was eventually diagnosed with Generalized Anxiety Disorder as well, and the biggest cause of her anxiety was her kids. It terrified her to let Jas or me leave the house. I could only go to school and straight back home. Jasmine was only small—she had just turned three when Leo died—so Mom quit her job to stay home. That, in turn, stressed my dad; not only were we financially strapped, but he was also having to come home to do the cooking and cleaning because Mom couldn't manage it."

"It's said that there is no grief like that of losing a child. I can understand why it was so difficult for her. That must have been really hard on your dad, though. He was grieving too."

"Mom never came out of it. Jasmine was raised by a zombie, but I never blamed my mom. I knew she loved us and that's why it was so hard. Jasmine started Junior Kindergarten the following year and Mom was obsessive about dropping her off, picking her up, and calling the school throughout the day to make sure Jas was all right. By the time I was sixteen, we were in such a financial hole, I started working after school at a coffee shop to help my dad out. It wasn't much, but it eased a bit of the financial stress. In turn, though, my absence while I was at school and work made my mother more anxious. That cycle continued until I was eighteen and ready to go away to college.

I was accepted to play baseball on scholarship and study chemical engineering. I thought if I could get a good job, I could support my family and things would be okay."

"Your brother would be proud of you." My words cause him to tear up again. I want to reach out to hold his hand or something, but that feels out of line, given how we left off our previous encounter.

"Well, I didn't get the chance to fix things. A month into my third year of college, I was walking across campus when two police officers approached me. I was afraid I had unknowingly done something illegal, but when they asked me to come with them, I agreed. They made me go all the way to the police station with them without answering any of my questions, so I had a feeling in my gut that something was wrong."

"Oh, no."

"Indeed." His lips form a tight line and he swipes at his eyes. "When we arrived at the police station, they informed me that both of my parents had died. I guess they had some work done on their furnace and the gas line was jolted, causing a leak. They never installed carbon monoxide detectors in the house, which is ironic, given Mom's anxiety. Luckily, Jasmine was having a sleepover at her friend's house that night, which would be a miracle on a normal day given how anxious my mom was about Jas being anywhere but home, but on that night, it saved her life. Jasmine's friend's parents dropped her off the next day after they couldn't get a hold of ours. Jas walked in and found them sleeping in the bed—but they weren't sleeping."

"Poor Jasmine. That must have been traumatic."

"It was. We didn't have any other family, so child services took her. I couldn't sit back and watch my baby sister go into foster care after everything she went through. So, I dropped out of school and looked into finding a job that I could start earning money at right away. I was lucky enough to be hired by a mortgage broker who took a chance on me. He taught me everything about the industry, and within eight months, I petitioned to become Jasmine's legal guardian. With the amount of money I was making, and having a stable address, the court approved my application. Jasmine came back to live with me, and she's been with me ever since."

"Wow. Your parents would be so proud of you, too. You realize that, right? The most important thing in the world to your mom was her family, and you did everything you could to make sure Jasmine could go somewhere she was loved and cared for. That's not a small thing."

"It was the right thing to do."

"It might have been the right thing, but that doesn't mean it was the easy thing. You exceeded the call of duty for a twenty-one-year-old. You're a good man."

"I couldn't imagine not having Jasmine in my life. She's my sun and moon and stars, and there's nothing I wouldn't do for her."

"So, you've been raising Jasmine for the past decade, all while working full time and opening your own business?"

"Yeah, but I wouldn't say I raised her. She raised me just as much."

I take a second to study the appearance of this man in front of me—not his physical looks, but his honesty, integrity, and vulnerability. He is beautiful. "You don't have to answer this, but the day I came down to your office, I was curious about your business name. What does it mean?"

His face lights up with his beaming smile. "My brother's name was Leo, my father was Ari, and my mother was Cynthia. It took us a while to come up with something to honour all three of them, but Jasmine and I settled on Arileia. A-R-I for my dad, L-E for Leo, and I-A from my mom's name."

"That's beautiful, Zach."

The sound of the curtain being pulled back jolts both of us from our conversation. Dr. Ross, who had seen to me earlier, returns with a clipboard and a serious expression. His presence ratchets up my panic level, and I send Zach a pleading look. Thankfully, he understands what I'm relaying without words.

"I'll wait outside." He exits the makeshift room, pulling the curtain closed behind him.

Dr. Ross proceeds with his medical report, and as expected, nothing of note showed up in my bloodwork. Just when I'm hoping I'll get the green light to go home, he lobs a curveball at me. "Miss Levy, I can imagine how difficult today was for you after being a victim of sexual assault in the past. If you'd be open to it, I'd like to refer you to a psychologist, so you have someone to speak to about this."

No, no, no.

My stomach plummets. Not only at the mention of my past, but because Zach is on the other side of the curtain. If he heard, he'll never speak to me again. He was vulnerable and opened up to me about his past, and this is how he finds out about mine? He'll be so disgusted.

Again, tears start streaming down my cheeks without permission.

Dr. Ross positions himself at the head of the bed, looming over me. His voice is a stark contrast to his imposing stance. "I understand that you're a youth counsellor, Zara. I'm sure you, of all people, can appreciate how important it is to speak to someone about these things."

I'm not brave enough for that. Airing my past for others to know what happened, it's too... shameful. It's embarrassing, and I don't want people pitying me. My clients are a fraction of my age, and they've dealt with far worse things. If they can manage, I better figure out a way. "I don't think that's necessary," I mumble, struggling to fend off more tears.

Why are you such a lunatic? Pull yourself together. No one wants to hear your pathetic sob story.

The disappointment Dr. Ross feels is clear from his dropped shoulders and sombre expression, but no one can be more disappointed in me than myself.

"It's your decision, but I want you to know the option is available for you. Let me know if you change your mind. Opening that channel of communication for the first time is often the hardest step, but it might help to process everything."

I am well aware how hard that first step can be. Most kids who come into my office are forced there, and our first several appointments are often silent or little more than surface talk. I'm not strong enough to open that channel yet. All I can manage is to say, "Thank you."

With no word on potential discharge, Dr. Ross excuses himself and Zach's terrified face re-enters the room.

He doesn't need to say anything to confirm he heard what was said, but he does. "Zara... I..."

"Don't. Whatever you heard, just don't. You shouldn't even be here."

"No, that's not what—"

"Please, just go. I'm disgusting, I know. I told you from day one that I wasn't the girl for you, but you kept insisting, and now you know the truth."

"That's not—"

"Go." I barely choke out that final word before my panic starts overwhelming me again. Whatever cocktail they gave me in my IV has worn off, and I'm unravelling faster than a ball of yarn in a room full of kittens. "Please, go."

"I'll leave because I don't want to upset you, but when you're feeling better, I'd like to continue our conversation."

Why can't he leave you alone? He can do so much better. Don't waste his time. He should know by now, you'll never be normal. You'll always be poor broken Zara.

Zach leaves, and I'm left staring at the swaying curtain as a reminder I pushed another person away. It's my thing. It's easier than people finding out what I really am. My brain is in a constant battle of needing to be alone, yet wanting people around, versus being around people, but wanting to be alone.

I'm lonely. But I don't feel like a worthwhile addition to anyone's life. I'm doing everyone a favour by keeping to myself. Quinn is better off without me. My sisters learned long ago that it's easier to ignore my existence. Everyone at work is going to find out what happened with Patrick and know I'm a magnet for trouble. Not that they had any respect for me before, but that will be impossible now. My parents tolerate be because they're obligated to, not because I add value to their lives. Zach is better off moving on. He's already been through so much.

Poor broken Zara. Boo hoo. Get over yourself, already. You're not strong enough to handle this life. You're not valuable enough to be worth anyone's time. You're not smart enough to benefit anyone. You will never be enough.

A nurse enters my space when she hears the rapid beeping of my heart monitor and finds me sobbing into my hands. As if my level of mortification could increase any more, here I am, making a fool of myself again. The tawny-skinned nurse with raven hair piled high on her head shouts something out into the hallway before rushing to my side. She fiddles with the IV bag I'm still attached to, just as an unfamiliar doctor pushes aside the curtain.

The new doctor has a heavy Nigerian accent and rushes an introduction to me as she gives the nurse instructions. My sniffles and sobbing provide a snot-fuelled soundtrack as another nurse enters.

Good grief. There must be more critical patients to deal with than someone who can't stop crying over stupid nonsense. You're a burden to everyone.

I can't get my emotions under control, and I don't have a good reason why. It's clear to me I'm being irrational, but that doesn't make it any easier to rein in the looming panic attack. Unable to control it, the doctor orders a dose of benzodiazepines, which lulls me back into a state of calm.

They also make me feel exhausted, and after the turmoil of the day, I drift off into a semi-conscious sleep, still on alert and aware of every movement around me. One could technically call it sleep, but it's not the least bit restful.

When I wake fully, Dr. Ross returns to inform me he'd like to keep me overnight for observation. A combination of the trauma from earlier, two serious panic attacks, and my refusal to call anyone to come sit with me or take me home, he's not comfortable letting me go. I'm not being held as a prisoner, but I'm not going to put up a fight either. What's waiting for me at home? My wilting ivy and cheap wine? Hardly worth rushing home for.

I accept that I'm safe here and resign myself to spending the night. There's no way I'm calling my mom or Quinn to come save me from this mess. No one can save me, anyway. It's not their job, and I'm beyond saving.

Saturday morning around 9:30, Dr. Ross comes back in to speak to me about being discharged. He's uncomfortable sending me home alone, but I insist I will be fine and again refuse to contact anyone. I promise I'll go pick up my car, go home, and follow up with my primary care physician in a few days—something I should have done long before now.

Within the hour, I'm a free woman. Free from the hospital, but still imprisoned by my thoughts.

The lady at the nurse's station calls a taxi for me to return to the office building, which the doctor graciously offered to pay for since I don't have my purse. I need to pick up my keys, phone, and wallet from the office so I can go home.

Home is safe.

I'm relieved to have a middle-aged woman as my taxi driver because I was panicking at the thought of being in a vehicle alone with an unfamiliar man. It's unfair of me to judge all men based on the actions of a few, but right now, I can't stop myself from feeling paralyzing fear at the thought.

We pull up in front of my office building and the lady drives off without another word. It's not until she's out of sight that I realize it's Saturday. I already knew that, but, for some reason, it didn't cross my mind that the office would be closed.

Now what do I do? My keys and phone are inside. I have no money and no way of getting home. Even if I walked, I'd have no way to get in.

After an unknown number of minutes, since I don't have my phone and possess no concept of time, I stroll down the street toward other businesses, hoping an answer will come to me.

I woke up thinking today would be better than yesterday, but that's not the case. Sure, I haven't been nearly choked to death in my office and had my darkest secret outed to the first guy to show genuine interest in me in over a decade, but that doesn't make my current situation any better.

Just when I think the day can't get any worse, it starts drizzling. I run into a drugstore, which is the first open business I come across other than restaurants. I take a deep breath as I get inside, wiping the rain from my face. Everyone in proximity to the door is staring at me.

No one wants you here.

Breathe. I have nowhere else to go and it's taking every ounce of strength in me not to collapse to my knees in tears... again.

Everything is fine. Everything will be fine. I will be fine.

You're wearing yesterday's clothes. They probably think you've done 'the walk of shame'. Your hair is a nightmare, and you have bandaids all over from needles. Who knows what people think of you right now.

Whatever their reasons for staring, it's probably not the truth of what happened, and I'm not going to correct them. I need to come up with a solution. I keep my head low to avoid making eye contact with anyone and make my way to the checkout.

The cashier spots me and appears startled. "Are you okay?"

How bad is your hair that you're scaring people?

"Well, I'm a little embarrassed. Would it be too much trouble for me to use a phone? I need to make a local call."

I assume that if she agrees, she will make me use the drug store phone, but to my surprise, she pulls out her cell phone with a glittery white case. "Call whoever you want. I have free long distance." Her kind smile eases some of my anxiety, only to replace it with the sinking feeling of being pitied.

"Thank you so much. I don't know how to repay you."

"Just bring my phone back when you're done." She lets out a nervous laugh.

The least I can do is reassure her I'm not going to take off with her phone. "I will. Just give me one minute to call my mom and I'll bring it right back." I point to the corner near the photo-printing station.

My parents' phone number has been the same since I was a child, so I have no issue recalling it from memory. It rings five times, but there's no answer. I try again. Still no answer. I push down the panic once I realize they aren't home and try to come up with a new plan. I guess I have no choice but to call Quinn.

She picks up on the third ring. "Hello?"

"Quinny?"

You are a grown woman. Do not cry because your friend answered the phone.

"Zara? Why are you calling me from a different number?"

This is not the time for an inquisition, but I don't want to make her upset by ignoring her questions. "I don't want you to make a big deal of this, but I need your help. I'll explain everything when I see you."

"What's wrong? Where are you? What happened?"

"It's no big deal. Can you come pick me up? I'm at the drugstore near my office building." I glance over and the cashier is going about her business, not paying any attention to me.

"Are you okay?"

"Yes, I'm all right." That's not a lie, right? "I need someone to pick me up and I can't get a hold of my parents."

"Okay, Chica. I'm coming. Give me thirty minutes."

"Thanks. I appreciate it."

I walk back to the cashier and hand over her phone. She doesn't seem interested in what I'm saying, but I apologize for taking so long, anyway. Instead, she's looking at me with fascination, as if I'm a zoo creature.

She probably thinks you're a tramp, just like Patrick said.

I gasp. Patrick! Suddenly, every person in front of me morphs into a Patrick replica. That look of hatred he had is displayed on the faces of each person within view. All logic disappears and I'm reduced to a fit of tears, terrified of everyone present.

Everyone is laughing at you. You look like a lunatic. You are a lunatic.

Before anyone can speak to me or flash me another angry glare, I dash out the door, into the pouring rain. I lean back against the large windows, resting on the small ledge, and wipe the tears from my face that are mixing with rain. I'm so tired of crying. My eyes are dry from the number of tears I've shed over the past few days.

Quinn arrives with Tyler a short time later. No doubt, I look like a drowned rat in yesterday's clothes. Tyler pulls his 1991 Trans Am ASC up to the curb in front of me, and Quinn jumps out before the car is in park.

I can't tell if she's crying, or if it's the rain until she screams, "Zara! What happened to you? Oh, Chica. Who did this to you?"

"The... rain?"

"Your neck! Who did that?"

Instinctively, my hands cover my throat, wanting to hide whatever the alleged issue is. I turn to look at my reflection in the drugstore windows. It's spattered with raindrops, but I can see exactly what she's talking about. Around my neck is a hand-sized purple bruise. It didn't occur to me that there would be marks on me.

That's why everyone was staring.

I turn back toward Quinn and see Tyler standing beside her. Now we're all getting soaked. I can't even come up with the right words to explain what happened, so I stare at them both.

Tyler's eyes go wide the moment he sees the bruise. "Zara, who did this? Is he still here? I'm going to make him wish he was dead." He scans the parking lot with his fists clenched.

"No. No, he's not here. Can we get out of here? I don't want to have this conversation here. I can't get back into my condo, either. My keys are in my office, and I had the locks at home changed a few days ago. Can you take me to my parents? I don't want to bother you guys any more than I have."

"You're not a bother. You'll come home with us. If you want to go to your parents' later, we can take you, but please let me take you to my place so I can get you some dry clothes, and we can talk." Her voice is breaking as she continues, "I've been such a crap friend. I got so distracted by the wedding, I haven't been checking in much. I'm so sorry."

"No, Quinn. You have no reason to be sorry. This had nothing to do with you. But, please, can we leave?"

"Of course." She opens Tyler's passenger door, flips the front seat forward, and holds her hand out to encourage me to get in. After I climb in, she says, "Move over; I'm coming in."

"It's okay. You guys came all the way here to pick me up. You don't need to sit in the back, too."

"Zara, I'm coming in whether or not you move, so shove over, or I'm sitting on your lap."

I slide over behind the driver's seat. No sense in arguing with her. Tyler starts the car, and it sounds remarkably different from my little Prius. Regardless, I feel safe here. With them, I'm okay.

"That son of a..." Tyler shouts, after I've changed into dry clothes and recounted the events of the previous day.

Quinn is in tears, holding onto me for dear life. "He almost killed you. I can't even imagine how you're feeling right now."

"Not very good, to be honest, but I haven't had time to process everything."

"I'm so glad that guy was there to beat up that scumbag."

The colour drains from my face at the mention of Zach and Patrick, but for different reasons. Of course, I didn't mention who Zach really was—just that he was another employee in the building who heard me scream. I said I wouldn't keep things from Quinn, but I don't want to distract from her joyous wedding preparation with my pathetic attempt at a love life; an attempt that lasted less than two weeks and my irrational brain sabotaged before it could turn into anything.

"Enough about me. Please. I need to forget right now. Tell me how your wedding plans are going."

Quinn sends me a questioning look, but concedes to my request. "They're going great. We'll have a small wedding, since it's such short notice."

I feel relief at those words—fewer people to embarrass myself in front of.

"We'll only have about 100 people there, but that's perfect. Mostly family with a few friends and co-workers."

A hundred people is a small wedding? When she said small, I thought maybe twenty people. I should have known better because Tyler comes from a large, tight-knit family. Quinn only has her parents and little sister, but a lot of aunts, uncles, and cousins.

That's 100 people to see you make a fool of yourself because you can't do anything right.

Breathe. "Wow, that's great."

I must not sound convincing, because Quinn laughs.

"Don't worry, Chica; it'll be fine. It's going to be an awesome day. Can I give you a couple of jobs to do?"

"I was hoping you'd ask. I didn't want to pry, but I wanted to live up to the whole maid of honour title."

"Sorry. I didn't know if you'd be up to helping, so I didn't ask. Ty, can you grab the list I have on my desk, please?"

Tyler hands me the list Quinn has written in her loopy handwriting, and I skim over the outstanding tasks.

"I can book us nail appointments for Friday, and hair and makeup for Saturday morning. I can follow up with the photographer and DJ, too."

"That'd be great. See, you're killing this maid of honour stuff." Quinn shoves my shoulder, wearing a huge smile.

"I hope these bruises fade in time. I don't want to be standing up there with a yellow neck."

"Don't worry about that. We still have three weeks. Even if it were tomorrow, you still look beautiful." Quinn squeezes my empty hand.

As I set her notebook on the taupe sofa between us, I return her gentle squeeze. "I don't want people talking about what happened to me. I'd rather fade into the background."

"Everything is going to be fine, Zar. I get to marry this dreamboat," she says with a sly smile as she hooks her thumb in Tyler's direction. "That's all that really matters."

"Soon enough, you're going to be Mrs. Quinn Ochoa. That's so exciting!"

I really am excited for them. They are an incredible couple. Through thick and thin, they support each other. They have so much in common, and they love each other enough you almost get secondhand love sickness. Who knew that signing up for a free trial with a personal trainer could result in finding the love of your life? I wish I was that lucky.

It occurs to me out of nowhere that I'm going to have to make a police report regarding what happened with Patrick. Those were the last words the police said to me before the ambulance doors closed.

Quinn must notice my change in demeanour because her body tenses. "Hey, are you okay?"

I nod. "Yeah, fine. I have to go to the police station to make a statement. The thought of doing that again is overwhelming."

Twin lines form above the bridge of her nose. "I'll take you. We can go right now and get it over with, so you won't be stressed."

"I guess that might be the best option. If I delay it, I'll avoid it altogether."

She pops up from the couch, flashing a glance at Tyler, who is still standing protectively behind the couch. "Okay, if you're ready, I'm ready."

"I'll never feel ready, but I want to get it over with."

"Then let's go get it done and you can put this behind you." She reaches a hand out to pull me up from the sofa.

I take her hand and allow her to ease me into this next unpleasant event to add to the long list I've already dealt with.

Quinn and I walk into the police station, drawing the attention from a few officers. I'm self-conscious of the bruises on my neck, which I inspected in Quinn's bathroom before we left, and they are not pretty. The officers within my field of vision don't seem bothered by them, which somehow makes it worse. What kinds of things are they faced with that they're desensitized to neck bruises?

The Desk Sergeant asks how he can help us, and I freeze.

They're going to think you're a problem-causing damsel in distress, making issues out of thin air to get attention. No one will believe you.

My deer-in-headlights look must spur Quinn into action, because she quickly informs the Sergeant why we're here. He assures her someone will be out to speak with me in a few moments, but his neutral expression only boosts my anxiety.

When are you going to stop causing problems?

I sit in a blue vinyl chair with weathered wooden armrests affixed to the steel frame, and wring my hands together in my lap. My cuticles have been feeling the wrath of my uneasiness, so, of course, I continue to pick at those too. "Can we just go? Forget about this. I can't do this again."

"Hey, take a breath. You've got this, okay? The police asked you to come make a statement, Zar. You're not causing any trouble, and they're going to believe you."

I stare into my friend's blue eyes, wondering when she developed these mind-reading powers.

"All you have to do is tell them what you remember, okay? They'll do their own investigation and get it sorted out. You're helping, not hindering them. This isn't your fault."

It's always your fault. Poor broken Zara can't exist like a normal adult. Always needing to be coddled and...

"Zara Levy?" A husky female voice pulls me from my thoughts. The petite brunette introduces herself as Constable Olga Griggs. She's got a fierceness in her eyes that says you don't want to mess with her.

Quinn puts her hand on mine as I get up. "It's going to be okay. Tell them what you remember. I'll wait right here." Her gentle smile still has no effect on my nerves.

I nod anyway, before rushing off behind Constable Griggs.

She opens the door to an interview room, and the sight of it sucks the air out of my lungs. Most people go their entire lives without ever seeing the inside of a police interrogation room, yet here I am for the second time, on both occasions, as a victim.

Forever a victim, Zara. A tax on the police officers, doctors, and taxpayers. You're a waste of everyone's time and money.

I pause at the door, take a breath and tell myself it will be okay. *I'll* be okay.

Constable Griggs does her best to put me at ease. "We'll start when you're comfortable, and you can tell me what you recall. I'll leave the door open, and if at any time you need to step out for a moment, feel free. You are not in trouble here, and I know it's difficult, but I'm here to help."

Her words, though helpful, seem rehearsed. I realize she's used to seeing people like me. Victims who have been violated in various ways and have survived to tell the tale. I can't blame it on her that the justice system isn't effective, and I'm confident this will be for nothing. Victims are left living with the trauma, and perpetrators sit in the naughty corner for a little while. Nothing about it is fair.

Regardless, I spend the next ninety-five minutes relaying the events of yesterday morning to the best of my ability. I explain my professional history with Patrick and about him being fired, but I mention nothing unrelated to our confrontation yesterday. I figure that's up to the police to investigate and not hear my second-hand account surrounding his at-home issues and career failings.

I tell her how I made Zach's acquaintance, but again, don't go into much detail. I ask if he'll be in trouble for hurting Patrick. Constable Griggs said she was certain there wouldn't be any repercussions for Zach because he was stopping a crime in progress and didn't have time to wait for police to arrive. Even though I can't handle facing Zach again, I'm glad he won't be in trouble because of me.

When we wrap up the interview and Olga confirms she has everything she needs, she says, "I'll call you if we have any other questions, but I think it should be an open and shut case. He'd be stupid to not plead guilty."

"I don't have my phone, but I can give you my friend Quinn's number until Monday."

She tilts her head. "Are you staying with her?"

I'm ashamed of this whole situation, so my mousy voice squeaks out, "Well, my house and car keys are in the office, along with my phone, so I can't get home right now. I'll have to wait until the office opens again on Monday."

"Yeah... that's not happening. Can you stick around for a bit longer? I'm going to get this sorted."

"Oh, don't go to any trouble. It's fine."

"It most certainly is not. You were assaulted in your workplace, where you do very honourable work, spent a night in the hospital, and now you can't go home? Not on my watch. Wait in the lobby with your friend, and I'll come back to speak with you as soon as I can."

A short time later, Olga returns to the lobby, looking quite pleased with herself. "Let's get you home."

I peek up at her from the corner of my eyes. "How will we do that?"

"I phoned your boss, Mr. Stafford. He called the building manager, who has the keys to the front door and each of the offices. I'll escort you in to get your belongings when he arrives. Let's head over now, because he'll be there in about fifteen minutes." I'm not surprised she wouldn't take no for an answer and had complete strangers accommodating her request.

"Wow, thank you."

Always a hassle. Forever a burden.

Quinn interrupts my internal torment again. "I know what that face means. This is not your fault, and I'll keep telling you that until you believe it." She leans in to give me a hug. "Do you want me to come with you?"

"Thanks, Quinny, but I'll be okay. You've already wasted half your day on me."

My beautiful friend's face morphs in a split second as she plants one hand on either of my shoulders and glares at me through narrowed eyes. "Don't you dare *ever* think you're a waste of my time."

I'm increasingly uncomfortable standing in the heat of Quinn's gaze, so I pacify her with a terse smile and a nod. There's no conviction in either.

We say our goodbyes, and I walk out with Constable Griggs. Something about being under the watchful eye of a police officer makes me feel protected, yet I'm not sure I'll feel safe until I get back within my four walls.

As protected as I feel, nothing could have prepared me for the feelings that surface the moment I walk onto the tenth floor.

He's here. You're not safe. You can never come back here. Patrick is going to come for you. He'll be waiting, and next time, no one will come to your rescue. Go home. Home is safe.

I'm paralyzed with fear and can't walk through the door—well, where there used to be a door. Zach wasn't playing around because he broke the door down. This is the gap in the wall, formerly known as the door.

Constable Griggs must notice the fear wash over me, because she walks in and grabs my purse off of my desk. She hands it to me, physically turns me around, and says, "Let's go over here to check if you have everything you need."

I root through my bag to find my keys, check. Phone, check—though it's dead and has a gigantic crack across the screen. Great. On the bright side, I can go home.

Home is not safe without a phone. How will you call Quinn to let her know you got home? How will you call for help if you need it?

I ignore my anxious overreaction, but that doesn't make it feel less real—and tell Olga I am ready to go. We take the elevator back down and exit through the lobby doors. The building manager is waiting to lock the doors again, so I thank him for coming on his day off. He stares at the bruises on my neck, and I wish the Earth would swallow me whole.

Everyone can see how weak you are. They know you're a victim. A pathetic little girl who can't protect herself. You don't stand a chance.

I thank Olga, and she offers to take me to my car and follow me home, but I tell her it's unnecessary. I am sick of people fussing over me.

A moment later, I'm on my way home.

Home is safe—if your phone works.

It's now Saturday evening and I haven't eaten for a full thirty-six hours. I have a few groceries left, but I don't feel like cooking. Oreos it is. I've earned these.

After my phone is charged a bit, I text Quinn to tell her I made it home safely and assure her I will give her my spare key. I decide not to turn a quick update into a whole phone call because she'd feel obligated to ask how I was feeling and so on. My efforts to put the last few days behind me will not be derailed by a phone call with an insightful eighth-grade English teacher. Texting—an anxious introvert's favourite invention.

I'm a few minutes into the next episode of my favourite nostalgic TV show when I hear a knock at my door. I'm not expecting anyone, and I've already texted Quinn that I was home—she wouldn't show up.

He's here. Patrick found you. No one is around to save you this time.

I tiptoe to the door, trying not to make any sound, so if it is Patrick, I can pretend I'm not home. When I peer through the peephole, I see the last person I would expect.

Zach is standing in the hallway when I open the door, and I am thoroughly embarrassed by my appearance. I'm wearing running shorts that display my hairy legs, a sweatshirt that's at least three sizes too big, my hair is in a topknot, and I haven't brushed my teeth. Zach is standing there looking like a GQ model, dressed in jeans and a pullover sweater. At least at this moment, my external appearance matches my inner character. Ugly chaos. Will this be what it takes for him to see me for who I am?

"Hi." He's staring at the bruises on my neck. I gather they hadn't quite developed yet when he saw me in the hospital.

What do I say in reply? Our last two encounters didn't end well. Actually, a vast majority of our interactions haven't ended well. Thanks to me.

"I know you weren't expecting me, but I've been texting and calling all day and you didn't answer. I wanted to make sure you were okay."

"I'm fine." Another lie.

He agonizes over his words. "I brought you some food. I wasn't sure if you had eaten. No pretence, whatsoever. You can keep the food, and I'll leave."

"Thank you."

He looks defeated but passes me the bag of food. It smells heavenly, whatever it is, then huffs a sigh with his eyes focused on my neck. "I guess I'll see you around."

"Zach?"

"Yeah?"

"Would you like to come in and eat with me?" My offer catches us both by surprise. Just forty-eight hours ago, I was running away from him, refusing to get in his car, and here I am, letting him come into my home. I'm a hot mess, my condo is a mess, and in all likelihood, I smell like a goat, though not a fraction as cute, but something compelled me to ask him in.

"I'd love to, if you're comfortable with that."

Without another word, I open the door wider and direct him inside. As he steps inside, he's taking everything in. I'm mortified by what he's seeing right now, but I don't have the emotional capacity to defend how things look—myself included. My poor housekeeping skills, terrible personal hygiene, lacklustre socializing skills, and magnetism for trouble should be enough for him to leave.

Please don't leave.

Why would he ever want to stay? He could have any woman he wants; he will not settle for you.

The silence grows increasingly awkward until he speaks. "This is a nice place. I like it."

"You don't have to fake nice, Zach. It's a disaster... and so am I. I only got home a short time ago."

"Oh, did you go out today?" He shifts his weight while looking at his feet.

"Not really." I blurt out the entire unedited scenario about the drugstore scene, the police station, and my broken phone before I can stop myself.

"Oh, shoot. Zara, I didn't realize. I should have gone back and grabbed your phone and keys yesterday. I could have brought them before I left."

When he mentions leaving the hospital, I'm reminded of why I asked him to go and the shame washes over me.

He heard your secret. He must think you're disgusting and only came here because he pities you. There's no other reason he would be here. Not after how you treated him.

"Can you give me a minute? I'd like to go clean myself up. I wasn't expecting company." In actuality, I need to go hide for a few minutes. Compose myself. Too bad I'm more complicated to compose than anything Mozart ever created.

"Yeah, of course." He walks toward the kitchen. "I'll get the food out."

I rush into the safety of my bedroom, close the door behind me. As soon as I enter my ensuite and catch a glimpse of myself, I'm more mortified than I was. This bruise is repulsive. How can he even look at me right now?

In hopes my long locks will cover some of the offensive bruise, I pull it out of the elastic and comb it with my fingers. I brush my teeth, throw on some deodorant and perfume, then go to change my clothes. I don't want him to think I'm dressing up for him, so I grab a pair of cotton leggings and a T-shirt. A bra is a necessity with this shirt—curse this modern torture device.

I emerge from my room a moment later, trying to push the disgrace I feel to the back of my mind. That's where my most frequent thoughts hang out and like to pop up at inconvenient times.

Zach is in the kitchen, pulling food out of the bag he brought. "I'm a vegetarian and wasn't sure what else was good, so I just went with what I knew."

I stutter step after tripping on the edge of my area rug. "A vegetarian?"

He chuckles once I'm steady on my feet. "Yeah. Is that a deal breaker?"

This guy thinks after all of my nonsense that him being a vegetarian would ruin our chances? Oh, buddy, I took care of that three encounters ago. "Not at all. I'm a vegetarian too, so I was just surprised."

He issues his gorgeous head-tilting smile. "You just keep getting better and better, Zara Levy."

That actually makes me laugh. An abrasive one-note laugh. "Don't be ridiculous. After the conversations we've had, I'd say it's fair you've gotten a good glimpse at the mess that is Zara Levy. It just gets worse, the longer you stick around."

After setting the final container on the counter, Zach stares at me, with his shoulders dropped. Meanwhile, I'm carrying so much tension in my body, I'm practically wearing my shoulders as earrings.

"Everyone is messy. You just think your mess makes you unworthy. All I see is perfection."

"I'm the farthest thing from perfect. I'm damaged goods," I choke out, reminding myself that he is aware of my past. Granted, he doesn't know much, but the fact he knows anything is enough to make me burst from discomfort.

He doesn't leave, though. He walks toward me, stopping before he can touch me, but the heat in his eyes says he wants to. "You are not damaged goods."

"I guess you aren't familiar enough with me yet. If this"—I point to my neck—"and my history you overheard don't convince you, I'm sure spending a bit more time with me will have you running."

"I wish you'd give me a chance to prove to you that there's nothing wrong with you."

"Zach, I'm trying to save you the trouble. I don't want you feeling like you need to rescue me or take care of me, always saying these sweet things. I realize what I am. You haven't figured it out yet."

He takes one more step toward me, this time cradling my hands in his. He looks into my eyes. "No. I know what you are, but *you* haven't figured it out yet."

Those words hit me like a Mack truck. For the first time in my life, I actually want to kiss someone. If he knew the whole truth, he'd never want to kiss me, and I admit to myself I can't deceive him.

"Uh... should we eat?"

A wry smile reduces the intensity of Zach's gaze. "Yeah. I got pineapple fried rice, spring rolls, green mango salad, and vegetarian pad thai. I hope you at least like one of those, but I can get something else if you don't."

I'd be hard-pressed to find foods I enjoy more than his selections. "This is amazing. Thank you. And thank you for the Oreos. Turns out, I did have to survive on them."

"Well, I'm happy to keep you alive." His eyes jolt open wide. "Sorry, I just mean..."

Obviously, the situation with Patrick bothers him more than he lets on. "I'm sorry you got involved in everything." Now my appetite has disappeared, because I'm riddled with guilt and overwhelm. Nothing destroys my desire to eat like a reminder of my near-death experience and dragging other people into my mess. I set down my plate before I put anything on it.

"I'm the one who's sorry. The other night, I pushed things too far." He sets his plate down, also with nothing on it. "Did you go to work early to avoid me?"

My guilt over not being honest versus the urge to lie and hide my shame are at war with one another. "It's not that simple."

"That's a yes, then." He scrubs his hands over his face. "I'm sorry." His eyes are closed as he utters those words, appearing as though he's having an internal battle, too.

I want to ease some of the guilt he's carrying. "It wasn't your fault. I just freaked out because… I'm pathetic." Zach tries to speak, but I stop him before he can. "No, I am. When you kissed me… ugh, this is so embarrassing… that was my first real kiss." I cringe as I say those words because, at twenty-nine years old, that reality is pitiful. Sad. Shameful.

The look of shock on his face makes me sick to my stomach. I knew he would be appalled. Who wouldn't be?

"That is not what I expected. Now I feel even worse." His words come out in a staccato as he runs his fingers through his messy hair.

There you go, making everybody feel bad. People waste their time worrying about you and feeling horrible for hurting your fragile feelings. Everyone is better off without you.

Now I'm crying because I'm ashamed. "I don't want to make you feel bad. I—"

"Wow. I need to wrap my head around this. That should have been a special moment for you, and I took it without even asking." He stands and marches toward the door. He says something about leaving and it not being my fault, but I can't hear him through my tears. Each tear representing a pound of shame and guilt I have been carrying around for so long. The tears may pour out, but the shame feels heavier than ever.

Everyone leaves because you're not worth the effort. Poor broken Zara.

The door closes, and I collapse onto my sofa, crying myself into a state of exhaustion for the second night in a row. This

time, I lack medical intervention to put me to sleep, so I stay awake for hours, replaying all the reasons I hate myself.
    My brain's favourite soundtrack.

Yesterday passed in a blur. I was so repulsed by the sight and smell of the food Zach brought, I threw it out. I want to forget everything about him. His captivating green eyes, his perfect smile, the way he smelled, the way I felt when he touched me—including the irrational, overwhelming fear. All of it. Every thought of him needs to disappear.

Whether he meant to leave me drowning in shame when he left, I'm not sure—the small, rational part of me says he didn't—but that's what happened. Logical or not, I never want to see him again. I'm mortified I confessed to him, only for him to run away. That was the exact reaction I was scared of all these years. That's part of the reason why I put off dating for so long, because I was worried no one would understand. The longer I waited, the stronger that fear became.

I've been on dates, but never beyond a first because I was afraid to admit the truth to anyone; they'd see me as a societal leper. Afraid that letting someone in to see how broken I was, they'd run off without looking back. Zach made those fears a reality when he walked out the door.

On top of that situation, reminding me how useless and pathetic I am, Mr. Stafford called last night to inform me I can have the next three days off. So I'm home with nothing to do, nowhere to go, and no one to talk to. Even my ivy is sick of hearing my whining. Not to mention, I'm out of Oreos, and since I threw out the takeout, I need to find some sustenance somewhere. I also promised Quinn I'd call for hair and spa appointments and handle the DJ. That means I have to go out, and I have to make phone calls. Both of which I don't feel capable of doing.

Useless. Pathetic. Unwanted.

One step at a time. I'll start with a shower and see what I feel up to accomplishing next.

Showering should be a normal everyday activity, but my brain convinces me it's an impossible feat, zapping what little energy I have. I sit on my bed wearing a towel for thirty minutes before my energy reserves fill up enough to get dressed.

Once that's accomplished, I need another break, but I'm hungry and can't wait around for my mind to catch up with my stomach's needs.

A few affirmations, attempting to convince myself I can leave the safety of my home, and I'm walking downstairs toward my Prius.

In a somewhat uncharacteristic move, I left without an exact plan where I was going, so I sit in the driver's seat looking at the map app on my phone, searching for food options. I settle on going to the grocery store so I can buy decent food options and won't have to go out for the next few days. One and done.

Once I'm parked outside the supermarket, I can't get out of the car right away because I have to prepare for potential conversations or unlikely scenarios that could occur inside. Ten minutes pass before I work up the nerve to venture through the doors.

My desire to avoid small talk is almost painful. I've lived in Bracebridge for years and despite my efforts to keep to myself, I've still become familiar with people around. The worst part about living in a small city is the propensity for running into people you know.

Naturally, because I'm a hot mess with no capacity to speak to anyone, I spot three people I know browsing the aisles of our local grocery store. Etiquette may dictate that I speak to them to be polite, but anxiety dictates that I keep my head down and pray they don't see me. The simple act of avoiding people exhausts me and by the time I cash out, I need a nap.

I did it. I survived the grocery store. On my way home, my mother calls, which is unusual because she normally waits for me to call her.

Something is wrong with your dad. He's been in an accident. There's no reason your mother would call unless something catastrophic happened.

"Hi, Mom."

"Darling. Are you okay?" She sounds like she's been crying. This can't be good.

"I'm fine. Just taking a few days off work. You caught me on my way home from getting groceries." I try to keep my voice neutral and not betray the panic I'm being swallowed by.

"Zara Rihanna Levy, don't lie to your mother." Her harshness causes my hands to clench around the steering wheel.

What have you done to upset your mother?

"I... I don't know what you're talking about, Mom. I'm sorry for whatever it was."

"You were attacked at work and you didn't think to call me while you were in the hospital?" She's using her Minnie Mouse voice again. Despite her tears, that tells me she's angry.

"How... There was no reason to bother you. I was fine. How did you find out?"

"Noa and Lexi are friends with Quinn on social media, and she posted that something had happened to her maid of honour. Lexi asked Quinn, who was reluctant to tell her anything, but Lexi can be persuasive. Then Lexi called to tell me. You should have called. I don't care how old you get, you're always my baby."

Now everyone knows you're forever the victim. There will never be a time in your life when people don't pity you for being so pathetic. Of course you're a bother.

My heart is pounding in my chest as I fight to maintain my composure. A panic attack while driving is not ideal. Everything is fine. I'll be fine. Breathe. "There was no reason to call, Mom. Honestly, I stayed in the hospital overnight so they could monitor me, but I slept most of the time." I'll avoid mentioning that I cried myself to sleep after being heavily medicated.

Mom blows a long breath into the phone, making it sound like she's driving through a tunnel with her windows down. "I worry about you, my darling. You can't keep going on like this."

Trust me, I've thought about putting myself out of my misery more than I'd ever admit to anyone. As much as I try to implement strategies to improve, I always seem back at Square One. Now I've turned myself into such a pathetic mess, not even my workplace wants me around. Romance is out of the question. I'm a burden to my family and only friend. What's the point of going on at all? What's the purpose of being an independent woman when you can't contribute to society in any way, shape, or form?

I pull into my parking lot, easing my car into its assigned spot. Instead of my mother's words reducing me to tears, I am angry. Defensive. Disappointed. I wish I could feel numb; instead I'm stuck feeling too deeply.

Those feelings cause me to speak to my mother in a tone I've never used in my life. "This is exactly why I choose *not* to bother anyone with *my* problems. I can't make enough effort or do anything right, and I'm tired of feeling guilty on top of everything that goes on in my brain. It's exhausting defending my worth to *myself*. I don't have the energy to justify myself to anyone else."

I shut off the car, not realizing that the call doesn't end, it just switches to my phone, so I hear my mom's voice from my purse, but can't make out what she's saying.

"Hold on; I can't hear you," I shout into my canvas shoulder bag tossed on the passenger seat. Curse this technology for not hanging up. Now this conversation is going to be awkward on top of frustrating.

Finally, I place the phone to my ear and explain what happened.

She groans, inching my frustration level upward. "No one thinks you're a bother. I only said that you can't carry on this way because I'm worried about you. This isn't normal."

Does she really think those words are helpful? I'm well aware I'm not normal, and I'd give anything *to* be. What else does she want me to do?

"Mom, I've got to get my groceries inside. I'll talk to you soon. Love you."

When logic prevails, I see my mother's good intentions. Unfortunately, logic is never my dominant feeling and is overridden by anxiety, which convinces me my parents are better off without me before I get to the door. My bags of groceries are heavy as I march up the stairs, but they're nothing compared to the crushing weight of disappointing everyone around me.

You don't benefit anyone and serve no purpose other than to stress people out. You're selfish for forcing them to deal with you. Do everyone a favour and leave them alone.

I struggle to unlock my door with tears pooling in my eyes; my earlier anger giving way to dispiriting sadness. Safe to say that's my "comfort zone", though it's not comfortable at all. I wipe the tears from my eyes as I set my groceries down on my kitchen island, and my phone lights up again. A text message.

Though I don't want to look at it, a nagging thought forces me to see who it is. If it's Quinn, I'm going to give her a piece of my mind for posting my private business on social media. Okay, no I won't, because I can't bear her being upset with me. Even so, I'm angry.

It's not Quinn, though.

Zach: Can we talk?

About how you proved the fears I've carried around with me for over a decade? About how you made me feel even more pathetic than I did before? What could he possibly want to talk about? Whatever it is, I know my answer.

Zara: No.

Thursday morning, I wake up later than usual. I spoke to Mr. Stafford yesterday afternoon, and we agreed I could return to work. He planned for me to have shorter workdays for the next few weeks, so I'm never in the office alone. He wants to meet with me as soon as I arrive at 9:30— my new starting time. This was my request because Zach starts at nine. I'm not leaving running into him to chance.

As much as I'd rather stay home, I have bills to pay that arrive like clockwork each month and don't care if I'm mentally incapable of facing adulthood.

Home is safe.

I made the phone calls for Quinn's wedding preparations on my days off, but it took me all three days to make three calls. When I texted Quinn to inform her of our appointment times and locations, she asked me to join her this weekend for a cake tasting. She's having a basic cake made because it's short notice, but she still wants it to taste good.

Wedding plans are coming along. My life is falling apart.

I walk into Mr. Stafford's office shortly after 9:30. He's seated on the near side of his desk with his legs crossed at his ankles and appears to have been expecting me. He gestures to a chair in front of him, "Please, take a seat, Miss Levy." He walks back to his desk chair.

Miss Levy? Unless we are in a staff meeting, he doesn't call me that.

The man is going to fire you. He sees how useless you are, and you've been getting by because everyone is afraid to hurt your feelings. Poor broken Zara.

My stress level pushes me to speak before Mr. Stafford can issue a fatal blow to my career—what little reason for living I had left. "I want you to know how sorry I am about what happened last week. I never intended to let the situation with Mr. Kennedy reach that point."

He looks stunned by my admission. "Zara, you did nothing wrong. I wanted you to come in here so I could apologize to you!"

"But Sir, you had nothing to do with what happened."

"Yes, I did. I had everything to do with it. Patrick was spiralling out of control and because I was afraid to be short-staffed, I let it slide longer than I should have. Beyond that, when I fired him, I didn't make sure he returned his keys, which allowed him to get into your office. Words can't express how sorry I am."

"I don't think you have anything to be sorry for, so consider yourself forgiven."

"Thank you, Zara. I've been beating myself up over what happened ever since I walked in to see the paramedics taking you away."

Heat floods my neck and face hearing that my boss saw me in that situation. In the chaos, I hadn't noticed him, but mortification doesn't begin to describe how I feel. "I'm so sorry you saw that."

He looks perplexed. Once again, I've left someone speechless with my stupidity.

If you weren't a joke already, you are now.

"Please, stop apologizing. You're lucky you survived—and yet you have the courage to come back only a few days later to continue to work with children who have been through similar experiences. If anything, you should be proud of yourself."

His words have me baffled, and I'm sure we've traded facial expressions. "I want to continue working with these kids. Their strength gives me strength. I have a lot of love for them." So please don't fire me.

Mr. Stafford places his elbows on his desk, bringing his hands together in front of his face. "Your passion for helping others is admirable, and it makes you incredibly effective in your job. The clients I spoke with while you were away told me how much of a difference you've made in their lives. I'm honoured we have you as an employee."

He's just telling you that to spare your feelings.

As much as I don't believe his words—not because I think he's a liar, but because I don't think I'm capable of anything positive—I thank him.

"I hope I'm not out of line here, but having worked in this field for so long, I notice these things, and I'm assuming someone has hurt you deeply in the past. Whatever that hurt involved, I want you to know that I think it's admirable that you've chosen to do the work you do. If you ever need to come to me with anything, my door is open."

The tears I've kept at bay trickle down my cheeks. "I appreciate that, Mr. Stafford. It's been an honour to work for you." A chuckle escapes my lips, earning a tilted smile from Mr. Stafford. "I really thought you were going to fire me."

"Fire? Are you kidding? You're a model employee, and if I may be frank, I'd be proud to have a daughter like you."

"Thank... thank you."

"One last thing I wanted to address."

Now he's buttered you up. He's going to give you the bad news. There's always bad news.

He continues, "I had a meeting with the other office managers in the building earlier this week, and we were all in agreement that it's time we had better security in place beyond what the property manager has after hours."

I'm frozen in my seat for several seconds. "Please don't tell me this is happening on my account."

"It's nothing you've done. We just want to make sure what happened to you never happens again. The gentleman from the sixth floor who restrained Mr. Kennedy was the one who brought it up. He proposed we all allocate a portion of our budgets to hire a security company, so we should have something in place within the next few weeks."

Poor worthless Zara. You can't protect yourself. It's not enough that you cost taxpayers money using police and medical services, now you have to cost the businesses here money too.

"There's never been an issue before. I don't think it's necessary."

"Perhaps not, but the lawyers and financial planners seemed eager to have security present during business hours. They're worried about client retaliation, so it will be to the benefit of everyone. I'm only sorry you were the one to suffer before we decided."

What am I supposed to say? It seems the decision has been made and I can't change anyone's minds. Pile on more guilt for not being able to protect myself.

"I'll let you get back to work now, but please, if there are any issues, come see me right away. Your new computer should be all set up, so if you'd like to take a few hours to make sure they have transferred all of your files, that's probably the best place to start."

"Sure. Thank you, Mr. Stafford."

With that, I stand up and leave. I walk toward my office on the opposite side of the floor, right past many pairs of leering eyes.

They're laughing at you—or worse, they pity you. Poor, helpless, incompetent Zara.

Before I reach my office, Mrs. Copeland stops me. I've come to learn that she loves to play office politics in addition to her gossip habit. While she is supportive when it relates to clients, I'm hesitant to speak to her too much. I know exactly why she's approached me.

"Zara, how are you feeling?"

"I'm fine, thank you, Erin."

"Such a shame about what happened. Poor Patrick must have been really suffering."

I go from looking at her to darting my eyes back and forth to scan the area. I'm waiting for the cameras to pop out to say someone is "punking" me. Ashton Kutcher seems like a cool guy and I admire him because of his efforts to fight against human trafficking, but alas, he's nowhere to be found.

My stance becomes rigid and my jaw clenches. "Not as much as I did with his hands around my neck."

If her facial expression is any indication, my words have surprised her. "Oh, yes. Of course. But it's heartbreaking how he was driven to take such drastic measures."

I am not okay with this woman painting Patrick as the victim when I'm standing in front of her with dark yellow bruises on my neck, thirty feet from where he tried to strangle the life out of me. Normally I'd avoid conflict since I'm skilled at creating it without trying, but not today. "You've been working here for a long time. You know how the human brain works, and you're intimately aware of how mental health can affect people's behaviours—but the truth of the matter is that Patrick knew that too. You can feel sorry for him, but don't do it in front of me!"

I spin on my heel and storm into my office, slamming my newly installed door. She has some nerve. She's welcome to her opinion, but I don't need to hear it. I'm sure she wouldn't like to hear mine about her right now.

She's going to tell everyone you're a loose cannon, and you yelled at her. They're going to think you deserved what Patrick did to you. Maybe you did.

The fear I felt last Friday comes flooding through me as if I'm still in that moment as soon as I sit in my chair. I think of Zach and how he rushed in to save me. He's not coming to save me now.

It's time for me to save myself.

Saturday morning at 11:00, I arrive at *Desirea's Sweets*. I brought change for the parking metre today, so I'm able to park along the main street in front of the bakery. Tyler dropped Quinn off so the two of us can spend as much time as we want together, and I'll drive her home later. As much as I'm happy to spend time with Quinn, the lingering knowledge that she shared what happened with my family has me on edge.

Quinn greets me with a python-like hug, then stands back to take in my appearance. I feel naked under her intense gaze, and imagine this is how a carton of eggs must feel before being purchased—is my delicate exterior intact, or have I been ruined?

Once I've passed her inspection, she smiles and says, "You look great, Chica. I've missed you."

"I've missed you too, Amiga, but you promised cake."

Quinn giggles. "I knew you'd be excited about this part. Tyler really couldn't care about the cake—if it were up to him, we'd probably have some kale and quinoa concoction with protein powder frosting."

"That sounds horrific."

"Now you understand why I asked you." She laughs as she drags me through the door that rings as we enter.

Of course, she only asked you because you're a fatso with an affinity for cake. It's not because she wanted to spend time with you.

We walk in and we're greeted by the bakery's owner, Desirea. She's a gorgeous woman who's about my age, with red hair and a sunny disposition that could blind you if you got too close. It's hard not to like her immediately.

After proper introductions, she invites us into an office area that has been set up for these types of consultations. There is a small table in the middle with five chairs around it. The walls are covered in pictures of the most amazing confectionery creations. I'm blown away by the art people can create with cake. I struggle to colour in the lines.

On the table, she has four separate types of cake, and the smell alone is making me salivate. She describes them as if they were each creating a Tinder profile. Quinn's found the love of her life, but I'm up for grabs.

We have a basic sponge with raspberry-lemon filling, salted caramel with dark chocolate ganache, maple pecan with French vanilla frosting, and a cookies and cream cake with crushed Oreos. Swipe right, please.

"How soon can we get married?" I blurt out.

Why are you such an embarrassment to yourself?

"Me or the cake?" Desirea asks.

"Oh, I meant the cake. Sorry, I have an addiction to Oreos." My face flushes as I adjust myself in my seat.

"So do I, to be honest. That's why I always offer this cake. I assume everyone loves them as much as I do. You seem nice, so I would have hated to turn you down." She laughs, holding her hand up to display her engagement ring. "I'm glad you meant the cake. I'm happily taken."

Everyone your age is taken. You're forever the odd one out.

Quinn chimes in, "Okay, you have to be open-minded here. We have to choose one the most people will like."

Don't screw this up for her.

To my surprise, we decide on the maple pecan cake. Desirea mentioned that it's a better option to make into a classy-looking wedding cake, and not everyone likes chocolate. I don't know those people.

We arrange for the cake to be delivered to the venue on Saturday afternoon before the ceremony starts. Quinn didn't have a preference for what it looked like, so she granted Desirea complete creative freedom, which seemed to surprise her. Quinn couldn't be further from a Bridezilla. She only wants to marry her man and eat delicious cake.

We knock a few other tasks off Quinn's to-do list by the end of the day. She seems to have everything in order. Taking the day to focus on Quinn's happiness and future has been a nice distraction from the turmoil in my life.

I haven't seen Zach since he left my condo a week ago. It doesn't make sense for me to miss him after I was adamant about never speaking to him again, but I do. I did the best thing for him, right? Telling him the truth was the smart choice?

You never do the right thing. You mess things up so often, you're one giant walking mistake.

Quinn breaks the silence in the front seat of my car as she asks, "What's on your mind?"

I stammer as I try to come up with a response. I'm terrible at thinking on my feet, and hate to lie, so I tell her, "Nothing, really. Work stuff."

"Well, that's not as exciting as I was expecting. From the look on your face, I could have sworn you were in love, but it's good to know you're passionate about your work." She laughs.

Love? I do not love Zach. There have been few people in this world who have ever made me feel as insignificant as he did, and that's saying a lot. I exist in a permanent state of insignificance. No, I do not love him, and he'd never love me.

"I love my work," I say in my best convincing voice. "Mr. Stafford had some kind words for me when I returned to work this week."

"Oh, Chica. That's great. I'm glad your boss recognizes your hard work. You give those kids your all."

"So do you."

"I do, but most of the kids I work with haven't been through serious trauma. There are always one or two, but my job with them is limited. I help them where I can, but I'm in no position to be guiding them through their issues. It takes a special person to do that. You are that special person, Zar."

"I'm just doing my job, Amiga. Same thing as every other working person."

"There you go, selling yourself short again. You don't merely show up to do your job. It was the career you chose. You went through years of schooling and training to do what you do. Give credit where credit is due. It wasn't an accident, and you didn't just settle for that job to pay the bills."

I check my driver's-side blind spot for no reason other than to turn away from Quinn. "It felt like the right thing to do. My job means a lot to me."

"Chica, it means a lot to you because you have an incredible heart and what you've been through has given you insight into things that most people never have."

I scoff. "Well, lucky me, huh?" There is no room for logic when my past is involved. Call my anger a misguided attempt at telling her I'm angry about her sharing what happened with Patrick. Of course, telling her without telling her. I'll never say a word.

"I don't mean it like that. You've taken bad things and turned them into good. I'm proud of you and find your strength inspiring."

"To be honest, I am sick of everyone talking about 'my good heart' or 'my inner strength.' It's a load of crap. I'm not strong. Everyone watches me as if I'm ready to crack, and you know what? I'm afraid that might happen! I don't want people to be proud of me because I'm a damn victim and I'm forced to live with that. I'm repulsive and unwanted." My tears are blurring my vision, so I'm grateful I've pulled into Quinn's driveway. I'm not safe behind the wheel like this. "Everyone patronizes me, giving me fake compliments to keep me from breaking, and I'm tired of it. I'm already broken, and the pieces don't fit back together."

Quinn's hand reaches over to mine. "Chica, can I ask you something?"

"I hate when you ask me that. I'd rather you ask and save me the inner torment of guessing what might come next."

"I'm sorry." She takes a moment to confirm I am listening. "If one of your clients came into your office and told you they went through the same thing you had, how would you respond if they said they'd taken that pain and used it to help others?"

My words get stuck in my throat. "I'd probably tell them how brave that is."

"You would, because it is. What else?"

"That taking constructive action to help others is important for dealing with the powerlessness trauma leaves you with."

"And who here takes constructive action every single day?"

"I... I don't know."

"Yes, you do. *You* take action. I'm not saying I'm happy for what you've been through—no one deserves those things—but I am happy that you're strong enough to help other people. One day you'll see how many lives you've changed because you didn't let what happened to you beat you."

"Quinn. I hear what you're saying, but I feel beaten. Broken, disgusting, ashamed. I can't turn those feelings off."

"Oh, Chica. I wish I could get rid of those feelings. You are not broken, nor disgusting, and you have no reason to be ashamed."

I blow out a loud breath.

"One day, you'll see how amazing you are. Someone else will see too."

"Ha! Now she's got jokes."

"I'm not joking. You've got so much to give, and one day someone will see that."

Zach comes back into my mind and I think about how I felt with him. Sure, I was full of fear because of my past, but mostly I was afraid to put myself out there and get hurt. He ended up proving me right.

You are unlovable.

I dry my eyes and thank Quinn for another one of her pep talks. After I leave her house, I return home with the voice in my head to a lonely night of existing. Sometimes, existing is the last thing I want to do.

The day has finally arrived. The past two weeks have flown by with no additional drama. I'm glad, because my stress level leading up to today has catapulted into the stratosphere. Once this day is over, I can go back to my meaningless existence.

I am scheduled to meet Quinn, Paige, and Ren at the hair salon at 11am. Apparently hair and makeup takes a long time to be done properly—I wouldn't know. Quinn has instructed me to wear a button-down shirt so I can get it off without messing up my hair and makeup. If someone hadn't already informed me of things like this, anxiety would have.

I grab the garment bag with my dress, my impossibly high heels, and my purse. I have a clutch for the wedding, and my everyday bag.

What if your dress rips right before you walk down the aisle? What if it gets cold? It is October. What if the heel on your shoe breaks and you're forced to choose between wearing one shoe, or no shoes with a dragging dress? What if the flowers make you sneeze? What if you vomit? What if you get so hungry, you faint?

Before I leave, I grab a mini sewing kit I picked up in a hotel that I've been saving for this very day, a black shawl and one of my work cardigans, some super glue, allergy and stomach medications, and a cookies and cream protein bar. I throw everything in my big purse, check for my keys, wallet, and phone. I'm ready.

When I arrive in front of the salon a short time later, I find a parking spot and go to wait at the front door. I'll never be able to calculate the amount of my life I've wasted by arriving at places unreasonably early. Quinn arrives about ten minutes later with her mom and sister.

We all greet each other, and I try to push down how intimidated I am when I look at Quinn and Paige. They're both about 5'8" with slender figures and long blonde hair. Then there's me, barely reaching 5'5", with curves to spare, dark brown hair and a nose that's slightly too large for my face. It's too late for an emergency rhinoplasty, so I'm going to have to work with what I've got. All I can hope is that no one will look at me.

After what felt like an eternity in a salon chair, the professionals have deemed me pretty enough to stand beside a bride. My "glam team" plastered enough product on me to make Honey-Boo-Boo cringe. I look at myself in the mirror and I hardly recognize the person staring back at me. This is what you call "the whole enchilada."

My hair is in an updo with a loose Dutch braid around my head like a hair crown, the length pinned into random curls at the back, with a few tendrils of hair pulled down around my face. I've been told this intentionally messy look is all the rage.

Quinn looks stunning. She, too, has a Dutch braid style, but they placed hers around the crown of her head, with her remaining hair down in loose curls. It looks both elegant and effortless at the same time; the perfect style for her.

Quinn beams at her mom, sister, and me, declaring, "Time to get hitched!"

I can tell how excited she is that her day is finally here. Their decision not to wait was the right one for them because they've been perfect together since Tyler corrected Quinn's squat form.

This day should be perfect for my best friend. I am going to shove down every negative or intrusive thought I have and focus on her. This is her once-in-a-lifetime day, and I intend to make it count.

Good luck with that.

We arrive at the wedding venue, which is a country club with a banquet hall. Quinn's father, Albert, and all of his lawyer friends have been members here for years. It's a stunning location, and because of the time of year, it's not busy with extra country club traffic.

We make our way to the bridal suite, where we will continue to get ready. I drag my garment bag to the corner, hanging it on a hook by the window, set down my shoes and clutch bag, then turn to Quinn. She's got this uncanny ability to move along with the tides of life, but I don't want her to settle today. I want to do everything I can to make her day everything she dreamed of, so getting her ready takes priority.

A quick check of the time says it's 2:45, which means we have seventy-five minutes until we walk down the aisle. Gauging by our trial run at the bridal boutique, buttoning up Quinn's dress will take half of that time.

Quinn wants a few shots of everyone getting ready, so after the photographer is done taking pictures of Tyler and his groomsmen, she comes in the bridal suite to capture some candid moments of us girls.

The photographer is taking pictures of Quinn's dress hanging on a special dress stand, her shoes, flowers, and other little touches she calls "micro-details", but then she focuses on us.

Keep your chin up so she's not getting pictures of your neck rolls. Stand tall so you don't look like a troll. Try to duck out of as many pictures as you can so they aren't all ruined.

Paige and I have wrestled Quinn's dress off the hanger and unbuttoned it so we can slide it onto her slender frame. We're pulling the sleeves over her arms when the photographer says, "Ya'll have some handsome gentlemen in there waiting for you."

Quinn blushes, and I've never seen that happen in the entire decade I've known her. "Did you see my groom? Did he look nervous?"

"Not at all. He looked as happy as any man I've ever seen on his wedding day."

Quinn's face lights up with a teary-eyed smile. I need to lighten the mood so she doesn't cry and ruin her makeup.

"I remember the first day you met Tyler, and you said you knew he was the man you were going to marry. Now you're here."

"I thought I was smitten—like a harmless crush because he was so handsome, but the more I got to know him, the more I became confident he was my guy."

"What was it that made you know?" I ask, buttoning one of the many pearl buttons on her dress. Tyler is going to resent this later.

"I can't really explain it. You hear all the time, people say, 'when you know, you know,' and it's true. He'd touch me in such a sweet way, and it felt like he shot lightning right down to my toes. He looked into my eyes when he spoke to me, and always knew what to say to keep me from second-guessing myself. Little things, but they felt like big things."

Her words hit me in the heart. I know. But I am also familiar with how it feels to have that person walk away without a backwards glance. Another subject change. "I think you're ready. Let me go slip into my dress, then we can get you down the aisle!"

"Okay, Chica. Holler if you need me to help you zip up."

Hopefully, you can still get your dress zipped up after the amount of brooding and Oreo eating you've done over the past few weeks.

I go over to the spot where I left my dress, and my first order of business is to transfer any essentials from my giant purse into this tiny clutch. I don't know how you're supposed to hold anything more than a lip gloss and a credit card in these things. Thank God I don't need a tampon. Who was the person who decided that when you're getting dressed up, you can't carry a big purse? I'll have to stuff my phone in my bra. Nothing makes for better wedding photos than the ol' square boob.

Next order of business is to squeeze myself into my body-shaper. There is nothing you can do to prepare your body for the onslaught of misery shapewear inflicts over several hours, but so help me if I have to stand beside the Ayala sisters having my picture taken—pictures that will be around for decades—I'll squeeze myself into this sausage casing for the day.

I unzip my dress, step into it, and pull it up around my arms. The neckline is even more "plunging" than I recall. It's scandalous. I don't like wearing things that draw attention to me, and I have a feeling with my girls out trying to join the party, they're going to grab some notice. Good thing I brought my shawl. The last thing I need is to have some creepy, drunk uncle leering at me.

Paige's help is needed to zip my dress before I return the favour. She looks as exquisite as I expected.

You look like you're about to be Photoshop's best customer. The only world where you're beautiful is the Planet of the Apes.

No, I'm not letting this get to me today. I have to focus on Quinn and forget about everything else. Be present in the moment and forget about the rest right now. Breathe. Easier said than done in shapewear.

I walk over to Quinn and she lets out an excited squeal as she jumps up and down. She's only wearing two-inch heels, so she can do that. To my chagrin, she thought it necessary I have four-inch heels, so my dress won't drag—a pleasant way of saying I'm too short for clothing designed for models. She's right though, because if it dragged, I guarantee I would trip on it. As long as I don't have to walk up or down stairs, or across cobblestone, I should be okay.

It's 3:54. The photographer snaps a few last-minute photos of various combinations of the girls of the bridal party, and then we're off.

Tyler's niece, Amora, is the flower girl, and she's prancing along in front of us, eager to take her turn walking down the aisle. Quinn is standing behind me waiting for Albert to join her when she says, "Look at Tyler's best man, Zach. I told you he was gorgeous."

My eyes shoot wide open and my heart rate speeds up. No, it couldn't be him. Zach is a common name. I've never heard Tyler mention a Zach before in the last four years I've known him. His best friend's name is Trigger. There's no way he's the same person.

I peek my head through the rectangular window in the door, and all the panic I was beating down the entire day rises to the surface. Breathe. Everything will be okay. No, scratch that. This is not okay. I am not okay.

Quinn is an expert at reading the emotions on my face. "Chica, what's wrong? Is it the crowd? Remember what I said. I'll rip my dress off so fast, no one will even notice if you fall."

"No, no, no. It's him. Zach," I say between gulps of air.

"What about him? You know him?"

I nod. "He… he knows."

Quinn squares my shoulders to face her. "What does Zach know? I don't understand."

"We work in the same building. He beat up Patrick. He… he kissed me, and when I told him he was my first, he ran away like I was some sort of pariah."

Just like you did to him when he kissed you. You got what you deserved.

"He what? I'm going to kill that bastard. All these years, I thought he was a gentleman. I am going to kill him." She pushes up her sleeves and opens the door like she's going to march down the aisle and kill him in front of 100 witnesses.

I grab her arm. "No, it's fine. I wasn't expecting to see him again; especially not here. It's fine. I'll be fine. I need to breathe and focus on why we're here. This is about you, and he doesn't matter." I wish that were true.

"Chica, after you guys walk down the aisle on the way out, you don't have to go near him again. I'll tell the DJ to scratch the bridal party dance, or you and Paige can switch partners so you can dance with Tyler's brother. Don't worry. I'm so sorry, I had no idea."

Bridal party dance? As in, everyone will look at you in the embrace of a man you want to hate but can't seem to stay away from?

"I can't believe it's him," I whisper to myself.

The music starts, and Amora is so restless, she swings the doors open in her very own "I'm here!" moment. The guests turn around to look in her direction as I duck behind the door. I take the last few seconds in relative privacy to compose myself. As Paige starts her journey, I give Quinn a hug and tell her how much I love her. My love for her will carry me down this aisle, and Zachary Haynes can go squat in a cactus patch.

I steady myself and turn toward the front of the ceremony room. The space is beautifully decorated with tasteful floral arrangements and ribbons in intricate bows. It's only about thirty steps to where I need to stand. I lift my bouquet up to an awkward height in front of me to cover my chest, then I amble past the spectators, toward the officiant. I make eye contact with Tyler, noting the joy on his face, and it makes me smile.

When I take my spot at the front, I realize how this bombshell could have been avoided if Quinn had a wedding rehearsal, but she didn't want me to be overwhelmed. That backfired, but once again, I'm the only one to blame.

I intentionally avoid Zach's eyes, aware one look would remind me how he made me feel when he ran out of my condo. I live my life comparing myself to scum on a shoe, and he made me feel even worse, so I have no intention of interacting with him and letting him ruin this day. He may have been as surprised as I was, but I will not let him wreck this wedding; not for me, and definitely not for Quinn or Tyler.

Quinn gracefully parades down the aisle with her father. She passed on a traditional veil, so her face is on full display—elation obvious across her features for everyone to see.

The moment Tyler looks in her eyes, he weeps. Seeing him evoke such emotion—such love—makes my eyes tear up as well.

Everyone is watching. Don't cry. You are an ugly crier. You'll make their wedding photos even worse.

I glance past Tyler because I could no longer restrain myself, and Zach's eyes are fixed on me. He gives me a shy smile before I look away to mask my anger and upset.

The officiant begins speaking to Tyler and Quinn about the sanctity of marriage and the weight of the commitment they are making to each other. Neither of them have a hint of doubt on their faces. The middle-aged man performing the ceremony is so exuberant, he makes the entire ceremony light-hearted and fun. He makes everyone laugh, gasp, and cry at various parts through the thirty minutes he speaks.

The ceremony speeds by, with Quinn and Tyler exchanging beautiful personal vows, and the officiant finally exclaims, "You may now kiss the bride!"

As he says those words, I find myself locked onto Zach's gaze because I couldn't resist the pull to look at him; he's trying to tell me something with his eyes. It would be logical for me to never want to hear what he's trying to say, but I'm drawn to him like gravity. I can't prevent it, I can't understand it, and I can't defeat it. My mind has waged some pretty epic battles against itself, but none have caused the conflicting emotions Zachary Haynes has.

After signing the marriage certificate, everyone in the room is cheering for the happily married couple as the lovesick newlyweds start the recession. Zach steps forward and holds out his arm for me to grab onto. I loop my arm through his, straighten my dress, and we start our march out the door.

"Zara, I..."

"Don't," I admonish. "Not now."

We walk the remaining distance in silence while I avoid eye contact with everyone by watching my own feet to ensure I don't fall. At least, not any more than I did for Zach before he squashed my heart like a bug. Good thing I didn't fall in love with him, but I'm aware that's a foolish notion for someone like me.

No one could ever love you.

After we've exited the ceremony room, we're instructed to form a receiving line to greet the guests. They line Zach and me up side-by-side. As the guests make their way through, greeting the wedding party, Zach introduces me to the first few people as "Zara, Quinn's beautiful best friend." He's trying so hard to get my attention, it nearly makes me gag.

My angry eyes are not effective, so after the eighth time he introduces me the same way, I turn to him and whisper, "Can you please stop? You're embarrassing me."

He gives me the same look he did the night he ran from my condo. That look, I assume, is disgust. Pity. Disappointment.

You are so pathetic. He thinks you're disgusting. He's mocking you in front of everyone.

My palms are sweating. I can feel the colour rising in my face. My heart is beating faster by the second. Once again, my unrelenting negative thoughts are spiralling out of control. I have to get out of here.

Before I can talk myself out of it, I take off running. I never would have thought I could run in four-inch heels, but it's amazing what unadulterated shame can accomplish. Where I'm running to is a mystery; I just run. Through doors, turn down hallways. By the time I am breathless, I don't know where I am. This place didn't look so big from the outside. Hopefully, I'm somewhere no one will find me.

"Zara?"

Hm. Apparently, I was not running as fast as the effort I exerted allowed me to believe.

"Zara, I'm sorry."

Without turning to face him, I snap, "Sorry for what, Zach? For letting me embarrass myself in front of you? For making me feel like persona non grata? Or for humiliating me?"

As he talks, I can barely hear his voice. "I'm sorry for all of it. Zara, I didn't handle it well when you confessed to me, but it had nothing to do with you." His voice grows louder, more determined. "I was ashamed that I took something special from you. I hated myself for doing that. You deserved so much better, but I came in like a caveman and took something I can never give back. You did nothing wrong. Please, you have to know that. I was only upset with myself."

Finally, I turn to face him. "It doesn't matter Zach. I told you already I was trying to save you from me. I know what I am. You didn't see it. Well, can you see me now?" I throw my hands up in the air and do a slow spin to let him see my disgusting form.

"I see you, Zara. There's nothing I see that isn't perfect. I've been calling and texting you for over a week, but my calls go to voicemail."

The fact he's been trying to get a hold of me is a surprise, but I blocked his number.

"I can't give you what you want. Please, leave me alone." This only ends in heartbreak for me.

He closes the gap between us as I stare into his hypnotic eyes.

"All this pushing me away, you fear something. I can tell you've been hurt in your past. I don't know who or what hurt you, but I could kill them for making you not able to see the alluring, fierce, sexy-as-hell woman you are."

In true Zara fashion, I'm crying, and he pulls me into his arms. After all the resisting I've done, here is the only place I want to be. He's stroking my hair, which must feel like concrete, trying to calm me down. Suddenly, he picks me up in his powerful arms and carries me down the hall, through a doorway into a lounge room—the room the groomsmen used to get ready. He sits down on a sofa with me in his arms, so I'm seated in his lap. My tears go from quiet droplets to heaving sobs because the tenderness of his actions overwhelms me.

I don't know how much he knows, but at that moment, I decide to let it all out. Something I've never done with anyone but Quinn, and even then, I only spilled my guts after drinking half a bottle of wine. Before I can change my mind, I blurt out, "He raped me."

Zach pulls his head back, but not as if he wants to get away; he's trying to look in my eyes. "Who? Zara, who did that to you?"

I take a deep breath, still too afraid to look at Zach's face. So, I pour my heart out, staring at my lap. "I was eighteen. It was a month before I left for University." I pause, afraid to continue, and release another sob.

"Shh, it's okay. You can tell me."

"My friend Jenna—well, I guess she wasn't really my friend—convinced me to go to a party at some guy's house. It wasn't my scene, so I didn't want to go. I was always very introverted and focused on school, but I thought Jenna was my friend, so I didn't want to upset her. I told her I would go but wouldn't drink, and I wanted to leave by eleven. My parents were happy I was going to do something 'normal' teenagers do, and they trusted me, so they told me to forget about a curfew."

I look at him now, and he's listening intently. I push down the fear and shame to continue.

"We went to the party at this guy Eric's house. He seemed okay at school, but I never really spoke to him. As soon as we got to the party, Jenna was off socializing, while I sat on the sofa wondering why teenagers think house parties are so much fun. I didn't see the appeal. By nine, I was ready to leave, but I couldn't find Jenna anywhere. I figured I'd go back and wait on the sofa until she came to find me. What's the worst that could happen, right?" I choke out another sob as the memories come back to me. "This guy, Christian, sat beside me and started talking. I knew him from school, but he was a year older, so he was already in college. He asked if I was having a good time, and I was honest, telling him I wasn't. He told me I should have a drink to loosen up. I was adamant, telling him I didn't want to drink."

I release a deep sigh and prepare myself for the hard part. I know by this point Zach is aware of where this is headed.

"He said he'd get me a soda, so I agreed. Naïve me, didn't think twice when he returned with soda in a plastic cup, so I drank it. Nothing seemed weird about it; it tasted fine. Christian said he wanted to show me something, so he took me by the arm down the stairs into the basement and I was feeling too dizzy to resist. I thought it was strange because no one else was down there. He led me into a guest bedroom, but I remember there was no window. It was only a bed in a room."

Before I can continue, I'm bawling on Zach's chest. He speaks for the first time in minutes. "It's okay. You don't have to continue."

"I need to get this out. You need to hear this so you realize why I'm not who you want." I have my sights fixed on a vase of flowers behind Zach's left shoulder because I can't bring myself to look at him. "I don't remember much after walking into the room. It's probably a good thing that I don't. It's because of that memory that it's a miracle I'm even in this room alone with you right now."

"Zara, I'm so sorry that jerk hurt you, but I never would."

I close my eyes so I can find the strength to continue and release a muffled sob. "My next memory is waking up in the morning. I had the worst headache of my life; the lights were off, and it hurt to move my head, but I felt cold. I was lying naked on blood-soaked sheets."

"Oh, my God. Zara."

"I tried to make myself get up, but I couldn't. I looked around and saw a beer bottle on the bed that was also bloody. He… he…" Between the memory recall and the certainty Zach is repulsed by me, I can't catch enough breath to continue. To my surprise, Zach doesn't move. He stays right where he is, rubbing my back, comforting me. Deep breath. "I screamed for help until someone found me. Eric's mother was home and called 911.

She didn't even know I was there. Oh, God. So many people saw me like that. They saw what he had done."

"Zara…" He pauses for a beat, then continues, "If you think that makes me not want to get to know you, you couldn't be more wrong."

"No, Zach. You don't understand. He did so much damage, I can never have children. I will never be a normal woman. I'll always be broken." My head drops to look at my fidgeting hands in my lap. "His parents hired a fancy lawyer from Toronto, and he got off with three years probation. Can you believe that? Three years when he literally ruined my life." I'm practically choking on my words, trying to spit them out through my whimpering. "He ruined me. He destroyed me. On top of everything he had done, he took pictures of me and shared them online. I don't know how many people have seen them."

"That's where you're wrong, beautiful. You are not ruined—you're a fighter. You're not destroyed—you're a survivor. All that this has told me is that you are so much more worthy of love than I even realized."

"Are you crazy?" I scrunch my tear-soaked face, studying his expression for an indication of his sincerity. "I told you I've been destroyed from the inside out, and that's your response? You should be running. Far and fast."

"Let me make one thing clear: he may have hurt you physically; he may have hurt you emotionally; but you are not destroyed. You are still walking this Earth, using your experiences to help others who desperately need it. Let me make you see you are as deserving of the love you give to everyone else."

I draw in a breath. "I can't find words right now."

"Say you'll go on a date with me. An actual date. Not ice cream. I want to show you what you're worthy of."

I pause, attempting to decipher his words. Am I hearing him right?. I never imagined I would tell someone the truth of what happened to me, but I certainly never imagined anyone could accept it. "Okay. I'll go on a date with you. But Zach, you need to realize that I am not a normal woman. I'm warning you now."

"Normal is overrated. You're even better."

Zach waits with me while I make myself presentable. I wash off the makeup I was wearing and by the time I'm done, I feel three pounds lighter.

Everyone is going to wonder where you went. They're going to see you return with Zach, looking like a disaster. You know what everyone will think.

I steady my shoulders and walk out of the washroom to express my concerns to Zach. "Maybe we should walk back separately?"

"Not a chance. I'm not letting you get away from me again." He winks, telling me that was playful, and for once, logic outweighs anxiety.

Thirty minutes ago, I would have assumed anyone saying something like that was a possessed stalker, but when Zach says it, it sets my body ablaze. "I'm a walking disaster, though. My makeup is a mess and my hair is ruined. I don't want to embarrass you."

"First, you're even more gorgeous without makeup, so that's a non-issue. Second, you don't have a hair out of place, and I'd wager a category four hurricane couldn't make it budge."

I laugh because my "glam squad" used enough hairspray to single-handedly destroy the ozone.

"And third, I could never, not in a million years, be embarrassed by you."

Suddenly, I'm a woman possessed. It's like someone else has taken over my body and I can't control it. Without a single thought, I kiss him.

You don't know what you're doing. He's grossed out by you. He will not want to...

As fast as my anxiety appears, it's gone, and everything I am feeling is being transmitted through the lips of this wonderful man who ran me over with his bicycle and didn't give up on me. He takes the lead, exploring my mouth with slow, languid strokes, pulling me against him with one hand on each of my hips.

We pull apart, breathless, and Zach rests his forehead on mine with his eyes closed. "That was... unexpected."

Now you've taken advantage of him. Your biggest fear is the same thing happening to you, and you've done it to the one man who tried to understand you.

I step back so quickly I nearly fall as panic rises once more. How could I have gotten so caught up that I would be so inconsiderate?

Zach steps forward to grab hold of my arms and levels his intense gaze on me. "Whatever your head is telling you right now, tell it to shut up."

My heaving chest begins to slow. "How... how did you know?"

"I may not have known you for long, Zara, but I recognize that look you have before you pull away."

"I'm… sorry for kissing you. Just when I think I can't do anything more stupid, I surprise myself."

"Baby, are you kidding me?" A wide smile splits Zach's face, exposing his gleaming white teeth. "That was one of the best moments of my life."

My eyes widen, making my forehead crease—which is hard with my tight skin from the excessive amount of makeup I had been wearing. "What?"

He puts his hands on my cheek, eyes locked on mine. "That kiss. That kiss was everything I've been thinking of for the past month. I've dreamed about you when I was sleeping, when I was driving, when I was working. You have no idea how badly I wanted that, and the fact you gave it to me in the heat of the moment, whew, it nearly blew my socks off."

I chuckle, glancing at his socks for some stupid reason, as if he was being literal. How is he so effective at bringing me back from the brink of panic? All the other times panic took over, and I ran off or sent him away, if I had just given him a chance, would he have been able to reassure me? I'll never know, and I don't want it to be his responsibility, but I'm going to give him more credit than I have been. "You're ridiculous."

"I'd say smitten." He winks again, and I didn't know a single eye blinking could have such an impact on me. "What do you say we get back in there and tear up the dancefloor?"

"I'd say there's a snowman's chance in hell you'll get me on the dancefloor, but we should get back."

He pulls me in against himself and whispers, "Not even a slow song?"

His breath on my ear sends shivers through my entire body.

"Maybe if you earn it."

"Well, please tell me what I have to do. I'll do it twice."

I giggle as I hike up my dress and start running out of the room. My shoes are a major hindrance—as well as my lack of athleticism—so Zach catches me before I reach the door. He grabs me around the waist, lifts me up, and spins around. I'm dizzy when he sets me down, but not from spinning. He leans in toward me with a predatory stare. Without hesitation, his muscular arms have pulled my body into his, and his soft lips are caressing mine. I don't push him away, nor do I pull away. I live in the moment.

When we finally break free, Zach chuckles. "I don't think I can ever get enough of that."

As much as I would love to stay in this moment with him, today isn't about us. "Come on." I beam as I walk toward the banquet hall. "We're going to miss the food."

"We can't have that. My girl's gotta eat."

I freeze mid-step. "Your girl?"

"Sorry, that's probably too fast. It felt right."

I take a few seconds to consider what he said before replying, "I like it."

His incredible smile adorns his face as he takes my hand, and we return to the reception side-by-side.

I don't miss the looks from Quinn and Tyler as we return. Quinn smiles at me, then glares at Zach as though she's issuing a warning. Tyler shoots Zach a wink and a radiant smile at me. Zach and I part ways to take our seats at the head table, flanking the bride and groom.

After a meal and two glasses of champagne, the master of ceremonies, Tyler's friend James, announces that it's my turn to give a speech. The champagne has done nothing to quell my nerves, so I saunter to the podium with my heart hammering in my chest. I feel a gentle hand on the small of my back and turn to see Zach, who has joined me as support, and I couldn't be more grateful. How is it possible to feel so relaxed in his presence? Maybe relaxed isn't the right word, because I'm still standing in front of a hundred strangers.

Don't screw this up. People are recording, and this is going to live in history forever.

I swallow my nerves and look over at Quinn with renewed determination to do this for her. "Good evening, everyone. My name is Zara, and for those who don't know, Quinn has been my best friend for over a decade. Best friend might not be the right word, because really, she's been my support system, my cheerleader, and my inspiration. She was a light in my life when I needed it most, and not a day goes by I'm not thankful to Professor Abbott for forcing us to do a group project in our Developmental Psychology class. I stand here today, looking at the most beautiful couple I have ever seen, excited to see what the future holds for you both.

"Tyler, since you walked into Quinn's life four years ago, you've been an extension of my best friend, and I can never thank you enough for your kindness and generosity. When I see how you look at Quinn, I know she'll be loved and cherished, just as she deserves to be.

"I'm not a relationship expert, but I consider myself a Quinn expert, so Tyler, I have some advice for you. To keep Quinn happy, there are two magic phrases: 'You're right, Honey,' and 'Sure, you can buy that.'"

People laugh at my attempt at a joke and I take in the size of the crowd I am speaking to.

They're all watching.

My racing heart prompts me to cut out the last section of my speech about my wishes for their future. "May you both have a lifetime of happiness and love together."

I want to walk off and take my seat, but Zach grabs my hand, which brings me back to the present as he steps up to the microphone, radiating confidence.

"Hello, everyone. Thank you all for coming this evening. It's been such a great day to celebrate two of the best human beings I've ever known. My name is Zach, and I've been friends with Tyler since high school. To say I'm honoured to be his friend doesn't quite express how truly appreciative I am. I owe his parents a debt of gratitude for raising such a great guy."

Zach's speech continues for another minute as he thanks everyone for making the day so wonderful and wishes the couple well in the future. He holds my hand the entire time, keeping me pinned to his side.

"Last, I want to thank the bridal party for helping to pull this day off. Specifically Zara, who made this day unforgettable."

My cheeks are burning hot and I'm horrified he is drawing attention to me, but I'm touched by his words. I nod toward him and mouth, "thank you." He returns a swoon-worthy wink, and I can't help but smile.

"Now let's get this party started!" Zach declares as the music starts. Everyone turns back toward their tablemates, and it suddenly feels as if Zach and I are the only two people in the room. He leans down to kiss my forehead. "After the bride and groom have their first dance, I can't wait to get you on the dancefloor."

"Zach, I don't dance. I'm terrible."

"Do you trust me?"

As strange as it may seem, I say, "I do."

He blinks rapidly, making me realize my word choice, and I wish I could melt into a puddle. "Then trust me to lead the way. I won't let you fall."

Too late. I am falling. I'm falling hard.

You're going to end up hurt. You don't get happy endings.

The days of the week don't matter anymore. Zach and I have spent every day together for nearly three weeks since Quinn and Tyler's wedding. We meet up for a coffee/tea date every morning during the week, have lunch together in his office, and dinner in the evenings.

Our first official date—not counting our ice cream disaster—was the Monday following the wedding. Zach took me to an Italian place that makes homemade pastas and desserts. We picked up some items to go and went back to my house to enjoy our quiet meal. He may not have known me for long, but I'm amazed how well this man understands me. Without me saying a word, he knew I'd be more comfortable in my space. We've also visited a museum, watched a cheesy rom-com at the theatre, and browsed a vendor market full of cute, unique items.

He's mostly been coming to my place, which is fine, but tonight he's asked me to go to his house because he wants to introduce me to Jasmine. I told him about our brief encounter, but he wants the women in his life to get to know each other better.

He loves his sister more than anyone. If she doesn't like you, he's going to break up with you. You're going to be heartbroken, and this time, you won't be able to recover.

At 4:30, I plaster on some fake confidence and make my way to Zach's office, where we arranged to meet. Any other day, I hightail it out of work because I can't wait to see him, but today I'm apprehensive. This is a big deal.

By the time I walk into Zach's office, my nervousness subsides the second I see his smile. He gets up right away to greet me with a peck on my forehead.

"Hey, Baby. I'm wrapping a few things up. Then we'll be ready to leave, okay? Do you need to run home first?"

"I was thinking I'd drive home now, get changed, then you can pick me up when you're done. That way, you don't feel obligated to rush, and you won't be waiting for me to change."

"That makes sense. There's one problem."

He has changed his mind. He doesn't want you to meet his sister. He's not serious about you, so meeting his only family is futile.

"What's that?" I try my best to mask my growing stress level.

"If you leave now, I'll want to work twice as fast so I can have you in my arms again."

I give him a coy smile. "Get your work done, and I'll be waiting at home for you." After the words leave my mouth, I realize how that sounded. I backpedal. "My home. I'll meet you at *my* home if you're okay with coming to pick me up."

"I like how it sounded better the first time," he declares, still holding me in his arms.

"Zach, you're going to have to let me go, or I'll never get out of here and you'll never get your work done."

"That sounds fine to me."

"Don't be daft, you whacko." I laugh in return.

"Okay, fine. Have it your way—ever practical." He leans down to give me a quick kiss. "I'll see you soon. Drive safe."

"I will. Text me as you're leaving so I can be ready for you." I turn and walk out of his office, ride down in the elevator, and head out to my car. It's time to go home to mentally prepare myself for the evening ahead.

By 5:20, Zach is at my home. I told him I'd walk down to meet him outside, but he insisted on coming right to my door—always a gentleman. He casually leans on the wall as I open the door to greet him. The sight of him steals my breath every time.

It's only temporary. He'll figure out he can't fix you.

"Come in for a second," I plead.

"Gladly. Now I can do this." He closes the door behind him and scoops me up into his arms in a bridal carry to kiss me.

I almost get lost in his affection before I come back to reality. "You're too distracting." I playfully slap his chest until he sets me down. "I wanted to ask your opinion on something."

"What can I say? I enjoy being distracted by you. If you want my opinion on what you're wearing, you look incredible."

I wave off the compliment. "No, no. It's not that. I got your sister a gift and I want your opinion if you think she'll like it."

"Baby, you didn't have to do that. Jas is already so excited to meet you. She's been harassing me for the last week to have you over, but I didn't want to overwhelm you with too much, too fast."

"Well, still. I want her to like me. I... I'm so afraid she won't like me, and it will be a deal-breaker. I would never expect you to choose me over your sister."

"Wow, slow down. Jas is going to love you, so please don't worry. Also, my brain didn't choose you. My heart did and there's no changing it now."

I look up at him through my eyelashes, questioning what he said. His heart chose me? Does that mean…

No. He couldn't. How could he love someone so damaged? He's perfect; you're defective.

I push the thoughts out of my mind and turn to retrieve the gift bag from the counter. I'm so eager to get Zach's opinion because I've been doubting my purchase since before the artisan finished it. It turns out, collecting business cards at the vendor market came in handy.

He's going to think it's stupid. It is stupid. Jasmine is going to think you're trying to buy her affection, but she'll see that you're too broken for her brother.

I open the small bag, lift out the box inside, and open it to display the present for Jasmine. Zach looks startled.

"Is that—"

"Oh, my gosh. It's stupid, isn't it? I knew it was stupid. Forget it. Can we stop and pick something—"

"Baby, it's perfect, and she's going to love it. She's going to love you, even without the gift. Let's get going so you can see it's not as bad as you think. Everything will be fine."

At this moment, his voice is more convincing than my anxiety. Only for a moment.

As we're driving toward Zach's house, he looks nervous.

He's upset with you for buying his sister a presumptuous gift. You can't buy such a personal gift for someone you don't even know. You're so stupid.

"Is everything okay?"

"Yeah, everything is fine. I, uh, I need to tell you something before we get to my house."

Oh, no. He's going to tell you that things between you are over after tonight. Or he's in love with someone else. Or he has a pet python. Or he's a secret wild game hunter and his house is full of stuffed rhino heads.

He's a vegetarian. Don't be ridiculous.

You are the queen of ridiculous-opolis.

"Baby, I can see your mind spinning. Don't panic. It's just that… I couldn't find the right time to tell you."

"Spit it out before my brain spontaneously combusts, please!" I immediately regret snapping at him, but can't calm myself to apologize at the moment.

"I'm sorry. It's just that when my parents died, you know how it was because of the gas line being damaged?"

"Yeah."

"Well, after they granted me guardianship of Jasmine, my lawyer advised me to launch a civil suit against the energy company that caused the damage." He releases a sigh. "About three years after my parents' deaths, they awarded Jasmine and I a settlement."

"Okay. That doesn't fix anything, but I'm glad you got something for their mistake." I'm confused why he feels the need to tell me this.

"It wasn't just something. It was quite a bit."

I wait for him to continue, not knowing how much he wants to disclose to me.

"They gave us thirty-six million dollars."

That's an unexpected bombshell.

So not only is this guy a perfect physical specimen, a kind, generous, loving brother, and a hard worker, he's rich. What could you ever offer him?

"Baby, can you say something? I'm sorry I didn't tell you sooner."

"I'm just surprised, is all. It makes me wonder what I could ever offer someone like you."

We're driving down a secluded road when Zach turns into a gated driveway. He reaches up to press a button attached to his visor when the gate in front of us opens. Is this his house?

Your stock is quickly plummeting, and it wasn't of high value to start.

He stops the car inside the gates without pulling all the way down the long driveway and looks at me. "Someone like me?"

"Zach, you're perfection. You're handsome, an incredible brother, a fantastic friend, according to Tyler, and now you're telling me you're loaded? I was already convinced you were out of my league, but this... it changes things."

"It changes nothing, Zara. I'm still a man. A man with genuine feelings for you. No amount of money changes that, and what you offer is so much more than dollars and cents. Nothing is different between us from five minutes ago."

"As long as you realize I'm not interested in your money. I don't want a dime. Luxurious gifts and vacations don't appeal to me. I'm not that girl."

"Zara, I've never for one second thought you were one of 'those girls' you keep mentioning. Let's go inside and we can talk more about this later, okay? But it doesn't change a thing between us."

Zach drives the remaining hundred yards down the driveway, toward a large, white, contemporary home. It's two storeys and looks spacious, but doesn't qualify as an obnoxious mansion. He presses another button beside his visor and one door in his four-car garage opens. There is only one other vehicle inside—a pink Jeep—which I am assuming is Jasmine's.

Once he puts the car in park, Zach walks around the car to open my door and captures me in an embrace as I step out. He repeats, "Nothing has changed between us. How I feel about you isn't affected by net worth, okay?"

"Okay." I want to believe that.

A handsome, compassionate, thoughtful millionaire. He's going to break your heart. You are worthless.

I grab the small gift bag for Jasmine, now feeling even more self-conscious about gifting it to her, so I turn to put it back on the seat of the car.

"Don't," Zach commands. "She's going to love it."

"It feels pathetic after seeing all of this." I wave my hand around, taking in the immaculate garage space. The floor is cleaner than my kitchen counter.

He takes a half step back and releases a breath. "Zara, all this," he replies while waving his hand around in imitation of me, "doesn't compare to this." He points to my heart. "The fact you bought something for her that's so thoughtful and personal is better than any of this. I promise."

Before I can respond, the door to my right swings open, and a stunning blonde I recognize comes running out, squealing with excitement.

"I've been so excited to meet you!" she exclaims before taking me in. "I remember you! Ballet flats!"

I grimace, reminded of one of my many irrational moments. "Yes, that's me. It's nice to meet you officially, Jasmine. I'm Zara."

"Oh, I know all about you. Zach talks my ear off about you day and night."

That statement, which should be flattering, brings my anxious thoughts to the forefront again.

He told her. You trusted him with your secret, and he told her. She knows how damaged you are. She'll only see you as a victim now.

"Jas, can you give us a sec? We'll be right in."

"Oh, sorry if I interrupted."

"It's all right. I just want some alone time for a second." Zach waggles his eyebrows and lets out a mischievous laugh.

"Ew, gross. Okay, I'm going."

Once the door closes, Zach reassures me, "I know what you're thinking when she said I told her all about you, but I would never tell anyone what you told me—not unless you said it was okay. I would never betray your trust like that. She meant I talk about you all the time, which is true."

I breathe a sigh of relief.

He pulls me in for a kiss. "Let's get in there before she gets impatient."

We walk through a mudroom, where I hang my jacket and remove my shoes. From there, we enter a large, open-concept living room, dining room, and kitchen. The décor is tasteful—it doesn't scream bachelor. It's warm and inviting. Jasmine is standing in the kitchen, which would be any chef's dream.

You don't belong here.

"Do you want to take a grand tour?" Zach asks, interrupting the downward spiral I was headed down.

I consider his question for a moment, but my anxiety reminds me that I'll never belong somewhere like this. "Actually, I'd love to spend some time getting to know Jasmine, if you don't mind."

"Seriously?" Jasmine's perfectly shaped brows arch without creating a single wrinkle.

"Yes, that's what I came for. I... um, I brought you a little something." I pass her the gift bag, swallowing the lump in my throat. "It's nothing much."

"Wow, thank you! You didn't have to do that."

"Well, it's nothing exciting, so don't get your hopes up."

She pulls the box from the bag and opens it. I can't read her expression as she looks over her gift.

She hates it. She can't figure out what to say without hurting your feelings.

"It's okay if you don't like it. I won't take it personally." Yes, I will.

"No, it's not that. I really love it. This is so perfect... I'm just in shock." Her eyes water as she closes the gap between us to wrap me in a hug. "This is the most beautiful gift anyone has ever gotten me—and Zach bought me a Jeep! Thank you."

I chuckle, tension releasing from my shoulders, knowing she's at least pretending to like the gift. "You're welcome. I don't know if Zach told you, but I work with kids in the foster system for my job, and for many of them, family is an unfamiliar concept. I know you went through a lot when you were young, losing your family, so I wanted to give you something that honours all of them."

Why would you remind her of that horrible time in her life? Keep your mouth shut.

She's crying actual tears now. "I'm going to wear this every day for the rest of my life. I can't even explain how much this means to me." She leans to the left to peek around me. "Zach, you better not mess this up." She glares at her brother. "I never thought a bracelet could mean so much." She holds the bracelet in one hand and lifts her opposite arm in my direction. "Could you help me put it on?"

"I'd be happy to." I look down at the silver bracelet that has the initials of each of her family members and an infinity knot heart, representing eternity.

After I've clasped the bracelet around Jasmine's delicate wrist, she takes a second to look at it, then pulls me in for a Quinn-style hug. When she releases me, she says, "I've never had a sister, but I do now."

I glance over at Zach, and I've never seen him look happier. He's been silently witnessing the exchange between Jasmine and me, and I almost forgot he was here. When I see him beaming at us, I'm dying to know what he's thinking, but he doesn't give me any insight into his thoughts. All he says is, "Let's eat."

Together, we eat an incredible vegetable lasagna, and I learn that Jasmine watched a documentary on slaughterhouses five years ago, resulting in her commitment to being a vegetarian. Like a good brother, Zach went along with it, assuming it was a phase. But their decision stuck and there's been no looking back. They tell me about their time together and what they call "raising each other." Their bond is undeniable.

After we finish our meal, I offer to help clean up. After we finish our meal, I offer to help clean up.

Jasmine reminds me I'm the guest and ushers Zach and me off to have some time alone.

I hesitate because leaving her to clean everything up seems rude, but Zach walks over, kisses her on her forehead, just as I saw him do in our office building all those weeks ago. "Thanks Jas." Then he grabs my hand and pulls me away.

I giggle at his eagerness and shout, "Thank you," to Jasmine.

Zach leads me into an office, which reminds me a bit of Mr. Stafford's. There's a dark wood desk with a brown leather chair, a built-in fireplace surrounded by an entire wall of bookshelves filled with various biographies, classic literature, and reference works. Across from the desk are two comfortable looking wing-back chairs with a small round table between them. It's classic and beautiful.

My eyes finish their tour and land back on Zach.

"Do you realize how incredible you are?"

"I didn't even do anything." My face heats under his stare.

"Are you kidding? You charmed the socks off my sister, and while Jas is a nice girl, with women I date, she is not easily pleased."

I shudder at the thought of him bringing other women into his home to meet his sister.

You thought you were special? You thought you were the only woman he's brought here before? He's Mr. Perfect. He's not as pathetic as you. It's not like he's waited his whole life for you to show up.

"Wherever your thoughts are saying, stop them. Don't pull away from me."

It shouldn't surprise me how he's learned to recognize when I retreat into my anxious thoughts, but it does every time. "I'm thinking about all the other women you've brought home before." I shouldn't have said that.

He exhales a groan. "Baby, I didn't mean that. To be honest, we've lived here for five years and you're the only woman I've brought home."

"I find that hard to believe."

"Have I ever given you a reason not to trust me? I've never had the opportunity to show the woman I love my home before now."

I stare at him, considering this revelation he launched at me like a grenade. "The woman you love?"

"The woman I love. *You* are the woman I love. I love you, Zara."

"You barely know me."

"Yeah, it may seem crazy, but I've known since the moment I saw you that you were going to change my life forever. I fell hard and fast, and now I'm hopelessly in love with you, Zara Levy."

I'm trying my best to choke back my tears. This time, confused, happy tears.

He couldn't love you. There's no way. You're hopeless. You have nothing to offer. You are unlovable.

"Zach, you can't love me."

His expression falls as he drops his gaze to his feet. "Why can't I love you? I want to love you. I've never been so happy as I am now, loving you. It's okay if you're not ready; I'm not trying to push you, but I had to say it."

"I'm not even a little worthy of you." I've spent so many years ashamed and disgusted with myself, love never seemed to be a possibility.

"You are worthy of so much more than I could ever give you."

"No, I'm not. Look at what you've been through, and you're amazing. I struggle to get out of bed in the mornings and cry myself to sleep at night. You can't love me."

"Amazing is a stretch, but Baby, what I've been through has made me fear losing people and encourages me not to hold back with those I care about. It's made me not want to keep from saying what I mean. What you've been through, understandably, has made you fear people—fear any situation you don't have control over. What we've each been through has been completely different, so please, please don't feel you're doing anything wrong in how you deal with your past."

Wow. He's very insightful.

"But what if I never get better? You'll be sick of dealing with me one day. I know it." I swipe at a rogue tear trickling down my cheek.

"I can't imagine you being any better, but if being with you means helping you out of bed in the mornings and holding you while you cry at night, then that's okay with me."

A massive lump forms in my throat, making my next words difficult. "I... I love you, too."

His signature smile overtakes his face. "Say that again."

"I love you. Zachary Haynes, I love you. I think I've loved you since I first looked into your eyes. I was sure you were a serial killer out trolling for naïve victims, but I still felt like I would have followed you into a dark alley."

"You're crazy." He chuckles.

"I am. Clinically. And I might be a mess forever."

Without another word, he pulls me onto his lap, and we express everything we're feeling for each other through a passionate kiss.

My heart will belong to Zachary Haynes until the day I die.

t's Saturday morning and I wake up in my condo, alone. It's never felt as small or as lonely as it does now. After my evening at Zach's house, he dropped me off around midnight, and I could tell he didn't want to leave.

Even after our revelations to each other, I was still so afraid he'd change his mind about me when I told him I wasn't willing to have 'sleepovers' until I was a married woman. As usual, he surprised me. He told me he admired my integrity and respected my choice.

To be honest, the thought of intimacy terrifies me—even with Zach. Would he be thinking about my past, repulsed by me physically?

It's not possible for him to be attracted to you. How could he be, knowing that your body was so damaged, your uterus had to be removed? How can he be attracted to a woman who can never bear his children?

The panic is becoming all-consuming as my phone lights up.

Zach: Good morning, my love. I hope you slept well. Can I see you today?

I hold my phone to my chest and absorb his words. His love. He said he loves me.

This is going to end in heartache.

I may not know how long this love will last, but I owe it to myself to make an effort.

Zara: Bonjour, *mon coeur*.

Zach: Ooh-la-la, I like when you speak French to me. ;)

I snort a laugh.

Zara: I'd love to see you today, but I'm supposed to visit my parents.

Right away, my phone rings.

"Bonjour," I say, trying to be cheeky.

"Ah, oui, oui." He chuckles, and the sound warms my heart.

"How are you?" I consider asking in French, but I don't want to turn it even cheesier. Plus, my French accent is awful. It would ruin any appeal.

"If I'm being honest, I'm missing you like crazy."

"It's only been ten hours since you dropped me off."

"Ten hours too long. I don't want to keep you from your parents, but I can't imagine getting through the day without you anymore. Even Jas has been talking about you nonstop."

"Ha! I enjoyed my time with her, too." I pause. "Listen, I'm supposed to have dinner with my parents. Why don't you come with me?"

He doesn't answer for a beat. "Meet the parents? That's a big step."

I'm suddenly self-conscious and realize he may not be ready for that step yet. "Oh, I'm sorry. I just assumed—"

"Baby, I'd love to meet your parents. What time can I pick you up?"

"Really? You'll meet them? My mom is going to ask you more questions than a job interview, and my father will be most concerned with your golf handicap and favourite sports team."

"That sounds like a lot of pressure, but I think I can handle it. So, if you're serious, I'd love to join you."

My smile spreads wider than it has in a long time, despite the raging nerves over the reality of this leap in our relationship. "Wow, okay. Let me call my mom and run it by her. She'll say yes, but it's the polite thing to do."

"Of course, Baby. Call me back after you speak to her and fill me in on the details. In the meantime, I better go do some research on sports teams."

I laugh. "Just be yourself. They'll love you."

"I hope so, because I love their daughter."

"I'll call you back soon. I love you too."

After the call disconnects, I take a moment to absorb what feels like the start of a new life for me. Going away to University was supposed to be a fresh start, but it never felt like one because I was still repressing my trauma. I carried it around with me like a backpack, using it as a shield to not put myself out there. Once I graduated, I should have taken the opportunity to move somewhere else and start over, but my anxiety kept me from taking that chance. I stuck with what was comfortable. But this—with Zach—feels like something new.

I dial my parent's phone number, and to my surprise, my dad answers.

"Please, don't tell me you're calling to cancel dinner. Your mother will be heartbroken."

"No, Daddy. I'm coming. I wanted to ask if I could bring a guest."

"A guest, huh? Is this guest a male or female?" He pauses a second before I can answer. "Not that it matters."

"My boyfriend, Daddy. It's pretty new, so I didn't want to say anything until it was serious, but it is now, and I'd like you to meet him."

"Well, who am I to deny my baby girl? Bring the fella over, but he better prepare himself for a grilling."

"Don't scare him away. I really like him."

"You sound happy. That makes me happy. He better be one hell of a guy."

"He is. We'll see you guys in a few hours then. Just tell Mom I'm bringing a guest, okay? I'll surprise her."

"I like the way you think. See you soon. I love you."

"Love you too, Daddy."

I excitedly dial Zach's number as soon as I hang up with my father.

"So, when do I get to see you?" he answers.

"We're supposed to have dinner at five, and it takes about thirty minutes to get there. Can you be here around three, so we'll have plenty of time? I wanted to stop at that Italian place to grab something for dessert."

"I like the sound of that. See you at three."

Zach arrives at three on the dot. When he knocks on the door, I feel as if my heart will burst from my chest. I spent years with that feeling being caused by panic, but now it's excitement. I open the door to find him dressed in a casually sexy outfit—brown shoes and belt, dark jeans, a white button-down shirt and navy blazer.

"Hi." My words come out as a whisper because he's taken my breath away.

Without a word, he rushes through the door and pins me to the wall in my foyer to kiss me. He kisses me as if I'm his lifeline, and I'm becoming more and more convinced he is mine.

"Hi," he finally replies. "Are you ready? You look beautiful."

I'm dressed in a grey, one-piece, strapless jumper. It's somewhat form-fitting but not scandalous, and the tapered pant legs stop above my ankles. I've paired it with black heels and a black trench coat, which I'm already wearing, so Zach has no idea what's underneath.

"Thank you. I'm all ready. Let me check and make sure everything is unplugged and locked. I'll be right there."

"Okay, take your time."

As I make my way through my condo, he watches me check every outlet and window. He doesn't comment; he lets me go through my process.

"All right, let's go. Are you ready for this?"

"Baby, with you, I'm ready for anything."

Something bad is going to happen. You don't deserve happiness.

The entire way to my parent's house, Zach holds my hand as he drives. I've always felt safe in his BMW X3. It's a compact SUV, but feels like it's a sensible winter vehicle, which is important in Muskoka.

We pull into my parent's driveway, which leads to their bungalow on a small plot of land in Bala. I was born and raised in this house, and it will always feel like home. I don't have a good excuse why I stay away for such long stretches of time other than feeling like a burden to everyone forced to be around me.

I wait for Zach to walk around his SUV to open my door—not because I can't open it, but because he likes to do it for me, and I am not about to cancel chivalry. He grabs my hand to help me out and waits for me to steady myself on the gravel driveway in my heels.

With one arm holding the box of cannolis and eclairs we purchased, I loop my other arm through his and look up at him. "It's not too late to make a run for it."

He smiles in return. "Yes, it is. You're holding my heart."

Before we even walk up the few stairs onto the porch, my mother is barrelling outside like a freight train. "Zara! Oh, Zara, I've missed you." She pauses as she spots Zach. "Wow, who is this handsome young man?"

Zach reaches out his hand. "Hello, Mrs. Levy. I'm Zach. Zachary Haynes. Thank you for having me."

"Oh, nonsense." She smiles and pulls him in for a hug.

I send Zach a pleading look that says, "Please don't run away," but he's grinning and looks like he's enjoying the motherly attention. It occurs to me it's probably been a long time since he felt something like this.

My dad pops his head out the door. "Would you let them come in the house, woman? You're all going to freeze out there."

We all laugh, but my mom looks embarrassed. I try to distract her by pulling her into a hug and whispering, "Hi, Momma. I missed you too."

Mom takes the box of sweets from my hand. "Come, now. Zach, please mind the mess."

"No mind at all, Ma'am."

"Oh, please call me Alanna." We step inside and mom shouts as she walks back toward the kitchen. "Zara, you know where the coats go. Make yourselves at home. I have to tend to the food for a moment, then I'm going to come back to ask you everything there is to learn about you, Zachary Haynes."

"I look forward to it, Alanna."

I turn toward the entryway closet and Zach insists on helping me with my coat. As he pulls my trench away to expose my bare arms and decolletage, his breathing rate visibly increases. Score one for Zara.

In a breathy whisper, Zach asks, "Wow. Did you have to wear that here?"

I take his comment to be an admonishment, which is not the reaction I had hoped for.

He leans past me to reach for a hanger, and whispers in my ear, "I'm not going to be able to focus on anyone else with you looking this incredible."

Oh. "S... sorry. I wasn't trying to—"

"Shh. You look stunning. I'll just keep my thoughts to myself."

"You can tell me all about them later," I tease, eliciting a smirk and wide eyes from him.

My dad breaks the tension by walking over and abruptly asking, "What are your intentions with my daughter, young man?"

Zach freezes for a split second, then recovers. "Nothing but pure, Sir."

My dad lets out a boisterous laugh as he reaches out to shake Zach's hand with his right and simultaneously slaps him on the shoulder with his left. "I like this one."

The built-up tension in my shoulders releases. This is going okay.

Something bad is going to happen. Something bad always happens. You shouldn't have asked him here. You should have stayed home. Home is safe.

"I'm Frederick, but most people call me Fred. What did you say your name was, Son?"

"Zachary Haynes, but most people call me Zach."

My dad looks as if Zach's name has slapped him in the face. He takes a step back as Zach looks toward me, appearing just as confused.

"What's wrong, Daddy?"

"Oh, no, nothing. Sorry. I'm happy to see my baby girl so happy." He scrubs his hand on the back of his neck, which, I learned throughout my childhood, he does when he's uncomfortable. "Say, where did you grow up, Zach?"

"I grew up in the Bracebridge area. I left to play college baseball in Michigan for a few years, but returned home to be with my sister."

My father continues leading Zach. "What about your parents? Are they still in the area?"

Zach looks away for a moment, settling his eyes on me, then back to my dad. "No. I'm afraid my parents passed away years ago. It's just me and my younger sister now."

"I was afraid you'd say that."

"I beg your pardon?"

When he doesn't reply, I prompt, "Daddy, what's wrong?"

My dad blows out a long breath and rubs his stubble with his hand. He looks as if he's about to be sick. My father spent decades as a firefighter in Bracebridge and Muskoka—he's as tough as they come. I've rarely seen him get emotional.

"When you were a kid, were you in a bike accident with your brother?"

Zach's forehead creases, giving him a scowling expression. "Yes... I was. How would you know that?"

"My firetruck was the first group on the scene. They sent me to tend to your brother before the ambulance arrived. I tried to save him. I really tried." My dad hangs his head.

"You tried to save him? He died on impact. There was nothing you could have done for him."

"No, Son." My dad rubs his hands down each side of his face. "He was conscious. He kept asking where Zach was. I tried to get him to stay still, but he was so worried. I knew he was badly hurt, but his adrenaline must have kept him from realizing it himself." My dad has a lone tear trickling down his face. "I really tried. I tried to keep him still." Through his heavy breathing, my father adds in another bombshell. "I responded to the call with your parents, too."

Zach appears paralyzed. He doesn't speak, nor move.

I'm torn between hugging Zach or hugging my father.

Before I get the chance, Zach says, "I'm sorry, but I have to go." He turns to leave.

When his hand is on the door, I finally register what's happening. I plead with him, "Please, don't go. I love you."

Without turning his head in my direction, he says, "I love you, too." But that doesn't stop him from leaving.

He backs his BMW out of my parent's driveway and speeds away.

It was too good to be true. People like you don't get a happily ever after. Nobody wants you. You're not worth fighting for.

I collapse into my dad's arms, and we cry together. My dad keeps saying, "I'm so sorry. I'm so sorry. I shouldn't have said anything."

My mom appears back in the room, oblivious to what happened, only to find my father and me sobbing. "What happened? Where is Zach?"

"He's gone, mom. He's gone."
He left, and he took my heart with him.

I didn't think anything could hurt more than the physical and emotional pain I went through after being raped. After I was assaulted, I spent nine days in the hospital, had three surgeries to deal with the damage, and yet, I'd prefer that over this heartbreak. This fear—fear that the man I love has given up on us—is so much worse.

I haven't heard from Zach since yesterday when he walked out of my parents' home. I stayed the night with Mom and Dad because I didn't want to be alone, and I could tell my dad felt terrible.

After Zach left, my dad explained what happened the day of the Haynes' accident. He arrived to find Leo trapped between the car and a retaining wall. His spine was damaged, and he had internal injuries, but he was conscious. My dad tended to him the best he could until the ambulance arrived. Leo was fighting to get free so he could see his brother, but it took time for the firefighters to release him. By the time my dad and his team secured Leo to a backboard, it was too late for him. Leo lost consciousness in the ambulance and never woke up again. They pronounced him dead at the hospital.

My dad witnessed many people die during his career, but there were a handful that haunted him; Leo was one of them. Dad attended department mandated therapy afterward, which I was unaware of until now. He never mentioned his work to my sisters or me. He was always the tough, unbreakable dad we looked up to. Seeing him so emotional yesterday made me realize how strong he is.

So much stronger than you'll ever be.

Once my parents drop me home around noon on Sunday, I decide I need to talk to my bestie. I call Quinn, knowing she has returned from her honeymoon. I hope she'll want to talk my ear off about how amazing it was and distract me from my heartbreak.

Quinn deserves to be happy. She isn't damaged and broken. Anyone could love her. Unlike you.

"Hey, Chica. I was just about to call you!"

"Hi, Amiga—or should I say Mrs. Ochoa? How does it feel being back in the cold?" I try my best to sound upbeat but fail.

"Ugh, just as miserable as you'd expect." She laughs. "Everything was great, though. We had so much fun. I'll have to show you the pictures one day soon since you're not on social media. We can have a girls' day."

"That sounds perfect. I missed you so much. I could use some Quinn time."

"That sounds ominous. What have you been up to while I've been away?"

Breathe. She's your best friend. You can talk to her. "Well, you know Zach and I were together at your wedding, right?"

"How could I have missed that? You two disappeared together, then came back to the reception looking like walking, breathing, heart-eye emojis."

I laugh at the memory. "We kind of started dating, and—"

"I knew it! I could tell by the way you were looking at each other that you two were hitting it off. That's amazing, Zar. He's a real catch."

"Well, he's more like the one that got away." I choke on those words as they spill out.

"What? What do you mean?"

I continue to recount the events of the last forty-eight hours. I tell her everything from meeting Jasmine to taking him to meet my parents. She listens intently while I spill it all and takes her time digesting each piece of information.

"So, when he left, he said he loves you?"

"Yes."

"Chica, I know you're spiralling right now, but I think hearing that information is a lot to digest. You need to give him time. You need time to deal with things in your own way before you talk to someone else, so he's probably just having the same feelings."

"I get that. It's just the fact I haven't heard from him, and I have this nagging feeling this was the final straw. All the times I pushed him away, he came back. He made me feel something other than complete self-loathing and fear." I can't hold back my tears now, but at least I refrain from full, ugly crying. "And now I've lost him."

"He just needs time. Do you want me to ask Ty to call and check on him? Have you tried reaching out?"

"I haven't tried calling. If I call and he doesn't pick up, I'll get the answer I'm afraid of. I don't want him feeling like I forced Ty to call either. I'll wait it out, but if I don't hear from him in a few days, then I'll think about it."

"Okay. Keep me posted. It will all be okay."

"Thanks, Amiga. We'll talk later in the week and make a plan so I can see your pictures. Maybe your joy will be contagious."

"If it was, I'd cough all over you," she jokes.

We say goodbye, and once again, I'm left alone with my thoughts. I guess I'll sit here and wait.

I haven't heard from Zach for precisely sixty-eight hours. His office was closed this morning when I stopped by. I texted him once; he hasn't replied.

I'm trying to pretend the last several weeks of my life never happened. My specialty: try to block out the feelings and let them slowly eat away at my soul. This method is always more appealing than dealing with my emotions.

You don't deserve happiness. Happiness is for normal, undamaged people.

I try to focus on my work. It's now 11:10, and I have Chelsea coming in for an appointment in twenty minutes. I have my seven-year-old client, Isla, at 3:00 this afternoon. They are the two girls I love seeing the most. I shouldn't have favourites, but those girls have made such great strides in the time I've been working with them. It's hard not to feel an emotional connection with someone when you've watched them grow so much.

By the time 11:30 arrives, I've texted Zach once more, promising myself this will be the last time. I'll wait for him to reach out to me, though I've prepared myself for the likelihood he never will.

A knock at the door tells me Chelsea is here, so I shout for her to come in. She looks defeated, and it breaks my heart but makes me grateful she is here with me today.

"Hey, Chels. Come have a seat."

"Hi, Miss Levy. How are you?"

"Oh, I'm fine," I lie. "Tell me what's new."

Her demeanour shifts. Something is wrong. I make my way from my desk chair to the armchair beside the sofa and wait for her to continue.

"I've had a bad few days, I guess. I don't even know why."

"Well, let's try to figure that out together. That's what you're here for. If we expected you to figure out everything on your own, I'd be out of a job. We all need help sometimes."

"I know, but I want to figure it out. My feelings bury me and it feels stupid that I can't deal with them."

"Let's start by trying to pinpoint your feelings, and we'll go from there, okay? We'll look at each step, not the whole staircase. You'll get there."

We spend the next forty-five minutes dissecting Chelsea's feelings and struggles. So much of what she is dealing with stems from not having a family, and her fear of being alone, but then at the same time having severe trust issues, so it's hard to let anyone in. Everything she is feeling is understandable, and it's hard to help her combat those feelings when I see what her future looks like. It makes me angry with myself for taking my family for granted.

"Next time you get these big feelings, I don't want you to wait for your next appointment, okay? Call me, and we'll talk about it together."

"But what if it's not during work hours? Or if you're with another client?"

"You let me deal with that, okay? If you call and I don't answer right away, you'll realize why. But I promise I will call you back. I'm here for you, Chels."

"Thanks, Miss Levy. I don't know what I'd do without you."

Little does she realize how much I need her, too.

I came home from work Tuesday evening feeling drained. I want to have a long, hot bath, eat some Oreos, and forget about life.

How did everything get so complicated? I was barely keeping my head afloat, then I fell in love with a man who is unattainable for someone like me. Stupid.

I guess this is evidence that love is not for me. I don't deserve love when I can't even tolerate myself.

Two stacks of four Oreos each make for a high-calorie dinner—at least it's balanced—then after watching Miss Congeniality, through which I cry more than laugh, I go to bed early.

I'm lying in bed, but I can't shut my brain off to fall asleep. Anxiety and I are taking a stroll down memory lane, reliving embarrassing moments.

Remember your tenth-grade computer-science class when you tried to wear wedges to make yourself look more mature, and you ended up tripping on a chair, falling in front of the entire class? Then you went to guidance to withdraw from the class instead of going and facing everyone again. Or do you remember eight years ago when you went to buy groceries, and after the cashier scanned everything, your debit card wouldn't work, so you had to take everything to customer service to leave it there and walk out with nothing? Everyone in the lineup saw you. You made them wait for nothing. Or do you remember the time you were at the department store and you were so convinced that man was following you, so you farted trying to keep him away, then his wife walked around the corner and they both stared at you?

This is fun. Let's keep going. Remember when...

Wednesday morning, I wake up feeling as though I haven't slept at all. A frequent occurrence, but irritating, nonetheless. Maybe my under-eyes will help me carry my emotional baggage.

Once I'm showered and dressed, I opt to make tea at home. If Zach hasn't responded to my messages by now, he never will, so I need to minimize the pain I'll feel by seeing him.

To my surprise, there's a knock at my door. I walk over, and for the first time in my life, excitement makes me open it without checking to see who was on the other side.

That is a terrible mistake.

"Patrick." The sight of my furious former co-worker has all of my stress hormones boosting production.

"You didn't think I'd forget about our last encounter, did you?" he sneers as he pushes through the door.

"How... how did you find where I live?" I step back until I'm against the wall. The same wall Zach pinned me against to kiss me just days earlier.

"It's the age of the internet. Anything is possible when you're determined enough."

"Patrick, please leave." Fear is causing my voice to shake.

He rushes toward me and I let out a bloodcurdling scream as I run into my kitchen. I don't get the impression he's here to talk. My best chance for help is to be loud enough to concern the neighbours.

"Somebody, help!"

"Shut up, you stupid whore. You've ruined my life and you're going to pay. Worthless trash like you doesn't deserve to breathe." He sets his predatory gaze on my body. "I'll admit, though, you are pretty hot. Maybe we can have some fun."

He's going to force himself on you. If you don't fight him off, you're asking for it. You deserve whatever you get if you can't defend yourself.

"Patrick, you're going to have to kill me first." Perhaps I should have considered the consequences of my words beforehand, but I will not live through that again. I can't.

"That can be arranged," he growls as he tries to clamber over the island to reach me.

I know I can't get away, so I have to be ready to fight. The kettle is on the stove, so I grab hold of the handle, and as Patrick is climbing over the island, I swing the kettle around, bashing his face with the hot metal. That doesn't stop him—it only angers him. I drop the kettle on the floor after recognizing there is barely any water left in it. It's useless to me with no weight.

My knife block. It sits on the counter beside my stove, behind me to my left, giving me a glimmer of hope. Maybe if I hold a knife, he'll back off.

But what if he wrestles the knife from your hand? He's stronger than you.

But what if you don't try?

I reach behind me to pull a chef's knife from the block. It's a sharp, six-inch blade; surely it looks intimidating. To my surprise, presenting the weapon makes Patrick smile. It's not a cheerful smile, it's a smug, self-satisfied smile, like a Cheshire cat. The cat's about to eat the canary.

Patrick reaches behind him into his waistband and reveals a gun. I have little gun knowledge, but I know enough to be certain that one can kill me.

What would Sandra Bullock do? SING. Solar Plexus, Instep, Nose, Groin.

I drop the knife, which Patrick seems to view as a sign of defeat. He lunges toward me, and I channel my inner Gracie Lou

Freebush. I kick Patrick as hard as I can in the groin, then connect the palm of my hand with his nose in an upward thrust before he can comprehend what has happened. It doesn't incapacitate him, but it stuns him enough that he drops the gun, and its momentum slides it across the floor behind me.

Get the gun. He's going to kill you. No one is coming to help you.

I don't want to turn my back on this maniac, so I step backward until the gun is at my feet, then bend down to pick it up, keeping my eyes on Patrick the entire time.

The weight of the gun in my grip feels unfamiliar and terrifying, but I've seen enough movies to know there's some sort of safety. I'm fumbling around with my right thumb, trying to find a switch. I slide a small lever on the side of the gun in front of the hammer. All those hours of TV watching pay off at this moment.

"Patrick! Stop! Or I'll shoot."

"You don't have the guts. You're a weak little girl." He walks toward me. For each step he takes, I take one backward to maintain distance.

My hands are shaking, my heart is racing, and I'm sure the sweat from my palms is going to make me drop this gun. I need to keep him at a distance. Maybe I can convince him to leave.

Then, the sweetest music I've ever heard; sirens approaching. Patrick doesn't appear to be as excited as I am—now he's got nothing to lose. He charges toward me and without enough time for the consequences to reach conscious thought, I squeeze the trigger.

Patrick collapses to the ground.

I vomit.

Seconds—maybe minutes—later, I can hear faint shouting and commotion around me, but between the thumping of my heartbeat in my ears, the tears in my eyes, and the bile vacating my body, I don't comprehend any of it.

I feel arms on me, but not affectionate, comforting arms. Arms that pull the gun from my hand and push me to the wall. I sob until I can't breathe anymore. My vision goes fuzzy. I blink; then my vision goes black.

Home is not safe.

I remember speaking to a police officer before paramedics ushered me off, but I have no memory of the conversation. Five hours later, I'm still in the hospital and I'm getting tired of this becoming my only hobby.

The police have insisted I call someone to come wait with me, but I don't want to bother anyone. It's not like I can call up Quinn, "Hey, girl. Can you come to the hospital and sit with me for a bit until the police decide whether to charge me with murder? Okay, great. Thanks."

I can't call Zach because he's been avoiding me, so I'm not about to attempt to elicit concern from him by whining about my violent encounter.

Everyone I know is at work. It's a weekday afternoon, for goodness' sake; I should be at work, too. Instead, I'm being heavily medicated and guarded by a police officer after murdering a man in my kitchen.

You're a murderer. Your life is over.

The medication is helping, but I'm not as numb as I wish I could be.

A man I recognize pulls the curtain aside to walk into my hospital room. Dr. Ross, whom I saw last time I was in this predicament, is caring for me once again.

He's tired of dealing with you. You're so pathetic.

"Good afternoon, Miss Levy. I'm Dr. Ross; I'm not sure if you remember me. We met a few weeks ago."

"I remember. I'm sorry for wasting your time. You must have better things to do." Pile on more shame. This situation got out of control again, and I'm the common denominator.

"Miss Levy, I assure you, making sure you are okay is top of my priority list. You went through quite an ordeal this morning. How are you feeling?"

"I'm fine." I'm not. "He… he said he was going to kill me after he 'had some fun' with me first. I… I didn't mean to hurt him." Thank God these meds are keeping me from turning into a blubbering idiot. Numbness is welcome at the moment.

"I believe you, Miss Levy, and for what it's worth, the police do, too. You were incredibly brave to defend yourself, and I'm sorry this happened to you again."

"I guess I'm a magnet for traumatic situations. We all get what we deserve."

Dr. Ross takes a seat in the chair beside my bed, and his mood shifts from professionalism to compassion. "Miss Levy, you didn't 'deserve' this, nor what happened in your past. What makes you say that?"

"I figure I have 'assault me' tattooed on my forehead or something." I default to my joke-away-the-uncomfortable-conversation method.

"The men who assaulted you, they're the reason you were assaulted. Not you. Those men bear sole responsibility for their actions. You didn't ask for it, and you didn't provoke it."

No one can know that. "Maybe I did."

"I don't think you did, and if you think about it, I'm sure you don't think that either."

I contemplate his words for a moment, but say nothing else.

But maybe you unintentionally encouraged it. You sent those men to their breaking point. You got what you deserved.

"Miss Levy, it says in your file that when you left a few weeks ago, you were to follow up with your primary care physician. Did you do that?"

I close my eyes and turn my face toward the window. Admitting the truth is embarrassing. My relationship with Zach distracted me so much, I felt like I was getting better. I should know better. Sporadic moments of joy do not heal mental illness. That's not the cure and I'm stupid for thinking it could be. "No. I didn't."

"Based on my medical opinion, you should speak to your doctor about medication for your panic attacks and anxiety. I also see signs of depression, so therapy could be a beneficial tool for you. There is help available; I'd like to see you use it."

I've considered medication in the past, but I felt like taking pills to control my brain made me weak. What kind of person can't handle their own thoughts? A pathetic one. Considering the position I'm in, though, I can't figure out how else to move forward. How does anyone ever recover from murdering another human? I can't even bring myself to each chicken because I feel too guilty.

You don't deserve to recover. It should have been you instead of Patrick.

Hindsight is always 20/20, right? In the moment, I was willing to do anything to protect myself, and did. But what do I have left to live for? Patrick was a father. He may have been estranged from his wife, but that doesn't mean she didn't still love him. What's my reason for living?

I don't know.

"I feel like I'm a bad person deep down, and medication won't fix that. Nothing can help."

"Those feelings are quite common with both anxiety and depression. I'm not saying medication and therapy are an easy fix—it takes time and effort to benefit from them—but you're a young woman and I'd like to see you live a happy life despite what has happened. Would you like a nurse to call your doctor to schedule a follow-up appointment?"

I release a shallow breath. "No, that's fine. I'll handle it."

Dr. Ross looks disappointed by my answer, but I'm not ready to face my problems yet. "Just think about it, okay? You don't have to handle everything yourself."

His words remind me of what I said to Chelsea yesterday. We all need help sometimes. Thoughts of Chelsea, Isla, and my other patients offer me a glimmer of hope for a moment. Are they my reason for fighting?

"I'll think about it." I look at the doctor's face but focus on the tip of his freckled nose to avoid his eyes. "Has my workplace been informed about what happened? I'd like to call and explain my absence."

"One more moment and I'll send the police officer in. I only know your next of kin"—he glances at his clipboard—"a Miss Quinn Ayala, didn't answer when we tried contacting her, but I'm not sure who the police have notified. You should consider adding another contact to your medical forms."

"I don't have anyone else." The reality of that statement hits hard. I could add one of my sisters or either of my parents, but I don't want to bother them. They've dealt with enough from me.

Dr. Ross directs another sympathetic gaze my way, and I've hit an all-time low of pitiful. People come into the emergency department in varying states of distress, and here I am, needing medication to cure my pathetic-ness.

"Take care of yourself, Miss Levy, but don't hesitate to come back if you need help again."

After the doctor leaves, the officer charged with making sure I don't attempt a great escape walks through the curtain. He is clearly unaware of the fact that my anxiety would cripple me before my feet even hit the floor. His youthful face looks serious but friendly.

"Miss Levy, would you mind if I asked you some more questions about what happened today?"

"No... no, that's fine."

"Thank you. I'm Constable Perkins, and the detective leading the investigation into what happened this morning has tasked me with taking your full statement."

"Okay, shoot."

Seriously?

"I mean, proceed." My face burns hot, and I can only imagine which stage of a ripening tomato I resemble now. Fluctuating from green and vomiting to red and mortified. Why isn't this IV concoction working?

Constable Perkins' face hints at a smile. I sure hope he understands I'm awkward—not a cold-blooded gun aficionado.

We spend the next forty-five minutes replaying the fifteen-minute window of time from this morning that has changed my life forever. Perkins asked if I wanted a lawyer, but I said I wanted to tell the truth. Whatever comes from that... who am I kidding? The potential repercussions of this morning's events could derail my life and I'll spend the next unknown period of time stressing over each possibility.

Once we've gone over the details frontward, backward, and sideways, I ask Perkins if they have notified my workplace. They have not.

World's worst employee. The co-worker exterminator, Zara Levy.

"So, what do we do now?" I ask, needing a hint at whether I'm headed to prison. "Do you take me to the station?"

"I don't think that's necessary, Miss Levy. We'll sort through the details and let you know if we have any further questions, okay?"

"So just, 'don't leave town' and all that?"

"Basically, yes. You aren't able to go home, though. Do you have somewhere else you can stay?"

Home is not safe.

"Right. I can call my parents and stay with them. Thank you, Constable Perkins."

I'm proud of myself for speaking to the doctor and the police officer without too many tears, but the second that curtain slides shut, I lose all control. I cry until I think I can't cry anymore—but I would be wrong. When I pull myself together, of one thing I am sure: I need my mom.

Both of my parents arrived to collect me from the hospital. Dad went to pick up some personal items from my condo, so I'd be able to stay with them until it's safe for me to return home. I'm not sure I ever want to return there. It's a harrowing reminder that nowhere is truly safe.

Since leaving the hospital, I've shifted into survival mode. As soon as my parents arrived to pick me up, the gravity of the situation hit me.

I killed a man.

I'm a killer.

Formerly, I was known as Zara, the youth counsellor. Now I'm Zara, the murderer. No one will trust me around children again. If I face criminal charges, my job will be gone. All this because of a situation I didn't ask for, but seems I deserved. For months, I was questioning my effectiveness at my job, and maybe this situation will force a decision to be made. This might be the end of my career and not give me the chance to take the coward's way out.

When I get settled at my parents'—my mom forcing me to stay on the couch instead of retreating to my childhood bedroom—I realize it's time to call Mr. Stafford. He's no doubt tried to get a hold of me by now. I fiddle with my phone with the cracked screen for several moments, but I can't handle reliving the day again, so I ask my mom to call him. Like a child having their mother call in sick to school.

Moments later, Mom returns with my phone and a tight smile. "The police already informed him of the situation. He said he feels terrible, and he's glad you're safe."

"It wasn't his fault. Did he say when I should come back to work?"

"Well, Darling, until the criminal investigation is sorted, you'll be on a leave of absence."

I may not have felt up to going into work today, but I wasn't expecting it to come to an abrupt end. My clients are going to be left to start over with someone new, and for some of them, that will mean undoing years of progress.

Pathetic failure Zara. They're better off without you.

Days go by. Without work to occupy my time, I waste my days sleeping and crying. I'm pretty sure it's Saturday, but I can't be certain. I've spent what I'm guessing to be three full days holed up in my childhood bedroom—a place that always felt safe, but now, nowhere does.

My mom has been bringing me food, though I haven't been eating much. I've cried myself empty and only hydrate to save the discomfort of dry mouth and burning eyes.

Today my lofty goal is to shower.

My phone lights up again, but there's nothing I can offer anyone, so I ignore it. Just as I have been for days.

Everyone is better off without you; Quinn, your sisters, your clients, Mr. Stafford, Zach. The best thing you can do for them is to walk away or disappear. You should have let Patrick kill you.

A short while later, Mom knocks on my bedroom door. "Darling?"

I don't lift my face from the pillow. "Yeah?"

"Zach is here to see you. He's been trying to call you for days. He's worried. Can I let him come in?"

There is no way I am letting anyone see me like this. I'd rather use vinegar for eye drops. "No. Tell him I was right. He should move on and find someone better."

"What on Earth are you talking about?"

"He'll know what I mean, Mom. Just tell him not to come back. He's better off."

"That's not true, but I'll tell him you're not up for a visit today."

There won't be any day in the future either.

A few hours later, I've showered and put on clean underwear. That's my accomplishment for the day, and it exhausted me to the point I need a nap. Naps are good. Sleep is good. I don't feel when I sleep.

My mother requested I come out to the dining room to eat with her and Dad for dinner. She's been taking care of me for days, so even though I'd rather hide in my cave, after my nap, I oblige.

Dinner conversation is forced, but it was kind of nice to get out of my head for a short time. After we eat, Mom insists on cleaning up—I don't offer to help—and I go back to my room.

I throw myself on my bed, lying face down on my pillow, wrapped in my blanket cocoon. Seconds later, there's a quiet knock at my door.

"Baby Girl, can I come in?"

"Sure," I mutter into my pillow.

My dad approaches with gentle footsteps, then I feel the bed dip under his weight. He places one hand on my calf, which is a simple gesture, but comforting. "How are you feeling? Really?"

I roll onto my back and sit up enough to prop myself on my elbows. "I'm fine."

"This"—he points around the room—"doesn't look fine."

"What do you want me to say?" I pause. "I'm not fine, not really. The circumstances don't matter. I killed a man. I'm a murderer and I can never take that back. It plays in my head on a constant loop and I think about how I could have done something different. I'm just a monster."

"No, Baby Girl. You didn't murder him," he says as calm as if he's stating the weather.

I tilt my head in confusion—like a puppy, but not cute at all.

Has Patrick somehow survived?

"He made the choice to come to your home with intentions to kill you, Zara. You did not murder him. You defended yourself by any means necessary. You survived. Now, I'm not saying that's an easy load to bear, but you have to recognize none of it was your fault."

"I pulled the trigger. I shot him in the neck. He bled to death in *my* kitchen. No one else did that. I did!"

"Zara, where did you get the gun?"

"It was Patrick's." His name tastes like battery acid on my tongue.

"Exactly. Before you had the gun, where was it?"

I stare down at my hands, recalling how the gun felt in my grip. I hated every second, but staring down the barrel of it was worse. "In his hands."

"Right, and where was it pointed?"

"At me."

"What you did, to fight that gun from his hands, that was incredibly brave. How strong you are; well, it inspires me every day. You need to believe in your own strength."

"I don't feel strong, Daddy." My waterworks start, once again making me hate myself more than I did five minutes ago. "I don't know how to move on from this. It feels impossible. I want everything to stop. I want the feelings to stop."

My dad takes me in his arms and lets me cry on his chest, just like when I was a little girl and skinned my knee. The problem, though, is that a skinned knee heals, and everything goes back to normal. Here, now, I can never go back to "normal."

"You are strong. Strength doesn't come from muscle mass. Your undefeatable character makes you strong. I'm so proud to call you my daughter, and I'm so sorry I wasn't there to protect you those times you needed me."

Now my dad is crying on me as much as I am on him. We hug each other and let all of our pent-up emotions pour out.

"Daddy, you couldn't have known. I'm all right. It's okay." I try to ease his guilt. None of this was his fault.

"See, Baby Girl. You are all right, and it *is* going to be okay." He smiles, though his eyes are filled with unshed tears.

"You're the best dad a girl could ask for. I hope you know that."

"I love you, and I'm always proud of you."

My dad and I sit in silence, sniffling and drying our tears. My phone lights up and for the first time in days, I decide not to ignore it. I don't recognize the number, so I assume it's the police calling me for a follow-up statement.

"I should take this. It could be the police."

"Okay. Mom and I are out here if you need us." He stands, hooking his thumb in the direction of the living room.

I flash my dad a weak smile as I answer the phone. "Hello?"

"Miss Levy? Miss Levy, it's Chelsea. Chelsea Wells."

"Hi, Chelsea. How are you?"

"You said I could call if I ever needed to talk."

"Of course, Chelsea. Are you okay?"

I hear a loud breath through the phone. "It's stupid. Ugh, I shouldn't have bothered you."

"You can tell me, Chels. Having feelings, whatever they may be, aren't stupid, and you are never a bother."

I spend the next thirty-five minutes on the phone with Chelsea. By the end of our call, I feel as if it were as therapeutic for me as it was for her. Our conversation made me realize it's time to take my life back.

Monday morning, I'm calling my doctor. I'll do it for Chelsea. I'll do it for myself.

Monday morning, I've already talked myself out of speaking with my doctor. It's been five days since M-day—Murder day—and I still haven't left my parents' house. I would be content never leaving again.

Nowhere is safe.

I consider Chelsea and how she has shown such incredible strength without the support of a family, and that motivates me to do something I never would have even contemplated days ago. I'm going to confide in my mom.

Sure, she knows what happened to me in the past, but I've never spoken to her about how much it's affected me. My mother looks at her children and grandchildren through a tinted lens, which makes things appear better than reality. I love her for that, but at this moment, I need her to see reality with me.

Granted, I can't say I haven't contributed to her perception of me because I've always tried to put on a brave face and pretend I was okay. Even when I was anything but. My mom thinks when I don't call for days or weeks, it's because work is overwhelming. I'm not sure how she'll take it when I tell her that's not the whole truth.

I steady myself on my bed-legs—like sea-legs but caused by an abnormal attachment to one's bed—and commit myself to baring my whole truth to my mother. If I'm going to get through this, I need help. It's okay to need help.

You shouldn't be bothering your mom with your problems. She has enough to worry about, and she's getting older and can't handle much stress. Don't be selfish.

No, it's okay to need help.

Mom is sitting at her desk by the window in the living room when I enter. Her long greying hair is draped down her back as she leans over whatever she's working on.

"Hey, Momma. Do you have a minute?"

"For you, my darling, I have as long as you want." Her giggle puts me a bit more at ease.

"I... I was just wondering if we could talk."

"Of course." She stands from her desk chair, gazing at me with concerned hazel eyes as she closes the gap between us. "You can come to me anytime."

"I know. The truth is, I've never been ready to talk."

"But you're ready now?"

This is a terrible mistake. She doesn't need this.

No, it's okay to need help. My thoughts are not trustworthy. I remind myself again that I have people who love me—even when I don't feel worthy.

"I am. But bear with me because I have no idea what will come out once I start."

"My ears are open to receive whatever you say. Do you want me to make some tea, then we can get comfortable to chat?"

A hot beverage is not going to soothe my soul. "I'm afraid if I don't start now, I'll lose my nerve." I take a seat on the left side of the brown microfiber sofa, holding a matching throw pillow across my stomach.

"Okay. Talk to me."

I blow out an anxious breath. "Where do I even start? I hate bothering you with this."

"Let me stop you right there," she says as she slides next to me. "I do not feel bothered. I don't know if you are aware of this, but for moms who spend so much of their lives raising children, when those children aren't at home anymore, it can be lonely. Not that we ever want our children to have hard times, but when they do, it means so much when they come back home. You never have to feel bad for confiding in me, okay?"

With a nod and teary eyes, I pour out my awful truths. "You know how every time we talk, you ask if I'm okay, and I say I'm fine?"

She nods, squeezing my hand tighter.

"Well, I'm not fine, Momma. I haven't been fine for a long time."

"I know." Her words are confident and matter-of-fact. This isn't a surprise to her. "I can see how you try to put on a brave front, but I knew you were struggling. As many times as I wanted to find a way to help, I knew you needed to decide in your own time. It's nothing to be ashamed of, Zara. You have been through some very hard things, and you've done your best to navigate beyond them."

"But I'm not beyond them. I was raped, destroyed, assaulted again, then murdered a man in the one place I felt safe. It's too much. I'm so ashamed and constantly overwhelmed by fear. My mind is always in overdrive. It's like I make this ongoing list of things to do, not to do, or wish I hadn't said or done; the list keeps getting longer and longer, and it's being read start to finish, on a loop. 'Good' things I do never get added to the list."

"Well, I'm no expert, so how do we go about fixing that? Do you have any ideas?"

I take a beat, questioning if I should ask her to go with me to my doctor. If I don't do it now, I may never take the chance again. "I think I need to see my doctor." It's amazing how I can feel so embarrassed in front of a woman who changed my diapers and taught me how to use a spoon. I've never felt so helpless in front of her.

My mom surprises me when she says, "I think so too. If you want, I'll come with you so you're not alone. I realize this is hard, Zara, but you deserve so much more than suffering in this mental prison. Let's launch a prison break."

Her words make me laugh. I don't know if even *Michael Schofield* could get me out of this one.

Before I lose every ounce of nerve I have, I ask, "Can you stay with me while I call?"

"I'll stay by your side forever if you need me."

And just like that, I pick up the phone to call my doctor's office, unsure of what the future holds, but feeling hopeful.

You can't get rid of me that easily.

My mother accompanied me to my doctor's office earlier this week. I sat in Dr. Holloway's office and cried for an entire hour, but she patiently sat and listened, even though she's a general practitioner and had people waiting in the reception area for their appointments. We've decided on a treatment plan which includes medication—at least for the short term. I hate the idea of taking it, but I will try because I can't continue down the path I am on.

It's been two weeks since M-day, and aside from going to the doctor, I haven't left my parents' house. If being a functioning adult wasn't necessary, I'd happily stay here forever. To make myself less of a burden, I've at least been helping my parents out around the house, but that doesn't make up for the upheaval in their lives I've caused. Returning to my condo isn't something I'm ready for, though. It's possible I'll never be ready.

I'm lying on my bed after spending a few hours helping mom rearrange living room furniture to clean underneath everything. I'm pretty sure her determination could have moved the furniture on its own, but she asked me to help, so I obliged. My muscles are sore from the physical labour, but it's nice to feel something beyond emotional turmoil.

My stomach sinks when I hear the doorbell. Hopefully, it's Jehovah's Witnesses, because they're lovely, and they don't come with any background knowledge of what's happened in my life. I don't particularly want company—and I certainly don't want a pity visit.

"Zara, can you get the door?" Mom shouts from her bedroom.

I drag myself to the door, stretching my aching muscles on the way, and without warning, fear overwhelms me.

The last time you opened the door, it had deadly consequences.

I'm frozen in place, standing in the entryway, when the doorbell rings again.

"Zara?" My mom is getting closer. "What's wrong?"

"I... I tried, mom. I can't. Last time I..."

The realization hits her. "Oh, Darling, I'm so sorry. I didn't even think. You never mind; I'll get it." She moves to the door swiftly, pulling the small curtain aside slightly, then glancing back at me before opening the door wide. Standing on the porch is a sight that hits me in the heart. Mon Coeur.

"Hi." Zach looks beyond my mother at my petrified face. He shakes his head and acknowledges my mom. "Hello, Alanna. I'm sorry to show up like this."

"No apologies necessary. Zara here was just a bit startled to open the door. Come in."

Zach's eyes widen in horror as he takes me in. "I'm so sorry, Baby. I didn't even think."

"No, it's…" I release a long exhale to steady my voice. His presence is like a harrowing reminder of all that's happened over the past several weeks. "It's fine. I have to get over it sometime, right?"

Zach stares at me, looking as though he's unsure how to respond.

My mother breaks the silence. "Well, if you'll excuse me, I was in the midst of rearranging my closet, so I'll be getting back to work. Zara, I trust you'll make Zach feel at home."

"Um, sure Mom. We'll be fine." My mother turns to walk away, leaving Zach and me standing in the front foyer. "Would you like to come in?"

"Is that okay with you? I'm sorry to show up, but I've been going out of my mind wanting to see you."

"Listen, Zach…"

"No, Zara. Don't do this. Don't pull away from me thinking you're doing me a favour. Please, I'm begging you." He strides forward, taking each of my hands in his and staring into my soul. "Let's figure this out together. We're better together."

The emotion in his voice makes what I have to say even harder, but I'm determined to do this for us. "No, Zach. We're not better together right now. I know you might not understand, but I promise you I am making a genuine effort to get better. I want to get better. But, for me to do that, I need to do it on my own. I need some time to focus on healing myself."

"Why can't I help you? Baby, I need you in my life. Nothing is the same without you." His voice is breaking as he reconciles what I am saying.

"I'm asking you to give me time to heal, so I can be better."

"You can't get any better. I love you, and I want to be here for you. God, I can't believe I was such a jerk, and I wasn't there when you needed me. I'm so sorry." He runs his hair through his unkempt hair, making me notice how dishevelled he looks. The past few weeks appear to have taken a toll on him, too.

"You have nothing to be sorry for. What happened was not your fault, but the reality is, for me to have a healthy relationship, I need to get my head on straight. I won't blame you if you don't want to wait for me to do that." My voice cracks because the possibility of losing him hurts, but this is something I need to do.

"How long do you think you need?"

He won't wait long. If you can't be what he needs, he'll find it somewhere else.

"I'm not sure. Weeks? Months? I'm really trying. I promise. This is something I have to do on my own, and it needs all of my effort right now. I still love you, and I'll always love you, but because I do, this is how it has to be right now."

"Of course I'll wait, Zara. I love you." Zach pulls me into an embrace, and instead of holding me together, I'm torn in two.

I feel selfish either way—whether I take time for myself to get a handle on my mental health, or if I stick by his side and let him help me. His willingness to wait tells me he does love me, and I hope I've made the right choice. Anyone could tell me they love me, but respecting me enough to allow me to do this for myself makes it clear. His love can't fix me, but it can be my reward once I fix myself.

"I'll be waiting for you the moment you're ready. That's a promise."

"I love you."

Zach leans down to plant a gentle kiss on my lips. This kiss is not full of passion and hunger like they were previously. This is a tender kiss full of love and regret. "I love you, too. Please, get in touch if you need me. I'll come running."

"Just don't come on your bike."

We both let out a laugh, which eases some tension. I notice he's back to holding both of my hands, and I am warring with myself, not wanting him to let go.

"That bike ride was the best decision of my life." He smiles and plants another kiss on my cheek. He drops my hands and turns toward the door. Unlike last time, I'm not begging him to stay—at least, not out loud. Internally is a different story.

If he walks out the door, he'll never come back. You're screwing this up, like you do everything.

When I close the door behind Zach as he leaves, I watch him walk down the steps to his SUV, and back his vehicle out of the driveway. I can't help but feel like I've let my heart drive off again.

I walk over to the sofa and collapse in tears. Not sobbing hysterics—but a steady stream of remorse pouring down my face.

This was a mistake. You've just lost the best thing to happen to you. Poor broken Zara.

It's been five weeks since I first saw my family doctor. I have been taking medication, but also attending therapy and being more mindful of self-care—eating right, taking supplements, and exercising. I keep waiting to wake up one day and feel "normal," but it hasn't happened.

The police confirmed I would not be facing any charges as a result of Patrick's death. They ruled it as self-defence, or "reasonable use of force" as they put it, and had no doubt if I hadn't acted, I would be dead. Some days, I still don't think that would be such a bad thing.

Despite the charges being dropped, I'm still not welcome back to work until my therapist signs off on my return. Not that I'm arguing because I couldn't bring myself to walk into the office knowing everyone would talk about me—or worse, fear me. Who wants to work with a murderer?

Chelsea and I have kept in touch, though in an unprofessional capacity that could have me losing my job.

That's a risk I'm willing to take, though, because she doesn't trust easily, and thrusting her onto a new counsellor is more than she can manage at this transitional time in her life. No one can make me feel guilty about that.

I've decided to sell my condo and stay with my parents for the foreseeable future. If I am going to move forward, I can't be doing it in the place I murdered a man. I did not envision being near-thirty and living with my parents, but here I am, sleeping in a double bed with *Backstreet Boys* posters on the wall.

Quinn has visited a few times, and while I appreciate her making time for me, I'm still struggling to feel worthy of it. I get the impression she doesn't know what to say or do when she comes over, but she continues to show up anyway. Every time Quinn comes to the door, my mother lets her in, because Quinn is not the type to take no for an answer. Yet, despite her determination, we feel more distant than ever. It's not her fault. I'm in protection mode—wanting to protect those I love. Protect them from me.

My sisters have also been stopping by regularly with their kids. Lexi's youngest son, Oscar, loves to come over to cuddle with me and we read books or watch movies. There's something comforting about his four-year-old innocence—the world hasn't beaten him down yet and I hope it never does. Even Sophie and Caleb have been stopping by between their endless extracurricular activities and although I still haven't seen them smile, I can see why my mom loves them so much. They sincerely are good kids. It pains me to think Zach and Leo were the same age when Leo died.

Zach.

I don't know how it's possible to fall so hopelessly in love with someone so fast—especially when you don't love yourself—but I managed to. I got caught up in the idea of fate and how we kept being pulled together. My irrational anxiety kept projecting onto him, expecting him to let me down, but it was wrong. I miss him so much it physically hurts, but I can't bring myself to drag him into my mess; I need to fix myself first. I can only hope that he waits for me.

Why would he ever want to wait for you? After all the times you pushed him away, this is the final straw.

No. I trust him. He has my heart.

I have a therapist appointment today, so I'm pushing myself to get ready. I still struggle to get out of bed and leave the house, but I'm improving. My anxious thoughts have diminished, and the depressive episode I was drowning in is much less severe.

My therapist, Dr. Windsor, has been great in helping me learn to process feelings as they come. I still, and perhaps always will, have issues with feelings I can't quite recognize to dispel with logic, but I realize that even ten percent is better than nothing. If I wake up and can't give one hundred percent, then I give what I can. Sometimes that's one percent, and other times it's ninety. Something is better than nothing.

I pull on my dark wash skinny jeans, a rust-coloured sweater, a black bomber jacket, and knee-high black boots. The ground is snow covered now that it's January, so I add a knitted hat, mitts, and a large plaid scarf. I shout goodbye to my parents and head out to my trusty Prius.

Once I arrive at Dr. Windsor's office, I wait anxiously in the reception area—yes, I anxiously await talking about anxiety. Fun, isn't it?

Who knows what we'll talk about today? Will we dive head-first into your psychological and physical traumas, or will we talk about whether you're making enough of an effort to help yourself?

"Hello Zara," Dr. Windsor says as I walk into her office after being called by the receptionist. "Take a seat and let's get started." Once I'm seated on one of the four teal-coloured armchairs placed in a circle around an oval glass coffee table, she continues, "So, how have you been the past few days?"

"I've been okay. Eating properly, doing yoga, and taking the supplements you suggested. I have been sleeping okay, but the medication seems to make me tired, so I still don't have a lot of energy. I've gotten out of bed every day, though."

"That's great. You're making substantial progress, Zara. I think we've come far enough that today we can approach the next big step."

"Bi... big step?"

Why is your heart beating so fast? You're having a heart attack. Maybe she'll make you play with those foam bats therapists use in the movies—you can't hit your therapist!

"Let me explain. You've made such great strides in the past few weeks, and normally I'd delay this longer so we don't derail progress, but I'm confident you are ready. Today, we're going to discuss forgiveness."

"Forgiveness? I don't understand."

"It's time for you to forgive the people who wronged you—who hurt you. This is such an important step for you to welcome new people into your life, and for your happiness, Zara. I know it won't be easy, but it's something I think you're ready to address."

It takes conscious effort not to scream my next words. "You want me to forgive my rapist? Or the man who tried to kill me?"

"I do. That doesn't mean you forgive the act itself, and it doesn't mean you forget about it and go hold their hands around the campfire, roasting marshmallows. You never have to see them again to forgive them. In this case, forgiveness means taking all of those negative feelings, putting them in a box, and shipping them back. It's different from repressing your feelings because you're going to address each one before you put it in your box, then you're going to let it go."

"I'm still not sure what you mean."

She slides me a notepad with a pen clipped to the top. "Here's where we'll start. I want you to write every feeling you've had as a result of the sexual assault. We'll start there." She holds out an empty tissue box. "Then we're going to discuss each feeling, process it, and put it in 'the box'."

"Okay." I take the pen and paper, and I write.

Shame.

Hatred.

Disgust.

Self-blame.

Worthlessness.

Anger.

Hopelessness.

I continue, having not realized how many negative emotions I was holding onto. When I'm done writing, I wipe the tears I hadn't even felt falling, and take a big breath. Wow.

Dr. Windsor and I spend the rest of my appointment addressing each feeling and placing it in "the box". By the time we're done, I feel more at peace than I've felt since before my encounter with Patrick. Maybe there is something to this therapy thing.

Strong and determined are not qualities I ever would have associated with myself, but as I sit across from Dr. Windsor, tiny bits of each are building within me like Lego blocks. I will not give Christian or Patrick one more ounce of power over me. They may have taken my self-worth, my energy, my time, my sense of security, my ability to trust, and my voice, but I am going to take it all back.

I'm a survivor.

My feelings box exercise at Dr. Windsor's office happened two weeks ago. I've returned three times since, having been scheduled twice a week. She's confident I am ready to reduce my sessions to once a week, and she encouraged me to return to work, at least part-time. It took me a few days to contact Mr. Stafford after Dr. Windsor suggested going back to the office, but once I did, he seemed supportive of the idea.

It's now 8:00am, Wednesday, January 22nd, and I've parked my car in the office building's parking lot. The last time I left here, about nine weeks ago, I was defeated, scared, and hopeless. I return today with a new resolve, and though I still have a long way to go, and recognize anxiety is something I will forever have to contend with, I'm ready. Ready to face what the future has in store—but mostly, I'm ready to give my all to these kids who need me.

I walk into the lobby and scan around, looking at this place that feels like a distant memory. It's more sterile than I remember. Intimidating with security personnel circling the space. Then I see him. This time he's not standing, waiting with his signature smile. He's seated in the coffee shop looking dishevelled, slumped over the table with his head in his hands.

He doesn't want to see you or speak to you. You ignored him. He's moved on.

My feet move without consulting my brain, and before I can protest, I'm standing in front of him. "Hi."

Zach lifts his head, and when he looks into my eyes, I feel my heart break all over again. He looks like he hasn't slept for weeks. His cheeks are hollow, showing he's lost some weight, and his skin looks dull.

What have you done? You don't do this when you love someone.

He blinks his eyes several times in a row, as if he's trying to determine if I'm real. Apparently, he's still not convinced because he reaches his hand out to place it on my arm. When his hand connects with me, he jumps up from his seat and wraps his arms around me.

"Baby, you're here. Oh my God. You're here. Zara. I..."

"Zach. I'm sorry. We need to talk." Every ounce of joy he had upon seeing me drains from his face, leaving me scrambling to clarify. "I mean, so much has happened since that day at my parents. I don't know what you want, or if you're seeing anyone else. It's not fair of me to walk over here being presumptuous, assuming that you've waited for me all this time, so we need to talk."

His face relaxes a bit. "Zara, there will never be anyone for me but you. I told you I would wait." He reaches down to grab his drink from the table. "Can we go up to my office and talk for a bit?"

"As much as I want to, today is my first day back since… first day back in a long time, so I need to go get myself settled. But we can go somewhere after work. Then we won't be rushed."

He sighs. "Okay. We can go to my place if you are okay with that. Jasmine won't be home."

"I'll meet you in your office after work?"

"How about lunch?"

I want to spend time with him more than anything, but I want to talk things through first. "Zach. Let's talk after work, okay?"

He leans in to hug me again like he never wants to let me go, and whispers, "I really want to kiss you. I've missed you so much."

My face heats feeling his breath across my neck and hearing his words. Is it possible to pick up where we left off after everything that's happened? "I missed you too." I reach up on my tiptoes to give him a peck on the cheek.

When I pull away, he's standing there with his eyes closed, like he's savouring how my lips felt on his stubbled skin. When his eyes open to look at me, I feel a sense of security I haven't felt for weeks—like I'm home.

Home is safe.

As I expected and stressed over, both Adele and Erin nearly tackle me as I step off the elevator and start asking me questions. I feel like a Kardashian, just worth many millions less.

They want to talk to the murderer. They hate you.

I stand there trying to steady my breathing and brace myself to say something when a voice that's saved me before chimes in. "That's enough ladies. Please let Miss Levy get to her office. I have briefed you on everything you need to know." Mr. Stafford turns to me. "Welcome back, Zara."

"Thank you, Sir. I'm glad to be back."

He smiles, deepening the wrinkles around his eyes. "I've emailed you some pertinent information you can sort through when you get the chance. Your clients were divided up and seen to by other counsellors, so I've forwarded their notes. You can spend the rest of this week getting caught up on everything."

"Thank you, Mr. Stafford. I'll get settled in and get right back to work."

My workday is slow and labourious. I'm stuck trying to reacquaint myself with the office and changes that have been implemented in my absence. It appears most of them have been doing fine in my absence. I transcribe the remaining notes into their dedicated files on my computer and feel nauseous reading the notes on Isla. I'm eager to see her again because I need to know she's okay.

The clock strikes 4:30, so I shut down my computer, lock up my office, and head down to see Zach.

Zach's guarddog slash receptionist, Candi, is a beautiful, umber-skinned, long-legged, twenty-something who seems to hate me. A sexy young secretary named Candi—nothing to worry about. So cliché. Thankfully, we don't see each other often. No such luck today.

My anxiety will not convince me I'm unwelcome here. Zach asked me to meet him, so I stride past Candi and knock on the door to his office. He's on the phone, so I wait outside the door. I hear him say the name Fred, but purposely try not to listen to anything else. Eavesdropping is not very becoming.

"Come in," his sexy voice calls.

When I enter, he's already walked around his desk to greet me. He grabs me in his arms again, and I submit to his embrace, eager to feel loved. It doesn't take long before the emotions overwhelm me and I start crying. I feel safe here, in his arms.

"Baby, what's wrong?" He runs a finger across my cheek but, otherwise, keeps his distance. "I'm sorry if you weren't ready for that. I shouldn't have forced myself—"

"No, Zach. That's not it at all." I smile. "Happy tears. I'm happy to be in your arms again. I missed you more than I even realized."

His award-winning smile—at least, it would be if I were in charge of smile awards—is back on his face as he scoops me up, bridal style. He seems content to carry me around like this, and I can't come up with a good reason I shouldn't let him. My arms are wrapped around his neck, my face pressed against his chest, and his heartbeat is the most melodic sound I've heard in my life.

He kisses the top of my head and sits down in his desk chair with me in his lap. This reminds me of the night I confessed to him at Quinn and Tyler's wedding. That was the first time he admitted he was falling for me, and I can't help but wonder how he feels now.

"You look good, Baby. You look happy." It's funny he would say that since I'm crying.

"I'm so sorry for everything. I'm so sorry I abandoned you." Guilt washes over me when he says I look good because I can feel his chest under his shirt and he's withered away.

"Shh. It's okay. It's okay. I wanted to be there for you, but I understood. You needed time. I just... I didn't know how much time you would need, and I didn't want to pressure you, so I waited for you to reach out. It was hard not seeing you for so long."

"I did need time. After what you learned from my dad, then everything with... you know... I wasn't in a good place. If I'm being honest, I was in a really dark place. I didn't want to live anymore." He startles at my confession, but I continue, "I started taking medication, and going to therapy. I'm trying to get better; really trying."

He squeezes me tighter. "I'm so proud of you, Baby."

"I still have a lot of work to do, but I've realized that I want to do it with you by my side." I peek up at him through my fallen hair. "If you still want me."

Without a word, his lips are on mine. Weeks of pent up heartache, upset and turmoil seem to melt away with each caress of his lips. I tilt my head back, allowing him to unload everything he's been feeling without needing to tell me. No words are necessary because I can translate what he's saying perfectly.

When we separate, he says, "Let me close up everything here and we'll head home, okay?"

The way he says "home" makes my heart skip a beat.

"Sure. I'll wait in reception until you're done." I smile at him—a genuine smile that feels foreign… and wonderful.

I'm seated in the reception area of Arileia Mortgage, scrolling through my phone—for what, I'm not exactly sure. My only goal is to avoid conversation. How did introverts avoid small talk before smartphones? I'll Google it.

Read. Oh, that makes sense. *Listen to music.* Do people still have Walkmans? *Join a monastery.* Seems reasonable.

Candi breaks the silence. "I'm surprised you're back here."

Dang it.

"Excuse me?"

"I said, I'm surprised you're back here. With Zach."

"Ohhh, kay?"

Please make it stop.

"I thought he hit it off with the blonde girl who was here last week. I didn't think you'd be back. But what do I know?"

Bile rises up my esophagus. He wouldn't; would he? He said there was no one else. I take a few breaths, trying to remember my coping mechanisms Dr. Windsor taught me. Healthy coping mechanisms. Things I have been telling my clients for years, but it's so much easier to tell than do. I stand up to walk out of the office, not yet sure if I'd leave or wait outside, but I don't get the chance to make that decision.

"Are you ready?" Zach stands no more than two feet away with his alluring grin.

"Um, yeah, I guess. Sure."

Zach's brows furrow as he studies me. "Is everything okay? You look like you're going to be sick."

Maybe because I am.

"I'm fine. Let's just go."

I glance back at Candi and she's shooting hatred at me with laser-beam precision. No. I will not fall back into assuming the worst and sabotaging everything good in my life. I can't have a relationship with Zach if I don't trust him, and he's given me no reason not to. We will have an adult conversation and sort this out.

Look at me being rational. Who knew?

We each drive through the iron gate at the end of the driveway, and while Zach pulls into his garage, I park my Prius in front of the house. The entire twenty-minute drive, I was replaying Candi's comments.

"I thought he hit it off with the blonde girl… last week." "I'm surprised you're back."

I try my hardest to push the thoughts out of my mind, but anxiety is a persistent bugger. It's hard not to question the conversation, but I have to consider the source. Candi doesn't deserve more trust than Zach. I know I have to ask him as soon as we get inside.

Zach opens the door to let me in once I reach the porch. He's out of breath. "I didn't want you waiting, so I ran. I'm out of shape."

If that's out of shape…

No, don't get distracted. Rip off the Band-Aid. "Listen, before we talk about anything else, I have to ask you something, and I want you to be honest."

"I'll always be honest." He tilts his head, waving for me to come inside.

Reluctantly, I step into the foyer. "Did you date anyone else over the past few weeks?"

His brows shoot upward, then back down, freezing his face in a grimace. "I told you there was no one else but you. You were on my mind every minute of every day. Where is this coming from?"

"Candi said there was a blonde in your office the other day, and I didn't believe her, but I had to ask. Did you have anyone in your office? I mean, we weren't technically together, so I have no right to be upset about it. I just want to know."

"Why would she say that? I haven't had anyo… oh."

Suddenly I wish I were a turtle, so I could retreat inside myself. Or maybe one of those lizards that shoot blood from their eyeballs. What a handy defence mechanism; way better than repression or denial.

"Last week, Quinn came to my office."

Relief floods my body; so much so I could melt. "Oh?"

"I was worried about you and I figured she'd heard from you, so she stopped by on her way home from work one day. She's the only person who has been in my office that wasn't a business appointment. Please believe me."

There's no stopping the smile that forms on my lips. "I do."

He takes two long strides to reach me, and without warning, he's kissing me. His lips are breathing life back into me. He's kissing me like he loves me more than oxygen.

I pull away from him because I have to know. "Do you still love me?"

"If you think how I feel about you could disappear in a few weeks, you're underestimating me. I love you Zara Levy. I love you so much, it hurt going so long without holding you. I'd give my last breath to see you smile, and I don't want to go another day without seeing your face as long as I live."

I giggle. "A simple yes would have sufficed." That confirmation feels like a soothing salve for my aching heart.

"I'm crazy in love with you. I understand why Tom Cruise was jumping on Oprah's couch." He shouts, "I hear you, Tom! I love this lady!"

His impression makes me laugh. "I love you too."

He holds me in his arms with my head pressed against his chest. I'm breathing in his scent, memorizing every note; lemon, ginger, bergamot... maybe basil. Whatever it is, it's perfection.

"Spending weeks without hearing those words was torture." He shifts uncomfortably before asking, "I don't want to pressure you, but do you want to tell me what happened?"

"I... I can. If you need to know."

"No, Baby, I don't *need* to know, but if you want to tell me, I'll listen."

If you tell him, he's going to hear how you killed a man in your kitchen. He will never look at you the same again. It will change his perception of you forever. He won't love you anymore.

Despite my anxiety, I declare, "You know what? My therapist says it's good to talk about it with the important people in my life, so I think I should explain what happened."

"Okay. Do you want me to order food now, or after we talk?"

"After. I may not have much of an appetite right after I get through this, so waiting a while for food isn't a bad idea."

He cringes at that statement but adjusts his facial expression to a comforting smile.

I spend the next fifteen minutes giving him the play-by-play of that life-changing morning. The entire time, Zach appears to be repressing the urge to upchuck on his presumably expensive sofa. I'm not sure if he's sick over the situation, or the fact that he's alone in his house with a murderer.

"Gracie Lou Freebush?" Of all the things I said, this is what he questions.

"If you've never seen *Miss Congeniality*, you won't get it, but she saved my life."

"Well, then I'm forever indebted to Miss Freebush. I can't believe you went through that." He pulls me close. "God, I'm so glad you're okay. You're amazing."

"I couldn't be less amazing, but I'm feeling better. The memories will haunt me for the rest of my life, but I'm learning how to cope with them." I turn to look him in the eyes and release an exhale. "I want to talk about the day you left my parents. We haven't discussed it, and I want to know if you're okay."

His eyes dart from me, off into the distance and back again. "Sorry I left you like that. I should have handled it better."

"No, I understand it was hard to hear."

He stares straight ahead, and with an unblinking gaze says, "For seventeen years, I thought my brother died on impact. I know it may sound horrible, but that brought me some comfort thinking at least he didn't suffer. He was my other half, Zara. We did everything together. We could practically read each other's thoughts, you know? Hearing that he spent his last minutes alive calling for me, and I was there but couldn't help him—knowing that I didn't even hear him—it was too much, and I freaked out."

My heart breaks hearing him process the bombshell my dad unintentionally dropped. "Zach. I may not understand how you felt in that moment because I didn't live it, but I get that it was hard for you. Give me a chance to be there for you, and I promise I'll give you the same chance, too. I love you, and if this is going to work—if *we* are going to work—then we both need to learn to trust each other and have to stop running away from working through things together."

He manages a weak smile, which quickly disappears. "I do trust you. At that moment, I just didn't want you to see me weak."

"I wouldn't think you're weak because you loved your brother so much. It only confirms to me that you are incredible. You have compassion and empathy because you've been through impossibly hard things and didn't let them destroy you."

"That sounds like exactly how I would describe you."

I squeeze him a little tighter, knowing how close I came to never having this chance again. "They nearly destroyed me… and I can't say it won't affect me in the future. For now, let's try to get through one day at a time."

"One day with you is better than a million without."

I jerk my head back to look at his face; my own eyebrows threatening to weave themselves into my hairline. "Were you formerly a player, because you seem to have a thousand and one lines?"

"I'm not feeding you lines. Just being honest."

With that, we sit on the sofa, me in his embrace, reacquainting ourselves with each other. At this moment, I feel like I can survive anything.

Zach and I have been inseparable for the past six weeks. If we're not working or sleeping, we're together or on the phone with each other. I often go over to his house after work, and we cook together or order in.

We've also been on a few double dates with Quinn and Tyler, which has been nice. There's nothing awkward about it because the guys have been friends since High School and Quinn and I since University. We've now had a full play-by-play of everything G-rated on the Ochoa's honeymoon. Quinn and I have heard endless high school baseball stories from the guys, through which I learned that Zach's nickname is Trigger because of his ability to hit a target when pitching. I never imagined one day I'd have a boyfriend who was as close with Quinn and Tyler as I am. It almost feels too good to be true.

Jasmine has been around little because she is finishing up her semester at school. She and I have become fast friends, and she's convinced me to go shopping a few times. Me, shopping?

I never thought I would go to a store—a place with actual people—on purpose to find clothing for myself. Not only that, but actually enjoy it.

Beyond that, my condo sold, and the closing date passed last week. I hired a moving company to go in and pack everything up for me. Quinn and Tyler packed the rest of my clothing and essentials to move to my parents', and everything else was put into storage. I don't know how long it will be before I find my own place again, but for now, I am trying to establish a new normal.

Work has been fine since my first day back, but Isla looks as if she's gotten smaller since I saw her last. While she opens up to me about her feelings, she still doesn't discuss her foster home life. Her little face breaks my heart every time I see her because she looks like she's carrying the weight of the world on her tiny frame.

I'll be seeing Isla in about twenty minutes, and I've been obsessing over how to get her to discuss her home life without shutting down. It's time to get creative. I put my plan in place and hope we can make some progress today. I want to see her cherubic little face light up.

Isla strolls into my office and, without a word, proceeds to the sofa. It's as if she marches in on autopilot saying, "assume the position." But today, I have something different planned for her.

"Hey, Isla, Sweet Girl. Why don't you come over and sit at my desk today?"

She studies me for a moment. "I can sit at your desk?"

"Sure thing. You're going to be the grownup today."

Her excitement is palpable, and I don't have the heart to tell her growing up isn't always as glamorous as you think it is when you're a kid.

"Okay! What do I do?"

"Well, you're going to take this paper and markers I have for you and draw a picture while you ask me questions. You can ask me anything you want, and I'll answer, but I want you to draw me a picture of what makes you happy."

"Oh… okay. I can do that." She climbs up into my grey fabric chair. I've raised the chair as high as it goes, and she still looks small sitting at my large white desk.

She picks up a black marker without hesitation, pulls the cap off, then draws with her tongue peeking out of her mouth. She looks as if she's concentrating so hard, but surprises me by saying, "So, Miss Levy. What brings you here today?"

I stifle a laugh. "I'm here to talk with my favourite grown up in the entire world, Isla."

She giggles, and it takes everything in me not to burst into happy tears. "Why is Isla your favourite grown up?"

"Well, she's so smart. She makes me laugh. She's always honest with me, and I'm so glad we're friends."

Her expression changes for a moment. "What if she wasn't always honest with you? Would she still be your friend?"

"She'll always be my friend, no matter what." I give her my best reassuring smile, knowing that this can get off track quickly.

Her shoulders relax. I will not push or guilt her into telling me something she isn't ready to say, so I wait for her to speak.

"Do you have a boyfriend?"

I'm surprised by the abrupt subject change, but I play along. "Yes, I have a boyfriend. His name is Zach, and he works in this building."

"He does? Maybe I can meet him one day."

"Maybe. He's very nice. I'm sure you'd like him."

"Is he handsome?" Her cheeks turn an adorable shade of pink.

I lean in, dropping my voice to a whisper. "He's the most handsome man I've ever seen."

Her hand flies over her mouth and we both start giggling.

"What does he look like?"

"Well, he's tall, has green eyes, dark blond hair, and let's not forget handsome."

Her giggle is contagious and I can't stop myself from joining her again.

She turns serious. "Do you love Zach?"

"Yes, I love him a lot." No hesitation.

"Will you marry him someday?"

"I hope so, but we'll have to wait and see."

"Well, if you love him, why don't you get married?"

Kids have an uncanny knack for simplifying things. I appreciate that about them. My nephews Ethan and Oscar give brilliant advice because *The Paw Patrol* can solve everything.

I don't know how to explain in an age-appropriate way, so I respond, "He hasn't asked me to marry him."

She twists in the chair, staring at her drawing. "When I meet him, I'm going to tell him to marry you."

"Why do you want me to get married?"

"I like seeing you happy." She pulls a cap off of a blue marker with her teeth and sets back to work on her artwork.

This beautiful girl, who has been through unthinkable horrors, is concerned with *my* happiness. I'm not sure I could love this child any more than I do.

"I am happy. I want my friends to be happy too. Are you happy?"

She's colouring furiously, but continues, "I'm sad a lot."

A strange sensation I can't name hits my entire body at once. As if I'm starved of oxygen. "What makes you sad, Isla?"

"I'm sad I don't have a family, and I don't think Miss Deborah likes me." She doesn't break her concentration on her drawing.

"What makes you think she doesn't like you?"

"She makes me sleep in the basement."

That statement makes my heart rate speed up. I don't know right away if it's a result of anger or upset—probably a combination. Breathe. No, it's anger. Pure anger.

Trying not to jump to conclusions, I ask, "Do you have a bedroom in the basement?"

She's still focused on her drawing, avoiding eye contact, but she continues talking. "No. I have a sleeping bag. I'm not allowed to sleep upstairs because I wake up too much and Miss Deborah gets angry."

Yep, it's anger. A near-blinding rage.

"How long have you been sleeping in the basement?" I hope it's only been a short time—not that it's okay for even one night.

"I don't know. Since I was six." She shrugs, but then panics when her eyes dart up to meet mine. "She told me not to tell. You can't tell, or she'll be so mad."

Thump-thump, thump-thump. It's hard to hear Isla's delicate voice over the pounding in my ears. Since. She. Was. Six.

How could you have failed her so epically? Why did you not push this before now? This is all your fault. You're terrible at your job and this sweet child is suffering because of it.

With considerable effort to control the shaking in my voice, I do my best to reassure her. "I won't tell, but I want to help. Can you tell me what else happens at Miss Deborah's house?"

"I... I don't know. I shouldn't tell."

"You can tell me. Remember, we're friends. I won't do anything to make Miss Deborah mad at you. I promise."

"Promise?"

"I swear."

Isla spends the next fifteen minutes recounting what life is like in her foster home. It takes every ounce of inner strength not to fly out of that room and to go savage on Miss Deborah. Isla has been getting the bare minimum to eat and drink, only allowed to bathe on days she is coming to see me and has to ask for permission to use the bathroom, forcing her to soil herself if she isn't granted access in time. They have refused her food after having accidents and forced her to do chores around the house to earn something to eat. She's living as a slave.

How have I missed this? I suspected things were not great in the foster home—sadly, a frequent occurrence in the system—but I had no idea it was so bad.

"Isla, I'm going to do everything I can to help you, okay?"

She looks at me with an expression I recognize from seeing on myself not too long ago—hope.

Our appointment ends and as Isla walks out the door, I say, "You forgot your drawing."

"It's for you." She smiles before disappearing.

I look at the paper that was a blank page an hour ago—now it holds a promise.

When the day ends, I want nothing more than to go home. I text Zach and tell him I'm leaving. Before the elevator has reached the main floor, my phone rings.

He doesn't give me a chance to speak. "Baby, what's wrong?"

"I need to crawl into bed tonight. Today was a hard day."

"Is there anything I can do? Why don't you come to my office and we'll leave together?"

Alone: good. People: bad. Bed: good. Talking: bad.

"I can't today. I want to go home."

Disappointment is obvious in his voice. "Okay, Baby. Call me later, okay? I love you."

"Love you." For some reason, saying, "*I love you*" is too much right now.

He doesn't deserve this. He's been supportive. He's tried to help you. You don't appreciate him enough and he's going to get sick of it. He's going to leave.

I climb into the driver's seat of my Prius, throw my car into reverse, and once I'm clear of the neighbouring vehicles, I drive straight to my parents' house and climb into bed.

Home is safe; but not for everyone.

I've buried myself in my blanket cocoon since the moment I got home. My mind is racing, trying to deduce how I missed so many red flags with Isla. I should have trusted my gut months ago and had an investigation done, but I had nothing to go on other than instinct—the same instincts that make it an impossible task to choose broccoli or cauliflower at the grocery store.

You should have known better. You should have stood up for her. She was counting on you and you failed her. You are useless.

I feel like more of an epic failure than I ever have in my life. I've had kids in the past that have been dealing with abuse or neglect in their foster home, but it was always relatively easy to recognize the signs.

Have I become so attached to Isla that I didn't focus on her counselling as I should have? Was I so distracted by how much I love the tiny blonde-haired, blue-eyed girl that I left her to fend for herself? It wasn't bad enough the child lost her parents at such a young age, she has to suffer at the hands of the people charged with taking care of her too? This is why professional boundaries exist. To maintain objectivity. I'm not cut out for this job.

Several hours later, I'm eager to sleep after I become so exhausted I can't stay awake another moment. I don't call Zach, nor do I answer his calls.

You are a terrible girlfriend. You can't keep cutting him out. How much longer do you think he'll put up with this? He deserves better.

Thursday morning, I climb out of bed, shower, and get dressed for work. I throw on a pair of red ankle pants, a white blouse, a white blazer with black pinstripes, and black heels. The outfit is slightly out of my comfort zone, but Jasmine convinced me I was "working it". My hair is down and wavy—in desperate need of a haircut, and my makeup is minimal, as usual. I may appear as if I'm ready to face the day, but that couldn't be more untrue.

I arrive at work by 7:45, and it comes as no surprise my handsome man is waiting for me. He walks toward me with a tentative smile. The problem is, I don't want to sit and talk today. I want to get into my office and figure out what I can do for Isla. Chelsea is coming in today too, and I need to be sure I'm 100 percent focused for her and my other clients. I can't let something like Isla's situation slip my notice again.

When Zach reaches me, he pulls me in for a hug while he kisses the top of my head. His seven-inch height advantage comes in handy, even when I'm in heels.

"Good morning, Baby."

"Hey."

"Are you okay? I never heard from you last night."

"I'm fine. Yesterday was a hard day and, honestly, I want to get a start on things for today."

"Oh." The corners of his mouth drop along with his arms. "Okay. Can we meet for lunch later?"

"I don't know. Today is going to be jampacked, and I can't be distracted."

"Zara." He sighs as he runs a hand through his perfectly messy hair. "Don't shut me out. I understand if I can't help with work problems, but please don't disappear on me again."

"I'm not disappearing. I'm just doing my job!" My volume causes a few other patrons to turn and stare at us.

You're an embarrassment.

"I know your work is important to you. I just thought I was too."

His words hurt; they hurt because I know how I've hurt him, and suddenly my anger is put back into perspective—I'm not mad at him; I'm mad at myself.

"You are." I'm once again filled with shame because of my misplaced emotions. "I love you, but this is something I have to do. I have to fix this mess I've made."

"Can I help somehow?" He cradles my chin in his palm to keep my gaze on his.

"No, I'll figure it out. I have to."

"I know you will, Baby. Just remember you're human and you have limits."

Limits because you are useless and can't do anything right.

I choke back the tears threatening to pour out. Not now. "I know, but I have to try."

He kisses me briefly—an "I'm here for you" kiss—and we part ways to each start our respective workdays.

When I arrive upstairs to the tenth floor, I get settled into my office. Then I send Mr. Stafford an email requesting a few moments of his time so I can figure out what to do for Isla. I'm hoping he can point me in the right direction.

Surprisingly, Mr. Stafford emails me back within twenty minutes, asking me to come to his office. I walk over, avoiding

Mrs. Copeland and Adele on my way—they have been like bloodhounds chasing a scent since I returned. It's been weeks. Get over it.

I greet Mr. Stafford after he gives me permission to enter his office, and thank him for seeing me on short notice.

"Of course, Zara. What can I do for you?" He gestures for me to take a seat.

"Well, it's my client Isla Harding. I had an appointment with her yesterday, and as I expected, she disclosed some serious issues at her foster home."

"What issues?" His warm eyes settle on me, giving me the courage to speak up on Isla's behalf.

I tell him the horrible realities of the situation, watching as his face twists and contorts with each revelation.

He lets out a deep sigh. "Any one of those things would be an issue, but all of them together is definitely grounds to have a case worker investigate."

"Yes, I was hoping you'd sign off on that for me so I can submit it today. I recognize it often takes them days before they can schedule a drop-in visit."

"I will. You fill out the form and send it to me. I'll sign it and forward it on to the appropriate office."

An ounce of relief eases some of the guilt and emotional turmoil I've been carrying for the last twenty hours, but it still doesn't solve anything. This is the first step. "What do you think the chances are of her being removed from the foster home, Sir?"

"Well, the foster parents have to be notified of the agency's intent to remove the child and given a reason for the removal. The foster parents then have the right to contest the decision. Sometimes, if an agreement can't be reached, a case conference is required. If that happens, they may require you to give a statement."

Nausea pools in my belly. "What happens to Isla during the time the case conference is happening?" I'm afraid to know the answer.

Mr. Stafford sighs again. "Unfortunately, the child remains in their current placement until they decide."

No. I promised her I would help her and that Miss Deborah wouldn't find out.

You've failed her again. You made a promise and you're going to break it. She trusted you and you betrayed her. You're useless.

"Mr. Stafford, if they find out that she spoke to me, things could go downhill very quickly for Isla. I can't put her at risk."

"I'm afraid that's the system, Zara. Our reach is limited. You have to hope her foster parents don't argue with her removal."

"Nobody enjoys having a pay cheque ripped away from them without notice. Of course, they're going to protest! What kind of system offers protections for abusers, but not for the kids?" My voice rises in both volume and pitch as I speak.

"I understand it's frustrating, Zara, but it's all we can do."

"There has to be another alternative. This can't happen."

Without waiting for a response, I exit Mr. Stafford's office to return to mine. I'm determined to find another solution. Before my first client arrives, I need to do some research. Then I'll need to compartmentalize. Isla's problem is critical, but my other clients deserve my exclusive devotion. Nothing like this is ever going to slip by me again.

After my second client for the day leaves, I go back to my computer to see what else I can do for Isla. It turns out we can remove her and place her in a therapeutic setting or a permanent placement. Maybe I can request she be placed in a medical setting to help with her social anxiety and night terrors.

Knock, knock.

"Come in," I call, not realizing time got away from me.

"Hi, Miss Levy," Chelsea says as she slinks her way to the sofa.

All of my instinct alarms are blaring. Something is wrong, but I am struggling to trust these instincts. "Hey, Chels. What's up?" I make my way to the armchair by the sofa.

She doesn't speak; she only cries.

"Oh, Chels. What's wrong? Talk to me." I'm having a hard time not pulling her into a hug and crying with her.

She sniffles. "Everything. Everything is wrong. Nobody wants me and soon I'll be out on the streets. I won't even be able to see you anymore. Yeah, it's still a while away, but I can't stop thinking about it. Sometimes I think I'd be better off dead."

I thought yesterday defeated me, but hearing those words from Chelsea has pushed my feelings of complete and utter failure to a new low.

You don't deserve to be caring for these helpless children. You're a failure at your job. Broken people can't fix people. They need someone who can aid them, not drag them down. That's all you ever do—drag people down.

"Chelsea, I'm so sorry. How long have you been feeling this way?" My effort to compose myself is for not because my voice is cracking.

"A few months."

Months. She has been feeling this way for months? What kind of counsellor are you when your client is feeling like she's better off dead, and you don't notice? She didn't even feel comfortable enough to tell you. What does that say about you?

"Oh, Chels. Let's sort out these feelings and see what kind of practical steps we can take, okay? I will do whatever I can to make sure you never spend a day on the streets. I know I'm your counsellor, but once we aren't seeing each other here anymore doesn't mean I'll disappear from your life."

My words seem to comfort her a little. I remind myself that even ten percent is better than nothing. A little hope is all she needs.

Chelsea and I speak at length about everything, and we decide on some steps she can take. She is going to look for an after-school job and save her money so she will have something to fall back on when she ages out of the system. She's going to focus on school so she can get a scholarship to help pay for college and try her best to develop some friendships, so she won't feel so alone.

As our time draws to a close, she looks a bit more confident.

"Hey, Baby. Oh, I'm sorry. The door was open." Zach peeks his head in from behind the door. Chelsea hates closed doors, so we always leave it ajar.

"Zach, what are you doing here?"

"I figured I'd bring up lunch. I thought you'd be done by now." He turns to Chelsea and continues, "I'm so sorry for interrupting. I'm Zach, Zara… I mean, Miss Levy's boyfriend."

"Hi, I'm Chelsea."

His face lights up with recognition. He's heard me mention her before, though we've never discussed her situation.

"It's nice to meet you, Chelsea. I'll let you two finish, and I'll wait out there. Sorry again."

"We're done," Chelsea blurts. "You don't have to go. I'm leaving."

Zach steps into my office holding a pizza box. "Would you like to stay and have lunch with us, Chelsea?"

Her face looks as surprised as mine. "Oh, no. I don't want to interrupt."

"You're not an interruption, Chels. Zach and I would love to have you stay and eat." I shoot him an appreciative glance. I wasn't ready to say goodbye to her yet.

"All right. I have to leave soon to get back to school, though."

"It's settled then." Zach sits on the opposite end of the sofa from Chelsea. "I hope you like vegetable pizza. I can run and grab you something else if you don't."

She giggles. "I do. That's great. Thank you."

Looking at these two wonderful human beings—both who have touched my life in such profound ways—and seeing them converse effortlessly with each other makes the anxieties from earlier in the day wash away. I realize they'll be back, but for the moment, I focus on here and now.

Zach strikes up a casual conversation with Chelsea that comes so easily, I gain more insight into her hopes for the future than I ever did in the countless hours of counselling. She wants to become a social worker so she can help kids who have become lost in the system like she has. I recognize that drive she has to use her own trauma to pay it forward in a job that is hard but needed.

Once we finish eating, Chelsea jumps up, looking so much happier than she did when she walked in my door. "Thank you for lunch, but I better go."

"Okay, Chels. Remember, you can call me if you need me." I'm sad to see her leave. It was nice to spend time with her in a more casual manner.

"Thanks, Miss Levy. Thank you for lunch, Zach."

"You're welcome. Maybe we can do it again sometime," Zach replies. "It was nice meeting you."

"You too. I'll see you next week," she says in my direction.

I almost utter the words, "I love you," but I stop myself. That would be a legendary breech of professional conduct. "Take care, Chels."

Once she leaves, Zach moves toward me. "I missed you."

I rebuff his advances, not in any mood for physical affection. "Zach, I appreciate that you brought lunch and invited Chelsea to stay, but I said I wanted to focus today. There's still a huge issue I need to deal with, and I was going to work on it through my lunch break."

"Sorry." He looks down at his empty paper plate like a scolded child. "I figured you needed to eat, and I didn't see you last night. It never occurred to me you'd be upset over me trying to feed you."

"I'm not upset. I'm stressed out, and I wanted to work toward a solution. This job, it's not about me. Other people's lives are at stake and—"

"Shh... I'm sorry, okay? I'll respect your work boundaries from now on, but sometimes when you have a problem, the best way to find a solution is to take a step back and look at the bigger picture."

Something about him offering advice right now angers me. There's no reason why, but it does. "Thank you, Socrates. Thanks for lunch, but I need to get back to work."

"Fine, I'll leave you to it. I love you."

How can anyone love you? How can you love anyone else? You don't even love yourself.

"Love you, too." I look down, embarrassed by my behaviour but unable to change my focus right now.

With that, Zach leaves my office and I'm not confident he'll ever want to return.

For the second evening in a row, I fall asleep without seeing or speaking to Zach. I can't help but feel like he's upset with me—he didn't call to say good night.

You've finally pushed him too far.

I'm the only person to blame. His wellbeing and emotions deserve to be prioritized over adult tantrums and irrational outbursts of anger. So why can't I stop myself?

This is what I feared all along; medication wouldn't help because I'm just a horrible person.

Instead of sleeping, I stay awake, replaying pivotal moments of my life over the last few months. Moments with Patrick, Zach, Chelsea, Isla. Only one of whom I can no longer disappoint.

I may have dozed off briefly, but by the time the sun rises through the pink butterfly curtains of my childhood bedroom, my eyes are burning. Today is going to be another hard day.

After I shower, I get dressed for work and throw my hair up in a bun. My energy level is already depleted.

My intention is to arrive early, so I have an opportunity to speak to Zach. I need to apologize for how I reacted. I need to make things right.

As I walk through the lobby, I scan the area, and I don't see a pair of captivating green eyes anywhere.

Something is wrong. He's always been here early to meet you, even when you don't agree on meeting. He must have gotten in an accident on his way to work. What if he's bleeding to death on the side of the road and no one knows? Or what if something happened at home and he is all alone, so he can't call for help? This is wrong. He's hurt, and no one is around to help him.

I scramble to pull out my phone and dial Zach's number with shaking hands.

He's not answering because he's dead. It's the only rational explanation. This is your fault.

My phone says it's 8:07am, so maybe he's already in his office. I rush to the elevator, pressing the button for the six[th] floor more times than necessary, but I have to relay my panic level to the elevator.

When I arrive on his floor, it's quiet. Too quiet.

Knock, knock.

Nothing. No sounds coming from inside the office. No one is here yet.

Call the police. Look up the local news and see if there have been any accidents reported this morning. Text him. Call him. Call Tyler. Call Jasmine. Alert the troops. He must be located.

I send off a few text messages in rapid-fire succession. I try calling Zach three more times. Still no answer. It's abundantly clear to me in this moment that I can't survive losing him—he is my reason for living. I'm succumbing to panic when the door from the stairwell opens and Zach emerges.

Relief floods my entire being as I run toward him. I wrap my arms around his neck but feel a noticeable absence of his arms around me. I pull back. "What's wrong?"

"Zara."

He used your first name. Something bad is going to happen.

"What are you doing here?"

People only say that when they don't want someone around and can't think of anything nicer to say.

"I wanted... I wanted to apologize."

He takes a small step back. "What are you apologizing for?"

"I'm sorry if you feel like I'm shutting you out. It's never my intention. I've spent the last decade of my life shutting everyone out except Quinn, and even she can't help me with work issues, so I just dive into them headfirst. I get too involved, and I can't help it—"

"Zara, it's okay. I'm aware your work is hard and other people are counting on you. But you told me you wouldn't disappear on me again, and I can't help but feel like it's happening with the first hard thing to come your way."

I take a moment to process his perception of events. "You're right. I'm sorry. I don't mean to push you away." The feeling of disappointment and total defeat nearly crushes me. Without conscious thought, my eyes are blurring with tears.

Can't you ever keep your eyes dry around this man? There's so much wrong with you, you're no value to anyone.

He finally returns my hug, and for a split second I feel like everything will be okay, but that feeling is short-lived.

"Can you come over tonight so we can talk?"

He's going to break up with you. You're more trouble than you're worth.

His words startle me, but I choke out, "If you're going to break up with me, get it over with. We don't need to drag it out and make it a big thing."

He chuckles. Actually chuckles as I fight off tears. "Baby, I'm not breaking up with you. I love you, and I know we can handle this."

I arch my neck to study his face. It's as if each time I look at him, I'm seeing him for the first time in a new, brighter light. "You're sure? You're not going to lead me there under false pretenses, then break my heart?"

"I'd be lost without you."

Relief helps combat the defeat I have been suffocating from. "Okay."

He laughs before kissing my head. I hear the elevator doors open and out comes Candi, who has just witnessed Zach's chaste display of affection. If I had any doubt she hated me before, she puts that to rest.

"Maybe save the PDA for inside the office, boss?" Candi spits. The girl has some nerve to speak to her boss like that.

"Oh, good morning Candi. We were just saying goodbye." Zach smirks. It's obvious he couldn't care less what she thinks. She's lucky she still has a job after she tried to drive a wedge between Zach and me several weeks ago.

I don't consider myself a petty person, but on this occasion, I can't stop myself. Candi's glare doesn't deter me from showing Zach how sorry I am with a lip-searing kiss. "I love you so much."

The teeth-baring grin he gives in return reaches his eyes, creating the most irresistible smile lines. "I love you too, Baby. I'll see you after work."

And with that, I walk past Candi, avoiding her death-stare, and make my way upstairs with a smile of my own. A smile that only remains long enough to remember the issues Isla is dealing with at home.

Who are you to carry on with your life and try to be happy when you've neglected this poor girl and made her suffer? You are heartless.

I will figure this out. I will find her a solution. I will make this right.

For the next hour, I avoid what I should do in order to focus on a solution for Isla. Mr. Stafford agreed to meet with me again to follow up with our conversation from yesterday. I have a new proposal for him.

"You want to have her placed in a therapeutic facility?"

"It's the only reasonable option. We can't prove neglect without an investigation and then her foster parents could put Isla in even more danger while we wait for paperwork to process. It's unfair, and I can't let her suffer more than she has."

"Her current issues won't be a sufficient reason to have her placed in a facility. They are reserved for extreme mental health issues that deem a person a danger to themselves or others."

I exhale and slump in my chair. "I don't know what else to do. Her only other option is to be placed into permanent care, so unless someone adopts her, she is stuck there. I don't understand how this system can think any of this is okay!"

"The best option at this point is to send a case worker in to witness conditions firsthand. Isla is their only foster child now, so unfortunately we don't have other eye-witnesses, but Social Services will try to get to the bottom of everything."

"Not fast enough." I stand to leave. "I'm sorry, Sir. This isn't your fault, and I appreciate your help, so I apologize. I feel trapped. Bound by an ethical duty to report the problem, but afraid reporting will only make things worse. The system makes me angry sometimes."

"I know what you mean. Your caring nature makes you great at this job, but we have our limitations. Some things extend beyond our reach and we have to focus on what we can change."

I leave Mr. Stafford's office without another word. This is not beyond my reach. I refuse to let this go and allow Isla to become a victim of the system. Even if I have to work all weekend, I will find another way. I made her a promise and I intend to keep it.

I see to my clients for the rest of the day, use my lunch hour to research options for Isla, and look at different cases and precedents set. So far, I've come up with nothing.

You will not be able to fix this. She is going to be stuck in the house being neglected and abused, and eventually shrink until she is nothing.

Why can't I do anything right?

Being given a key to someone's house might seem like a small thing, but as I pull into Zach's gated driveway and into my dedicated garage space, it feels like a huge step. My workday finishes thirty minutes before his, so I stopped to grab some groceries on my way to his place, and now I'm going inside to make dinner.

By the time Zach enters twenty minutes later, I have a skillet of Shakshuka simmering on the stove. It's one of my favourite egg dishes, but I rarely make it for myself.

"Wow. This is a magnificent view." Zach is unbuttoning the collar of his navy dress shirt, his tie already tossed aside.

I chuckle, but have to tamp down the lingering fear that he's upset with me for taking over his house in his absence. Anxiety and logic are at a war with each other, as per usual. "Dinner's almost ready. You can go change if you want."

His arms wrap around me from behind as his lips trace a path from my ear, down my neck. "That can wait."

"Zach." My pathetic attempt to act like I'm not interested while I'm cooking only makes him chuckle. His chest rumbles against my back, and it sets every nerve ending in my body alight. "You're distracting me."

"Mmhmm. I like distracting you." He spins me to face him, then teases my lips with his.

Instead of being in the moment, allowing myself to fall into a blissful make-out session, I can't stop myself from recalling the first time he kissed me. We've come a long way since then, but I don't know if I'll ever let myself become absorbed in a moment of ecstasy without also recalling my failures. Of which, there are many.

Zach pulls away. "What's wrong?" His green eyes stare down at me with concern.

Why do I keep ruining this?

Terrible girlfriend. Terrible counsellor. Terrible person.

"Why do you put up with me?" I can't think of a good reason. I need him to explain what I can't figure out.

His concern disappears when he smirks. "It's obviously hard for you to believe, but you're pretty amazing." He kisses the corner of my lips. "Beautiful, funny, and the most selfless person I've ever met." He lifts me up so I'm seated on the counter. His lips trace a delicate trail across my jawline. "You're everything, Zara. If I have to spend the rest of my life proving that to you, I will."

Something about the mention of a lifelong commitment does the opposite of ease my mind.

"You're going to get tired of me. This"—I wave my hands around my head—"is exhausting. It exhausts me, and it will exhaust you someday too. Even on medication, I'm still failing at everything."

Zach wraps his arms around me, leaving me on the counter, and resting his chin on my shoulder. "Oxygen will fail to be useful before you do."

I let out an abrasive one-note laugh that startles us both. "You're so wrong. I've been failing at work... failing my clients. In an epic way, mind you. I suck at this girlfriend business, and no matter how hard I try, I can't seem to get anything right."

An alarm starts beeping and only then do I realize the stove was turned on all this time. I push Zach aside and hop down to rush over to the stove, fanning away the smoke billowing upward. "See! Ruined. Everything I touch is ruined." I remove the skillet from the heat, using a dishcloth to protect my hands, which fails... also epically. "Ow!" I drop the skilled with all of its contents into one side of the double sink, and turn on water to run over my burning hand in the other.

"Let me see. Are you okay?"

I shake my head, choking back tears. Another thing I fail at. I end up with soaking wet shirt sleeves, ruined dinner, tears pouring down my face, and an overwhelming confirmation that I'm useless.

Everyone is better without you.

Zach pulls my hands out from under the water, cradling my burnt hand in another dish towel. "Baby, I'm sorry."

Through my tears, I mutter, "It's my fault. Not yours. It's always my fault. Everything is my fault." My willingness to live and stand both disappear at the same time. I sink to my knees, pulling my hand from the towel, using my hands to cover my ashamed, tear-soaked face. Maybe the tears will work as a burn salve.

Zach drops behind me and yanks me into his lap as he leans against the island cabinets. "Baby. Baby, listen to me." He puts his hands on my face and wipes a tear from my cheek with his thumb. He holds me, so I have no choice but to look into his eyes. "I don't want some flawless woman you've decided I'm deserving of. I love you. I love you just as you are. Flaws and all. I love that you always put other people's needs ahead of your own—not because you feel obligated, but because you want to.

I love that you've dedicated your life to understanding people who don't have it easy, and you do anything you can to help. Even though it's hard, you get up every day and try. I even love that whenever we go out, you always know exactly where the bathrooms and fire exits are, or how you have something for every scenario in your giant purse."

"But, I… I'm broken." I hide my face behind my hands again, but he gently tugs one away.

"Zara, we're all a little broken. What matters is that we love each other with our broken pieces. We can get through anything together."

"Not anything. Work is a mess. You can't fix that. I've screwed up so bad, the only solution is to adopt them myself, which I'd do if I thought for one second I could be a decent mother figure." I regret my words as soon as they pour out. Another reminder of how broken I am. I can never be a mother. "You deserve better. I love you enough to see that."

"What are you saying?" His embrace becomes loose.

"I'm saying I won't stand in your way of having everything you want and deserve." My voice breaks as I continue, "I'm not the woman to give you that."

"Baby, don't you see that would break me? You see things from a different perspective. You hold yourself to an impossible standard that no one could achieve. What I see is the love of my life."

"Zach…"

"No, don't push me away. There's nothing that we can't fix. We can pick up takeout. I'll buy a new pan. I've got first aid cream for burns. Everything else we'll figure out."

I can't even look at him. He makes it seem so easy, but it's not. "You don't get it. These are today's problems. Things I've ruined *today*, but tomorrow will have new issues. More things I'll fail at. More ways I'll screw up."

He lifts me off his lap, then brings himself to stand. I grab his offered hand to join him. "Wait for a second." He spins and bounds down the hallway toward his office.

You've finally pushed him away. Poor broken Zara. Never enough.

What does he want me to wait for? I doubt he has the cure to crippling anxiety and depression in his home office.

He may have told me to wait, but I'm exhausted from the effort of trying to be an adult today. I walk to the mudroom, planning to put on my shoes and leave.

A shaky voice from the mudroom door says, "I was hoping you'd wait."

I glance behind me, not wanting to commit to making eye contact, but nearly trip on a pair of Zach's sneakers when I realize he's down on one knee.

He raises a small box toward me. "I didn't want to do this like this. I had a whole, elaborate plan worked out, and I was waiting for the right time. But this—this is the right time for you to understand exactly how much you mean to me. I'll never give up on you, and I'll never leave your side. You are beautiful, intelligent, motivated, and stronger than anyone I know. I'll spend forever trying to help you see that. You'd make me happier than I've ever been to have you as my wife."

Words fail me. My legs feel weak. My heart is pounding like the bass line for a *Guns N' Roses* song. "Zach..."

"Just be here with me, in this moment. Think about how great we are together, and don't, for one second, doubt how much I love you. I'll do whatever it takes to show you that you're the one for me. Please, say 'yes', Baby."

Tears are falling down my cheeks, but as my vision is blurring and I'm sure I look even more a mess than I feel, I fall down to my knees in front of Zach. "Okay. Yes, I'll marry you." As much as I don't feel worthy of him, saying no doesn't cross my mind.

He wraps his arms around me once again and captures my lips in a passionate kiss.

Is this real? Am I having some sort of detached episode, when I'll wake up in the morning and realize none of this happened?

Zach brings me back to reality when he pulls away and takes my hand in his. He slides the ring from the box and I look down to see a stunning square-cut diamond, surrounded by diamond flakes. It's vintage and beautiful. "This was my grandmother's ring. She cherished it almost as much as my grandfather." A tear trickles down Zach's face, which causes mine to up production. "When my dad met my mom, my grandma gave him the ring. So my mother wore it for twenty-five years. What do you say we give this ring a happier ending?"

I nod. "I'd like that."

The smile on his face is like one I've never seen before. His level of understanding and compassion is something I never thought I'd find. Never thought I deserved. But Zachary Haynes showed up in my life and changed everything.

By the time I leave his house hours later, we have a plan in place that will change alter the course of our lives, but the fear of the unknown takes second place to overwhelming love.

After spending the weekend preparing for our upcoming weekday wedding, Monday morning arrives too soon. As per usual, Zach and I meet in the lobby coffee shop, and we're both smiling so big, our faces might crack.

We step up to the cashier to order our usual drinks, but we've been doing this long enough, she remembers our order and just confirms. The cashier, Janette, stares at me with wide eyes and a creased forehead. "My, my. That's some rock you've got there!"

"Oh, thank you." My eyes drop to look at the display of freshly baked goods. Attention is uncomfortable.

You're being rude.

"I take it congratulations are in order?"

Zach slips her a ten-dollar bill with a huge smile I see reflected in the plexiglass surrounding the muffins and bagels. "That is correct. She's agreed to be the ball to my chain."

"That's so romantic," I mutter, earning a chuckle from Zach.

"You two have been in here for months making heart eyes at each other, so I knew it was only a matter of time before he put a ring on it." She pushes the money back across the counter. "Your order is on me today."

I'm embarrassed at the thought of other people watching Zach and me as we were having private conversations and getting to know each other. Why are other people so interested in the business of strangers? "That's not necessary. Thank you, Janette."

She insists, and rather than argue, we accept, but Zach leaves the money in the tip jar. We grab our drinks and go up to his office until I have to head to my own. At least there we can be away from prying eyes.

Candi hasn't arrived at work yet, so Zach unlocks the door, and we make our way into his office. We sit in the side-by-side chairs, setting our drinks on his desk. He's seated to my left, holding my hand and playing with my ring, twirling it around my finger.

"I can't wait to make love to you. I don't want to sound like a neanderthal, but God, I am excited about our wedding night." To me, his declaration comes out of nowhere. Bagels and sex don't seem related, but maybe I'm ignorant to a large subsection of the population who is privy to things I am not.

How are you going to be intimate with him? You have no clue what you're doing. How are you going to let him touch you when you're so damaged? He's going to be repulsed and disappointed. Just another way you'll be a complete let-down.

"Baby, come back to me. I can tell you're off in your thoughts again. Relax." He brushes his thumb over the back of my hand. "I don't want you stressing over it. I love you, and I want to make love to you, but everything will depend on you, okay?"

At this moment, I am so self-conscious. I'm humiliated. I spent the entire weekend dreaming about married life with

Zach, and never once did intimacy enter my mind. What kind of wife will I be if that's not even a thought? I'm so terrified of the idea, I wanted to avoid it forever. I can't even stop myself before I'm crying again.

"Zara, what's wrong? I'm so sorry, Baby. I didn't mean to upset you."

Honesty is necessary here—even if it's mortifying. I have to explain my fears. "I... I'm so afraid that you're going to see me on our wedding night, and I'll disgust you. You'll see what a huge mistake you made. I have scars from surgeries. What if I'm so messed up...?"

"Shhh." He tries to calm me as he pulls our chairs closer and puts his arm around my shoulders, leaning me into him. "I will never feel like I made a mistake; that's a promise. You could never repulse me. But mostly, I don't want to have sex with you, Zara; I want to make love to you. I want to be connected to you emotionally and physically. Please don't stress over anything else. I love you, and that's all I care about."

"But, what if...?"

"All that matters is that I love you. More than air. Remember that."

I'm trying to calm my hysterical breathing, again embarrassed by how I am reduced to being a blubbering fool in front of this man. He never fails to say the right thing to bring me back from the brink of panic.

"I love you too."

We both stand as I grab a tissue from the sunrise adorned box on Zach's desk to wipe my snotty tear-soaked face.

"I should get to work."

We both stand as I grab a tissue from the sunrise adorned box on Zach's desk to wipe my snotty tear-soaked face. "I should get to work."

He leans down to give me a kiss that helps to calm my panicked mind. "Okay, I'll see you at lunch?"

"Only a few hours away." I offer a weak smile as I exit his office.

Candi is at her desk when I exit and in the half-second I make eye contact with her, her face changes from disdain to excitement. "Oh, I'm sorry. Did he break up with you?" Her enthusiasm sets me over the edge.

I steady myself for a confrontation I never wanted, but she has pushed me to my limit. This is the last time I'm going to put up with her snide remarks. I'm standing up for myself. "No, Candi. He didn't break up with me. In fact"—I turn back to face her and lift my left hand—"he proposed, and these tears, they're tears of joy because I am so happy I get to marry him. So, whatever your problem is with me, you best get over it, because to him, I'm irreplaceable. A temp can replace you before lunch."

I storm out of the office without capturing her expression or waiting for a response. I said what I needed to say, and that's the end of it.

An awkward café encounter, a meltdown, and a confrontation are not the best ways to start the day, but so far, I'm managing. It's only just beginning.

The three clients I saw this morning are all progressing well. One was recently adopted and is adjusting to life in a family. It makes me so happy to see kids find hope again. For them to know what it feels like to be loved. Some of them have never felt that. If I had it my way, I'd make sure all of them knew that feeling. But as Mr. Stafford said, my reach is limited.

Zach and I rush to the courthouse at lunch to obtain a marriage license and schedule a marriage ceremony for Wednesday afternoon at 2:30. We only have a thirty-minute window, but that should be plenty of time. We've told our family members and friends to block out a few hours for us on

Wednesday afternoon, so everything is looking ready for our big day.

They were all shocked when I not only announced our engagement, but our plans for a hasty wedding. Not one person disagreed with our decision, though. Jasmine and Quinn both squealed with excitement.

I've spoken to Mr. Stafford to request Wednesday to Friday off. Zach has also rescheduled any client meetings of his own. My dress is ready and waiting at my parents' house. We've arranged for a caterer to come to Zach's house on Wednesday afternoon. Desirea from the bakery Quinn had her wedding cake made at was beyond excited to create an Oreo masterpiece for my big day.

Everything is coming together. I just hope it all works out according to our plan.

In two days, I will be Mrs. Zara Haynes.

It's Wednesday afternoon, 2:15pm. I'm at the courthouse surrounded by my parents, sisters Lexi and Noa, their husbands Lorenzo and Henry, Quinn, and Jasmine. Zach has yet to arrive, and I'm freaking out.

He's changed his mind. He doesn't want to marry you. What if he's gotten in an accident, and he's all alone?

Before anxiety takes over, the door opens, and my breath catches as I see the most remarkable human being I've ever known walk through. He's looking like a dream in his light grey, two-button suit, white button-up shirt, black bow tie, and shiny black dress shoes. He styled his hair perfectly for the first time since Quinn and Tyler's wedding. His green eyes meet mine as soon as he enters the room. I grin at him, and he expresses a smile that makes my knees weak.

Tyler trails in behind him and beelines for Quinn. If I weren't about to get married to a man I love more than life, I'd wonder if it was possible to love another human as much as they do. Now I know with certainty.

My groom stares at me in my A-line tea-length dress with lace detailing on the cap sleeves. It's simple, but pretty, and everything I wanted for a courthouse wedding. My shoes are my favourite nude heels, and my bouquet is a simple last-minute arrangement from a florist. My hair is in a loose updo, and my makeup, natural.

Zach strides across the room before pulling me into his arms for a kiss, but I turn my head away from him.

"Not until we're man and wife."

He grumbles. "Well, let's get this show on the road, then. I need some sugar from my beautiful bride!"

Everyone laughs, and I soak in the feeling of pure joy.

He looks back at me. "Are you ready for this?"

"So ready, Mon Coeur."

We proceed into the room where the ceremony will occur, which is an unremarkable space with wood panelling, dated pictures that look like thrift store purchases, twelve dark wood chairs, and a plain looking, white, metal arbour which seems a bit out of place for an indoor wedding. Beggars can't be choosers—there's only one goal for this day.

Zach turns to me one last time and gives my hands a quick squeeze. "I love you." He walks ahead to take his position at the front of the room.

My father and Quinn stand beside me, Tyler is standing at the front with Zach, and everyone else has taken their seats.

The faint music starts, and Quinn looks at me. "I knew one day someone would see what I did in you. You're amazing, and Zach is so lucky to have your heart. I love you."

"Thanks, Amiga. Now get down that aisle before you make me cry and mess up my makeup." We laugh together before she turns to make the twelve-step trek to where my future starts.

Once Quinn has made her way down the aisle, my dad and I follow. He kisses my cheek, tells me he loves me, then takes his seat beside my mom. I am now standing face-to-face with the man who captured my heart, knowing that after today, everything is going to change. At this moment, I may have 'what if' scenarios running through my mind, but the way Zach looks at me gives me courage to face them. The willingness to try. The strength to fight whatever might come our way.

Our officiant, an older man named Nigel with a slim physique, brown skin, and short, greying hair, welcomes us and begins the ceremony. When it comes time for our vows, he informs our guests we have written our own.

"Zara, I promise to love you above all others, to be faithful to you, honour you, cherish you and care for you with tenderness. I will always seek to strengthen you, comfort and encourage you. Let me be the shoulder you lean on, and the one on which you rest. May our lives intermingle and our love grow as we become one. You are my everything. I look forward to spending my life with you and accomplishing our dreams together. I look with joy to the path of our tomorrows, knowing we will be side by side, hand in hand, and heart to heart."

By the time he finishes speaking, his eyes are brimming with tears, and mine are leaking. To break myself out of the emotions I'm feeling, I joke, "How am I supposed to follow that?"

Everyone's laughter eases the pressure, and I'm able to continue. "Zach, you are my once in a lifetime—my miracle. May our lives come together and our love for one another grow each day as we become one. You are all I could ever need in my life—my friend, my love, my confidant, my everything. I promise to be faithful to you, love you, honour and respect you, encourage and inspire you, live by your side and cherish you. As time passes, trials may come, laughter will bless us, but no matter what we encounter together, I vow to make my home in your heart, from this day forward, as your ever-loving wife."

Only a moment later, we are exchanging rings, then Nigel utters the words Zach has been eagerly awaiting: "You may now kiss the bride."

Everyone in the room claps and cheers. My parents and Jasmine are crying as Zach leans me back so my left leg lifts into the air and he kisses me like a husband kisses his wife—well, at least how my husband kisses his wife.

Once we've signed all the paperwork—a decidedly unromantic end to the ceremony—taken a few pictures, and hugged everyone, we're ushered out of the room for the next bride and groom to have their shining moment. Zach and I leave hand-in-hand as husband and wife. Mr. and Mrs. Zachary Haynes.

Our family and friends come to Zach's house—our house—for a celebratory dinner. The caterers do an excellent job, and the food is great. They even take care of the clean-up, so we have nothing to worry about. We're going to be eating leftovers— including the cookies and cream cake—for breakfast, lunch, and dinner for the next few days.

After everyone leaves, the anxiety of what is supposed to happen next is overwhelming me. I could tell Zach was a little nervous too, though he tried to hide it. He leads me into our bedroom by the hand and gently places me on the bed. He places gentle kisses on my lips.

He looks in my eyes with his soft gaze. "Get out of your head, Baby. Stay focused on me. Stay here with me, in this moment. Let me love you."

And he does. He shows me how it feels to be loved. The entire day was emotional, but everything I am feeling, being loved by this incredible man, has my heart threatening to burst.

From now on, getting out of bed in the morning will be hard, but for a different reason than the past eleven years. I finally feel like I found my place in the world—in my husband's arms.

283

'm sitting in my office, where I no longer feel the fear I had for months, after spending the last four days in wedded bliss. Chelsea and Isla are both coming in for what will be their last visits to my office, though Chelsea isn't aware of that fact yet. I have to break the news to her.

A gentle knock on my door ratchets up my heart rate.

"Come in."

Chelsea walks through the door looking unnerved, but like she's trying her best to hide it. I hate adding to her anxiety.

"Take a seat, Chels," I tell her with a smile. "Thanks for coming in on short notice."

"Yeah, sure. What's this about?"

I steady myself as my own anxiety rises. "Well, Chels. I wanted you to come in today so I could tell you I'm no longer going to be your counsellor."

Her face falls. Her shoulders droop. She looks devastated. So much so, I almost feel bad about what I'm doing. Almost.

"Why? Did I do something wrong? I can fix it. Please let me fix it." Tears spring in her eyes and she drops her face into her cupped hands.

I rush over to sit beside her on the sofa and gently pull one hand from her face to hold in mine. "Oh, Sweetheart, you did nothing wrong." Just then, there's another knock at the door. This is it.

"Come in."

Zach walks in with Isla, followed by Ms. Faerber, who is a stunning woman with ebony hair and a smile that can set anyone at ease.

Chelsea looks confused. I am struggling to contain my emotions. Zach looks as self-assured as ever, and both Isla and Ms. Faerber are smiling.

Chelsea breaks the silence. "What's going on? Why are they here?"

Still holding her hand, looking in her eyes, I say, "Chels. I'm not going to be your counsellor anymore; I want to be your family."

I give it a second for what I've said to register before I can't hold back my smile anymore. Zach strides across the room and seats himself on the wooden coffee table in front of the sofa. Isla skips behind him, then climbs into my lap. I reach out and take one of Zach's hands.

"What do you mean?" Chelsea hesitates, glancing around from one person to the next.

"You remember Zach, right?"

"Yeah, your boyfriend?"

"Husband."

"You got married? I... I had no idea."

"I wanted it to be a surprise. We got married last Wednesday. A simple wedding at the courthouse. We didn't want to wait any longer."

Her blue eyes are pooling with moisture, but tears are no longer falling. "I'm happy for you. So, are you leaving because you got married?"

"No, Sweetheart, I'm not leaving. We got married because married couples have a stronger case for adoption. Well, and because we love each other."

She's still for a moment, as if she's deciphering everything I've said, but by her expression, I can see she's putting everything together. Her face goes from excitement to trepidation in an instant. After years of not being able to trust people and being let down, I can't blame her.

"Chelsea, Zara and I want to make you part of our family. We want to adopt you. What do you think about that?" Zach is much more direct, which I'm thankful for. I'm too emotional to spit it out.

I'm now crying happy tears. Chelsea looks at me for confirmation, and I nod. "It's true, Chels. We want you to be our family. We want to give you a home and love and support and everything you could ever need. You're such an incredible young girl, and I've loved you from the moment I met you."

"I... I... I..." She struggles to speak through her sobs.

Ms. Faerber gives me a nod when I look in her direction. I slide closer to Chelsea with Isla still seated in my lap. I take Chelsea in my arms and let her cry on my shoulder. A second later, Zach wraps his strong arms around the three of us, and I can hear his emotions taking over.

The four of us stay in our embrace for enough time, Ms. Faerber exits the room. At this moment, it feels like I'm home. Everything in my life led me to this, and though it was hard, I made it. I survived, and now I thrive.

We're all a little broken, but we're all deserving of love.

"My family," Chelsea cries.

"We're going to be sisters!" Isla exclaims.

We all laugh through our tears.

I look up at the framed picture on my wall—Isla's drawing from two months ago. A dark-haired woman, a blonde little girl with ocean blue eyes, and a handsome blond man with green eyes, all standing in a grassy field under a corner sun.

I kept my promise.

Home is safe.

THE END

If you enjoyed Zara's story, please consider leaving a review on Amazon and/or Goodreads. Your reviews help give me feedback so I can continue to learn, and also helps my books garner more attention from other readers. I would greatly appreciate your thoughts!

Read the continuation of Zach and Zara's story in **We're All a Little Overwhelmed**. The extended epilogue is a novella for which all proceeds are donated to Carter's Forever Rescue and Sanctuary in Bracebridge, Ontario.

Picture by Linaya, my daughter, Age 7.
Thank you for completing Zara's story perfectly.
I love you, Sweet Girl.

To my dear friend, Desirea, I can't thank you enough for giving me the courage to share this story with the world. Your endless support and cheerleading made this possible, and I'm forever indebted to you for pushing me beyond my comfort zone and trying to find a confidence in me I didn't have in myself.

To my "Bookstagram" friends, thank you for not only reading this story, but for your feedback and encouragement along the way.

Of course, I can never forget the support of my wonderful husband and children. They inspired a lot of this story. Zach is much like my husband with his tender heart and unrelenting support. A lot of the lines he says are things my husband has said to me over the years. It only seemed fitting that I wrote in our actual wedding vows for Zach and Zara's wedding. I also had to make the same joke as Zara to stop myself from crying so I could say my vows.

This story is deeply personal for me, and I sincerely hope that you either found some comfort in these pages or some insight into the anxious mind.

Regardless of what you took away from it, I hope you enjoyed it.

Please consider signing up for my bi-weekly newsletter at linktr.ee/burdenofproofreading, or following me on Instagram at @Burdenofproofreading.

I'm excited to continue to share stories with you all and greatly appreciate everyone for taking the time to read them.

Much love,
Tiffany

You may have noticed the Guns N' Roses theme throughout this book. The three novels in this series were all inspired by different musicians (amongst other sources of inspiration). As a teenager, I loved Guns N' Roses, and even named my first dog Mr. Brownstone. It seemed fitting that this story would pay homage to that love.

So, here's my epic GnR Playlist for We're All a Little Broken.

(All music Copyrights belong to Guns N' Roses or their label, and I do not make claims to any of the songs below. This list is merely to share my influences for the story.)

My World
You're Crazy
Street of Dreams
Down On the Street*
Too Much, Too Soon*
Right Next Door To Hell
I Don't Care About You/Look At Your Game, Girl

New Work Tune
I Don't Care About You
Don't Cry
Sorry
Out Ta Get Me
Since I Don't Have You
Patience
Think About You
Appetite For Destruction (Album Title)
Bad Obsession
Breakdown
Yesterdays
Human Being
Welcome To the Jungle
There Was a Time
Ain't It Fun
Reckless Life
It Tastes Good, Don't It?*
This I Love
Nice Boys
Heartbreak Hotel
One In a Million
Anything Goes
Knockin' On Heaven's Door
November Rain
Shadown of Your Love
Civil War
Shotgun Blues
Perfect Crime
The Plague
Used To Love Her
Better
So Fine
It's So Easy

Bad Apples
Attitude
Confession*
Estranged
You Could Be Mine
New Rose
The Garden
Sweet Child O' Mine

*Indicates song is not on Spotify at time of publication.
You can find the link to the entire playlist on Spotify through my
LinkTree at linktr.ee/burdenofproofreading.

Also By This Author:

You Are Enough Series:
We're All a Little Broken: Book 1 (Zara's story)
We're All a Little Overwhelmed: Book 1.5 (Zara's extended epilogue)
We're All a Little Guarded: Book 2 (Chelsea's story)
We're All a Little Tired: Book 2.5 (Chelsea's extended epilogue)
We're All a Little Scared: Book 3 (Isla's story)

This women's fiction series focuses on various aspects of mental health and overcoming trauma. It addresses anxiety, depression, panic disorders, miscarriage, adoption, grief and loss, racism, discrimination, and more, but in a light hearted way that will also make you laugh. The entire series is set in Muskoka/Bracebridge, Ontario.

Suburban Watchdogs: Long-time friends, Justin, Morrie, Brendon, and Josh, live in a small farming town north of the big city. When crime starts making its way onto their streets, the group of men brought together by circumstance, rather than choice, band together to keep their town safe. One movie night watching a good ol' gangster film is all they need to motivate them to take action, thereby forming the Suburban Watchdogs. If criminals think they can just waltz into the Suburban Watchdogs' territory without resistance, they are mistaken.

Justin takes matters one step further by adopting Karma. Karma is a... female dog, and she'll make sure you get what's coming to you.

Join the group of unlikely friends and their canine companion on their hilarious vigilante mission and laugh at the chaos and mayhem that ensues.

A New Leash on Life Series:
Coming Spring, 2022
Sixteen interconnected standalone romantic comedies; each featuring at least one new furry friend.